The Lost One
Wrath of the Tyrant

By
Nick Wickens

The Lost One: Wrath of the Tyrant
First Edition
Published by Nick Wickens LLC

Place of Publication: Killeen, Texas, USA

Publisher's Cataloging-in-Publication
(Provided by Cassidy Cataloguing Services, Inc.)

Names: Wickens, Nick, author.

Title: The lost one : wrath of the tyrant / by Nick Wickens.

Other titles: Wrath of the tyrant.

Description: First edition. | Killeen, Texas : Nick Wickens, [2023] | Audience: young adults, adults.

Identifiers: ISBN: 979-8-9876894-0-0 (Paperback) | 979-8-9876894-1-7 (Hardback) | 979-8-9876894-2-4 (E-book) | LCCN: 2023901951

Subjects: LCSH: Orphans--Fiction. | Magic--Fiction. | Dragons--Fiction. | Friendship--Fiction. | Wizards--Fiction. | Soldiers--Fiction. | Basic training (Military education)--Fiction. | Empathy--Fiction. | Self-realization--Fiction. | Resilience--Fiction. | Courage--Fiction. | Adventure stories. | Fantasy fiction, American. | LCGFT: Fantasy fiction. | Action and adventure fiction.

Classification: LCC: PS3623.I267 L67 2023 | DDC: 813/.6--dc23

"Success is not final, failure is not fatal:
it is the courage to continue that counts."

- Author Unknown

Table of Contents

Chapter One: Thief

On an island called Clearhallow, home to a noble and fierce army called the Dragon Knights, a troubled prince sleeps in his room. His sleep is fitful, which causes concern for me, the thief currently attempting to rob him. If he were to wake, I might be too busy fleeing to get what I came for: a piece of paper lying on his desk, a map with something written on the back of it. To most people, this parchment is of little to no importance. To me, it holds the only clues I have seen about my people, which are long lost to a war against Ma'roog, a monster who leads the Rul Coilband Tribe. He has only gained more power since the destruction of my village nearly thirteen years ago when I was four years old. Since then, I had to abandon my village of Likenhallow, and I've been a wanderer traveling between islands ever since. Now that I'm seventeen, I'm considered a legal adult. I miss my home island of Tiendys, but I find myself drawn to one particular island more than others. It's called Zir'gez, a small, abandoned island in ruins where I go to cope with the loss of my family and the destruction of my village, which the Rul Coilband Tribe destroyed, but then the other tribe, the Dragon Knights, came along and stole the only thing I had left connecting me to *my* tribe and *my* village. It happened a week ago. The Dragon Knights were on their way back from visiting another island. Their dragons needed a break, so they descended from the clouds on their fiery mounts to rest and landed on the island Zir'gez, where I had been living for the summer. They saw nothing wrong with taking a look around the island because it seemed to be abandoned. I stayed out of sight, closely observing them. They came across the ruins I was living in and stole the map—*my* map!

"No! Mother!" the prince yells as he sits upright in his bed, sweating.

I stand still, hoping that he'll go back to sleep before seeing me in the corner. No such luck. His eyes go wide, and the color drains from his face as he notices my blue eyes and a sliver of pale skin exposed through my black hooded mask.

"In-intruder! Guards!" the boy yells, as he moves to grab his battle-axe from beside him.

My knife lands in the wall right between two of his fingers, slicing his skin on the edges.

"Move, and this one goes in your throat," I threaten, holding up another knife.

The prince freezes.

"Good decision," I whisper.

I grab the map and run to the window.

"Hey lady, you can't have that," the prince says.

"Yeah? And who's going to stop me? Go cry to your mommy, little prince," I say.

A very large guard slams the door open, sword in hand, and calls out the prince's name, "Brezmard!"

"It's been fun, little prince. Don't steal my stuff again," I say, hopping out the window onto Nalrai, my dragon, who is waiting to catch me.

"We'll have pursuers. Get out of here," I say as I land on his back.

He takes off quickly. After a few flaps of his wings, I lay back and relax. After all, Nalrai is one of the fastest dragons in the world, outraced only by myths, as far as I can tell. I don't risk pulling the parchment out of the small sack I stuffed it in for fear the air would tear or blow it from my grip.

The Lost One: Wrath of the Tyrant

I've almost committed all the symbols on the back of the map to memory over the years. It holds an ancient, dead language I've been teaching myself through books ever since I located a translation guide in my library five years ago. The problem is, although I can translate the words easily enough, they still don't make sense. It's like some sort of story or riddle... or part of one. I hear an alarm bell going off in the village. As if that'll do any good. We're as good as gone already. After a few minutes, an unpleasant surprise rises up to meet me. A dragon and her rider appear right in front of us, pulling up from somewhere below.

"Halt, thief!" the female rider commands.

"How did you catch up with us," I yelp, drawing my sword.

"I took a shortcut," the dragon knight yells through the wind, pointing her sword at me.

"We flew in a straight line... there are no shortcuts," I say.

"I know this island, thief. There are no shortcuts, but there are air eddies. I can predict almost any air current and follow every fissure with my eyes closed. I know how to use your surroundings against you. Surrender," she demands.

"How about no?" I shout, slashing her arm with my blade as Nalrai rolls past her dragon, "Hmm. One against one? Home turf or not, I like those odds," I laugh.

"Really? What about one against a hundred?" she asks, right on Nalrai's tail, "All I have to do is stall you for a minute or so until my friends get here. I like *those* odds," she says.

"Get us out of here, Nalrai," I say.

"Unh-unh. I don't think so," she says, appearing in front of us again.

"Dive Nalrai! We can't blend in with the ocean so easily, but I'm willing to bet we can handle the waves and winds better than she can," I say.

"You sure that's a good idea? Prince Brezmard said you stole a map… on parchment. Last I checked, paper and water don't mix so well," the knight says with her dragon swooping past my head.

I duck to avoid her sword, then I shout back, "Waterproof sack! Maybe you should invest in one. It comes in handy."

Nalrai dives out of the clouds toward the ocean.

"Come on, Qombaryth," she says to her dragon, "Let's give this thief a hard time."

"Nalrai, when they get right behind us again, pull up. All we have to do is knock her off balance," I quietly tell my dragon while watching behind my shoulder, "Now!"

He spreads his wings wide, and I shove the butt of my sword into her chest hard, sending her tumbling off her beast, as she hangs desperately onto the strap of her saddle, with one arm bleeding profusely from the cut I got in earlier.

"And where do you think you're going?" the large guard from the prince's room asks, hovering above us on his equally larger dragon.

"Oh. Hey now… I wasn't trying to hurt anybody," I say to the guard.

Then I whisper to Nalrai, "I think we can still outfly them. If not, I'll have to rely on my combat skills to get away."

The injured knight struggles but climbs back onto her dragon's saddle, assessing the injury on her arm. My grip tightens on my sword as I yell into the air, "Unless you want more people to get hurt, let me go," I warn.

"That's not how this works. You don't get to make threats," the guard says.

The Lost One: Wrath of the Tyrant

I raise my sword, but someone grabs me from behind, sticking a needle into my neck. I can feel some sort of drug in my bloodstream, slowing me down. It must be a sedative. As I glance over my shoulder, I can see that it's the girl who injected it. I can't believe it… beaten by an injured science geek. Maybe I'm not as tough as I thought.

"N-not fair," I say as the world goes darker.

I wake with cuffs around my wrists and heavy iron chains hang from the dungeon's wall. My knees are on the ground, ankles cuffed tightly together, forcing me to kneel in front of the chief when he comes. I'm covered in a suit made from overlapping black dragon scales. They remove my matching mask and hood. When I started this mission, I had a single, long braid going down my back, past my shoulder blades that was tucked into my somewhat loose outfit, but now my blonde hair dangles annoyingly in my face. I try to blow it off, but it just falls back to where it was.

When did the braid fall out? I think to myself.

At this point, I'm almost tempted to chop it off the next chance I get. My attention goes to Nalrai. I can see him pacing in a cage. There are gnaw marks on the bars and burn marks on the ground around it.

"Who are you?" the prince asks calmly as he sharpens his ax.

"I'm nobody," I say.

"No, really. Where are you from, and what do you want with my map?" he asks.

"*Your* map? It's *my* map! You stole it from me!" I say.

"It's a map of Clearhallow. Where are you from? Clearhallow?"

I drop my head and say nothing.

"You must be. You have hardly any accent, and I saw no evidence of anyone currently living in the abandoned ruins of Zir'gez. So, you live on that island we found it on? Or were you just visiting? Or are you from Clearhallow?"

"Me? From Clearhallow? News to me," I say.

"No? You must be from somewhere. Did you just *spawn* from the sky?"

He smirks sarcastically as a smile tugs at his lips.

"You think this is funny?" I ask angrily.

"My apologies. This should be a very serious matter. You broke into my room and stole *my* map—with potentially dangerous information on it. You injured me and one of my knights. I need to know where you are from, so we can properly punish you," he says, with seriousness returning to his face.

"But I'm not *from* anywhere. I'm... a nomad, I guess you could say."

"There are no nomadic tribes left in the modern world," he says.

"No, I know that. It's just my dragon and I wandering. My village was destroyed when I was very young. He's kept me safe ever since, and we've lived wherever the food has taken us," I say.

"Destroyed? You're from a dead village?" he asks.

"Yes. As far as I know, we're the only ones that made it out alive, but I keep *hoping* that I'm wrong. I think the writing on the back of my map could be the key to learning if there was any evacuation point or safe place they could have fled to," I say.

"Then why is there a map of Clearhallow on it? My people have been here for hundreds of years. Your people couldn't have lived here," he says.

"I think the map is incomplete. The writing on the back doesn't make sense. There has to be more to it than just what's on that map. I assure you, it's harmless and has nothing to do with your village. I have no interest in your people. Now let me go," I say, annoyed.

"Who destroyed this village of yours?" he asks, examining his ax.

"A monster… the leader of the Rul Coilband," I say.

"Ma'roog?" he asks.

"Yes," I say.

"Hmm. You can't be much older than I am. Sixteen? Seventeen? And father never mentioned a northern village being destroyed in the last few decades. Did your village have a name? Was it close to here?" he asks.

"No, it wasn't near here. It's a journey of several days on a dragon, several weeks by ship. Look, I was barely old enough to speak when it was destroyed. All I want is to take my map and get off your island," I say.

"Did your people have any allies we could consult with?" he asks.

"Do I look like some sort of historian to you? I don't know! One of my earliest memories is of my father throwing me on Nalrai's back and telling him to keep me safe. I was *four*, okay? I don't remember."

"I'll have to consult with my father. I'm not sure if I believe you, but I'll see what I can do to get you released with nothing more than a warning. You hardly injured me. It'll be a matter of days before the wound heals. I believe a fine should be an adequate punishment for theft," he says.

"How are you going to fine me? I don't have any money," I say.

"We could flog you instead."

"You're going to flog me? That's *my* map. I haven't stolen anything. I don't see why I should be punished at all," I say.

"You said you could read what's on the back of the map?" he asks.

"Yeah. I found some old translation guide. Taught myself some sort of ancient language or something."

"What does it say?" he asks.

"You think I'm an idiot, runt? Why would I tell you? As far as I'm concerned, anyone who locks me up in their dark, smelly dungeon is an enemy," I say.

"An enemy who holds power over your fate," he says.

The heavy prison doors open.

"Prince Brezmard, your father wishes to talk to you," the large knight from earlier says as he enters the dungeon.

I guess he's the prince's private guard or something. I surely do not envy the hours he must pull being the prince's personal babysitter.

The prince smirks again and says to the knight, "You know what Norkuz? I think I like her. She's as stubborn and hotheaded as I am."

"Oh, I doubt that very much," Norkuz says.

"And Norkuz, guess what else? You're not the only one who calls me 'runt' anymore," the prince says, heading toward the exit.

"I see," the knight says, sounding more tired than interested.

Hmm... I think to myself, *Figuring out how often they change shifts might be useful if I have to escape and attempt to get my map back again.*

13

The Lost One: Wrath of the Tyrant

"Nalrai," I say after they leave, "Are you okay?"

He snorts, frustrated, then he gnaws on the bars of the cage. Nalrai is definitely not cut out to be a jailbird.

"I hear you Nalrai. I can't feel my arms, which makes escaping harder. That is, if I could escape in the first place. Never tried it before," I say, glaring at the chains going from my wrists and ankles up into the wall.

"I have a headache," I continue, "I think it's from that sedative they gave me. How long do you think they're going to keep us here?"

Nalrai huffs, puffs, lies down and curls up.

"Not very optimistic today, are you?" I tease.

I examine the chains as closely as I can. I wish I had experience with picking locks, but as it stands, I honestly don't have a clue how I'm supposed to get out of here.

"Okay Nalrai, I guess I'm with you. I hope the chief isn't too ticked off that I scraped his kid's fingers a little."

Chapter Two: Prisoner

7he light from outside is blinding when they open the dungeon doors. It makes my headache worse. I squint against it, withdrawing from the pain.

"Headache?" guesses a knight I haven't seen before.

"Killer," I say.

"Don't worry, that's the least of your concerns," he says, purposefully dropping the food he's carrying on the ground.

"If that's for me, I've had worse," I say.

"You haven't seen worse yet," he says.

He pounds his fist in his hand and flinches at me.

"Whoa! Hey now! Look, I'm all chained up. I can't hurt anyone from here," I say.

"Too bad you weren't chained up earlier. Maybe my sister wouldn't have gotten hurt. Luckily for you, she's okay, but I don't like it when people hurt my sister," he says.

"Sister? Oh... the one who drugged me. Look, I wouldn't suggest trying to get revenge, kid. I don't know much about your country, but your prince didn't look like he was going to just let anybody beat the living daylight out of me whenever they felt like it," I say, trying to get to my feet with these stupid shackles.

"I'm *friends* with the prince. I think he'll forgive me, but I'm not going to forgive you for Ak'dech's arm," he says, then he flicks some of the food from the ground onto me.

"Listen, kid, I don't think you want to do this," I say.

The Lost One: Wrath of the Tyrant

"Don't call me *kid*, thief," he snarls.

The young knight charges at me. I somehow get the muscles in my arms to work, and I pull down on the chains enough to get my legs under me. I swing forward, and both feet hit him in the chest.

"Huh, you should probably get that checked," I say, surprised that it actually worked.

I quickly wrap my right arm around the chain that's fastened to the wall and tug with all my strength. The wall crumbles around it, breaking the chain loose. As he kneels and bends over to catch his breath, I take his sword as he tries to recover. As hard as I can, I drive the tip of the sword onto the metal binding my feet together, breaking both chains and the sword, reducing its length to about two-thirds of what it was.

Oh well, I think to myself.

I turn away from the wall and grab the one intact restraint that is shackled around my left wrist, then I yank, using my weight to break the chain out of the wall.

"Not wise, thief," the knight gasps.

"What's that armor good for? I didn't hit you *that* hard. I can show you what a *hit* looks like," I say, grabbing the collar of his chest plate and raising my fist.

"Don't move," a deep voice commands.

It's Norkuz, the large knight again. He has an arrow aimed right at Nalrai. I relax my fist a little, but I don't let go of my prisoner.

"Nalrai, fire-blast!" I say.

"Ahhhh," Norkuz says, diving out of the way of Nalrai's flames.

I knock out the kid and run over to the big guy as he tries to roll back onto his feet. I send a kick into his neck, right under his jaw. He should be out for a while, but there is still a little bit of consciousness left in him because I hear him moaning. For now, these metal shackles are still digging into my wrists and ankles, and I think my friend Nalrai likes captivity even less than I do.

"Where are the keys?" I say to myself, looking around.

I notice that the guards don't have keys, so I guess I'm improvising. I pick up the arrow Norkuz was about to send into Nalrai's skull, and I try to pick the lock with it. After a minute, Nalrai starts to whine.

"Hold on Nalrai. I'm trying to do this with a splitting headache and no practice. Have a little patience," I say.

"What kind of thief doesn't know how to pick a lock?" a voice from behind me says.

I spin around, aiming the arrow at Norkuz's throat, which is hopefully sore from the previous hit, but he's more prepared this time. He catches my wrist before I can attack and twists me around, holding my arm painfully behind my back.

"Going somewhere?" he asks.

"Yeah. Away," I say, stomping on his toes.

"Ouch," he growls through his teeth, not flinching otherwise. Then he says, "I'll let you know right now, even if you get another lucky hit in, backup will be on the way after too much time has passed. Are you going to spare yourself the unnecessary pain of trying to fight through half a dozen Dragon Knights on your own? Besides, I don't think you know what you're doing trying to pick that lock."

"Okay, you win... stupid lock! But next time they send food down, could it be with someone who doesn't hold a grudge against me for getting in a fight with his sister?"

"Hm," he grunts.

"You know, you're good. Like, really good. No wonder you're the little prince's own personal bodyguard," I say.

"Yeah? Wanna tell me how you broke free?" he asks, all businesslike.

"It was easier than I expected. Must've had cracks in the wall or something," I say.

"Won't happen again," he says.

"Okay, Mr. Growl and Scowl. I wasn't *planning* on trying to escape, but things kinda changed when your buddy over there tried to attack me. Then you came in threatening my dragon, and it got worse from there."

"Really? I singed an eyebrow because of you and your dragon! You couldn't have surrendered *before* then? Maybe I would've been more likely to believe you," he says.

"Heeeey, I saw an opportunity, and I was already free. I just had to figure out a way to get Nalrai out of here, but what do you expect? I'm being held here because *I* got robbed!"

"I'll make sure to tell that to Nokk over there when he finally wakes up. Surely you understand you're not making this easy. You keep causing problems for us. This could've been a simple trespassing and theft charge, but you had to throw a knife at the prince and fight with the rest of us. Stop making it harder on yourself," he says.

"So you want me to just accept being locked up and have my freedom taken away because *I* was stolen from? It's not like I could go *ask* for it back! I heard what your little prince was saying when he took it. He wasn't going to give it up just like that, and I'm not going to sit here and take whatever punishment you come up with. I'm not even a citizen of Clearhallow! I don't follow your laws!"

"No, you're not from anywhere. You have no government for us to turn you over to. You live in your own little world without laws. Well, that's not how it works. Grow up, kid. Welcome to reality, where invading the room of a foreign nation's prince has consequences. In all actuality, Prince Brezmard was willing to overlook that and let you off with a warning, but you're not making it easy for him to convince his father. Do you understand how difficult you're making this?"

They put me in different chains, but at least these are less uncomfortable. I have more freedom to move around, but they have two knights posted inside the prison, watching me constantly. I was on the verge of figuring out that lock, so I think I could escape. I'm not so concerned about the knights either, as long as I'm not caught off guard again. It's very unlike me to be caught unaware like that, especially twice in a row, but I'd like to at least rest until my headache goes away. It's harder to concentrate through the pain. Besides, I'm not sure I could escape *with* the map, either. I better wait for a while and formulate a plan. I squint in pain as the doors open again and sunlight pours through once more.

"Sir Norkuz, the prisoner has barely moved a centimeter, " one of the guards report.

"Thanks," Norkuz says dismissively, walking straight up to me.

"You again. Don't you ever sleep?" I ask.

"Double shift... a favor for a friend. *What* are you?" he asks.

"What?" I ask, confused.

"*What* are you?" he asks again.

"I don't understand. Do you want me to say *thief*? Is this an admission of guilt?"

"No. The wall, the chains," he says.

The Lost One: Wrath of the Tyrant

"Oh. That. They were old... I guess. I'd say to ask your dungeon up-keeper about it, but I doubt you have one. This place is falling apart," I say.

"So what about my friend? He was wearing armor. He's young and healthy. His armor wasn't defective. So how did you break his ribs, especially while restrained like you were?"

"You sound like you expect me to know what you're talking about," I say.

"Do you *not*?" he asks.

"Not a clue," I say.

He stares at me, trying to tell if I'm hiding something.

"Don't do anything stupid," he says to me while turning and walking away. Then he tells the guards on his way out, "Keep a close eye on her. She's dangerous."

After a few more minutes, I get bored... really bored.

"You know, I have to admire your dedication. I've hardly seen either of you blink since that Norkuz guy left. Do you really think I'm *that* dangerous all chained up with no weapons or anything? He already established I can't pick a lock to save my life."

Neither of them respond. I frown.

"Well, they're no fun," I mumble under my breath, and then I say out loud, "I don't suppose your medical staff would know how to ease a migraine, would they? I think it's from that poison gunk... or tranquilizer... whatever your friend injected me with when I was captured."

"Tough luck. Your medic just left," one of them cracks.

"That Norkuz guy? Seriously? Is he the do-it-all knight?" I ask.

"Basically," the taller of the two guards says.

"Oh. Well, let me be frank with you. I'm not scared by much, but honestly, I find him intimidating. Is he really that scary, or is he just all scowly because I'm a prisoner?"

There's no response from neither of them. I sigh and groan. The door opens yet again, and Norkuz enters.

"You weren't gone very long," I say to Norkuz.

He pauses as one of the guards whispers something to him. He nods at them and says to me, "Prince Brezmard wants to ask you a few more questions."

"You have keys with you this time. I'm confused," I say.

"Prince Brezmard decided you might be a little more cooperative if you're comfortable," he says.

"You object?" I ask.

He glares at me and says, "To be honest, I'm pretty sure the only reason he thinks that is because you amuse him, and he thinks you're pretty."

"Ew," I grimace.

"Careful, that's my best friend you're talking about. I wouldn't want you to hurt his ego," he says quietly as he smiles a little, then breaks out into a full smile, shaking his head.

"What about Nalrai?" I ask.

"We can't risk having you two together. That'll make it too easy to escape, but we'll make sure he gets food and the chance to stretch his wings. Oh, and I have something for that headache of yours too. Chew on these," Norkuz says.

"What are they?" I ask, taking the leaves he holds out.

"Peppermint. I can't guarantee the headache will go away, but sometimes they help."

The Lost One: Wrath of the Tyrant

"You know what? I suspect you're actually a nice person under all that scowling."

"Do you really think I was hand-picked by the chief to protect his heir because I'm *nice*?"

I raise an eyebrow, hunch my shoulders and mumble, "If you say so."

Norkuz is uncomfortably close as he walks me to a gigantic dining hall. He keeps about half a step away from me as a constant reminder that if I try anything funny, he could snap my spine in an instant. The prince doesn't say anything as I enter, but he motions for me to take a seat. Norkuz unlocks and releases my shackles and stands beside the door, standing tall. The prince stares at me for a moment while I glare back at him in silence.

"Good evening," he says.

"Free me, and I won't bother you again," I say.

"I can't. My father is in charge, not me."

"Then *convince* him to free me," I growl.

"It's not easy to convince my father to do anything he's already set against. Freeing prisoners is especially difficult. Allow me to introduce myself properly, milady. I am Prince Brezmard of Clearhallow, commander of the noble Dragon Knights, and heir to the chieftain's chair," he says, as he stands and bows. "What, might I ask, is your name?" he asks.

"None of your business, runt," I nip.

"So you don't feel you owe me even *that* for the crimes you have committed?"

"Minor transgressions," I say.

"Perhaps that's how you see them, but here, they are a great deal more than minor transgressions. My father would rather see you executed, but I wish to see you free," he says.

"How knightly and noble of you to show such mercy," I snort, "Do you expect me to be impressed by you, Prince Brezmard? Should I be charmed by your manners and supposed good intentions?"

"I assure you, I'm not interested in charming or impressing you. You're not my type," he grimaces.

A guard bursts into the room and says, "Prince Brezmard, my apologies for the intrusion, but we've found something you should see."

Norkuz remains at the door as Brezmard follows the other guard into the hall.

"Where did you get this?" Brezmard asks me, as he returns with anger in his voice. Then he jams my dagger into the table in front of me, shaking with rage.

"It's a family heirloom. My father gave it to me as he sent me away," I say, confused by the anger he's trying to swallow.

"What's your name? Who was your father?" he asks.

"Why should I tell you? My family is dead!"

"This is the seal of the *chief* of Clearhallow! This is my family's symbol! You have no right to have this engraved on your dagger," he shouts, face burning red.

I pause, staring at him for a moment, and then I whisper, "My name is Arid Dho'zogg. I don't remember who my father was."

He grabs the handle of the dagger, yanks it out of the table, and says, "Here is your dagger and its *stolen* emblem, *thief*."

Then he spits on the ground as he offers it to me. When I reach for it, he snatches it back.

"Let's talk about this map that seems so important to you. What does it have written on it? What do you know about my island?" he asks.

"I don't care about your island, and the writing on the back mentions nothing of Clearhallow. It's only a part of a bigger map," I say, exasperated.

"You keep insisting it's *your* map—a clue to the whereabouts of your people. Why are you so sure that it has something to do with your island? Does the writing on the map mention them?" he asks.

"No, but eight years ago, my dragon took me back to the ruins of my village. A piece of the map was buried in a stone chest, along with other keepsakes. Nothing on it makes sense. All it says is something about seers and marks of the chosen. It could be some sort of religious writing, or the scribblings of a madman. Whatever it is, the rest of it could mention an evacuation point where my people may have fled to. I know it's a long shot, but it's all I have. It's the only surviving documentation from my village," I say.

"That's one *hell* of a long shot. In fact, many generations ago, my people had seers. They believed in magic and prophecy. Nowadays, all that is dismissed as nonsense, but maybe your people believed. However, I doubt old historical writings have anything to do with the current whereabouts of your village," he says.

"I know," I say quietly, "But it's all I have."

A loud explosion outside shakes the building. Norkuz has his sword ready in an instant, looking out the window.

"Brezmard," he says with a warning in his voice.

"What's going on?" Brezmard asks.

"I don't know who or what is attacking, but I see fire," Norkuz says.

"Would now be a bad time to mention that my dragon Nalrai is very particular about his flying companions? You see, it is rare to see an opal salamander dragon with a rider because they aren't usually very docile. They are hard to subdue, harder to train, but *very* loyal," I say.

I lunge forward and snatch my dagger out of Brezmard's hand. He draws his own sword reactively and says, "You couldn't escape last time. What makes you think this will be any different?"

I assess the situation. My dagger is my only weapon at the moment. It could take a minute or two for Nalrai to track down my exact location, and Norkuz has already proven to be tough.

"Doesn't seem like you're taking us seriously," the big guy Norkuz says as he takes a step toward me.

"As much as I'd love a duel," I say, "I have other plans. You can keep the map for now. I have more important things to worry about."

I run towards Norkuz, ducking under his blade as he swings at me, and then I dive through the window. I'm on the ground level, so it shouldn't be a bad fall.

"Follow her!" Brezmard commands.

I hit the ground rolling.

"Nalrai!" I yell, as I sprint away from the palace.

A moment later, Nalrai locates and flies to me. I grab hold of his saddle and pull myself up as he blasts past. I have the dagger, my dragon, and my life. My other weapons are expendable. I can steal new ones later. My freedom is much more valuable than anything I'm leaving here. As we speed through the clouds, I say to Nalrai, "See if you can find those wind eddies that knight mentioned. Use them, and don't hold back this time. You know that small island about fifteen kilometers from here? Let's go hide out there for a few days. Even if they track us there, we can blend in while I replenish my weapons stash."

Chapter Three: Dho'zogg

"Ah, Arid! Welcome back to our village! It's always a pleasure to see you! Tell me, have you any more stories of your adventures?" Kaz'gum, a familiar face asks while smiling at me.

"Not today, Lady Kaz'gum. How are your story-loving children?" I ask.

"Mul'gom and O'zom are quite well, though I'm afraid little Halzog has been ill. The physician says it's just a fever and will pass by soon. I can only hope he's right."

"Sorry to hear that. I'll drop by for a visit sometime, I promise. Surely I have *some* tales left to mention that'll lift Halzog's spirits for a while."

"That would be nice. Have a lovely stay, my dear," she says as she waves and continues on her way.

I quietly steal an apple as I pass through the market to my next destination with Nalrai close behind me.

"Morning, Mister Lulvom," I say as I lean against one of his carts and bite into the apple.

"Arid! Been a while since I last saw you here. What brings you to my shop this time? Weapons or information?"

"Both," I say.

"What do you need?"

I carefully examine a sword as I speak, "What do you know about the history of Clearhallow? Specifically, their legends of magic and seers?"

26

"I believe this is a more fascinating topic than you expect. When Clearhallow was first settled hundreds of years ago, they believed in such things as magic. Every generation had a counsel of seers, which were witches and oracles they said could see all of time: events of the past and predictions of the future. It would drive the seers to madness because they would have all of time going through their heads at once and couldn't distinguish which time was the present. With every generation of seers, there was always a being of powerful magic, a sorcerer, who could use their own skills to help tune out the chaos in the seers' minds. It's been said that the sorcerer would calm the seers by anchoring them to the present moment to help them keep their sanity, without taking away their oracle ability to see throughout time. Some say the seers died out, but the vast majority agree they never existed to begin with. They're often dismissed as fairy tales. Unfortunately, six generations ago, the disagreement between magical and scientific beliefs caused division and tore apart the people of Clearhallow, most notably, the family of the chief. You, my dear, may have an interesting history because at the time of this division, the name of the chief was Elok Dho'zogg, and he had two sons, Alruz and Miyan. His sons had different views on whether or not the seers existed. Miyan believed fervently they existed and wished to seek out magical beings who could aid them in times of war. His brother, however, was a skeptic, believing in science instead of magic. They were already at odds with each other, but this drove a further wedge between them. Eventually, the disagreement drove Miyan to gather all the people on Clearhallow who believed the old magical stories, and he led them away. They settled at the foot of Mount Tiendys."

"Are you *sure* the name was Dho'zogg?" I ask.

"As positive as the stories are, but take it with a grain of salt, Lady Arid. My tales of history are unreliable, considering my sources. They are stories passed by word of mouth by travelers and merchants. Anything with magic in it is particularly prone to misinformation," Lulvom says.

"Still, why haven't you told me this before?" I ask.

"You know why. You ask a question. I answer. You haven't asked the right question until today, which you have yet to pay for, by the way. And speaking of paying, there's a friend of mine who happened to notice that a handful of items at his shop mysteriously went missing last time you were passing through. You wouldn't happen to know anything about that, would you?"

"Afraid not," I say, unsure whether I had anything to do with it or not.

"No, you only steal things that won't be missed, like an apple from a full cart, or coins from the pouches of the wealthier folk on the island," he hints again.

"I'll keep my eye out for anyone more troublesome than *I* am," I say, putting stolen coins on his table and sheathing my new sword.

"Feel free to drop by any time if you have more questions," he says.

I stop by Kaz'gum's house as promised. As I continue to braid her daughter's hair after concluding a highly exaggerated tale of a time I got into a fight at a bar on an island where travelers greatly outnumber actual inhabitants, O'zom asks, "Can you tell me another story?"

"I would, but you've heard all my tales. What about you? What adventures have you had since I last stopped by?" I ask.

"Me? None," she says.

"I find that hard to believe. After all, you are six, and six-year-olds are known for their adventures close to home," I say.

"I don't have any. I promise!" she giggles.

"That's a shame. I would have liked to hear *you* tell a story for once. What about you, Mul'gom? Halzog? Any tales to tell?"

"Only a boring one of the time I went fishing with the fishermen. As it turns out, I wouldn't like that job much at all," Mul'gom says while rolling his eyes.

"Like it or not, a fisherman you will be," Kaz'gum, his widowed mother, says sternly.

"Aw," he whines.

Halzog sneezes for the hundredth time but offers no stories.

"Attention! All who can hear me! We are Dragon Knights from Clearhallow! We are looking for an escaped prisoner. She is dangerous and should be reported immediately if seen! Arid Dho'zogg, surrender now! We *will* search these houses, and we will find you," a voice yells, echoing through the streets.

"Arid?" Kaz'gum asks, "Trouble with the Dragon Knights?"

"I've been in trouble before," I say.

"Not like this. They are one of the most formidable armies in all of Northern Vrarg, and their prison system is ruthless. It will not end well for you if you are captured," she says.

"*Recaptured*," I correct, "And I've heard *plenty* about them and their self-righteous attitude from travelers near and far."

"What did you do to offend them?" she asks.

"I took back what they stole from me. Lady Kaz'gum, I appreciate your hospitality, but I have another tale waiting for me. Get well soon, Halzog. Stay safe. I wish you all well," I say.

"No Arid…. not with these people! They could kill you!" O'zom whines, then she grabs my hand, as if she could stop me from leaving.

I gently push O'zom off my lap and stand, then I say, "They'll find me here anyway, and I wish to save you from property damage and possible charges of harboring a fugitive."

The Lost One: Wrath of the Tyrant

"Good luck, my friend," Kaz'gum says.

"Thank you."

"I repeat, Arid Dho'zogg, surrender yourself," the knight calls.

I step out the hut and climb onto Nalrai, and I already see someone I recognize. It's Ak'dech!

"Isn't she injured? Tough bitch isn't going to catch us again," I grumble to Nalrai as I draw my new sword and yell, "You want me? I'm right here!"

"No! Don't touch her!" a 12-year-old boy from the streets yells as he runs out in front of me, throwing his arms up as if he could stop a dozen knights from taking me.

"Gog'drac! What are you doing?" I yelp, surprised.

"Don't touch Lady Arid!" he repeats.

"She's a thief. She will pay for her crimes," the knight says.

"She's a hero! She saved our village. Not you. She fought off a gang of rogue warriors from the Rul Coilband while our neighbors didn't care enough to send knights to help! I won't let you touch her!" Gog'drac shouts.

"Stand down, little warrior," I say.

"No," he shouts and stands his ground.

"Gog'drac, it's okay. I'll be okay. I promise. I have a plan. Remember how I always get out of trouble? This time won't be any different," I say.

"Yes, it will. This time you're not facing a few dozen, Lady Arid. You're facing a few *thousand*," he says.

"You know, maybe they *should* stop teaching numbers in school," I murmur.

"What do *you* know? You can't count past your fingers!" he says, as he sticks his tongue out at me.

"Hey! I'm trying to keep you out of trouble," I retort, "And I *do* know that *eleven* comes after ten," I add.

"Yeah, and who taught you that?" he says with a smirk.

"Stand aside, child," one of the knights says, pointing a crossbow at the kid.

"No!" Gog'drac screams at him.

"Gog'drac, step back," I say, fearing for the boy's life.

The female knight Ak'dech storms up to her friend pointing the crossbow at Gog'drac and yells, "Zual, what are you doing?"

"He's in our way," Zual says.

"We don't *murder* children!" she says, "Lower your weapon," she orders.

"This prisoner is dangerous," he says.

"Lower your weapon," she repeats insistently.

"Gog'drac, listen to me. I appreciate your willingness to help, but I can handle this. Stand down. I don't want you to get hurt, and I'm sure your mother doesn't want you getting hurt either. Live to fight another battle another day, little warrior," I say.

He slowly lowers his arms and takes a few steps to the side.

"Run home, kid," the female knight says.

Then Gog'drac takes off running.

"How did you know where I was?" I ask Ak'dech.

"You realize it *is* possible to track a dragon through the air?" she says and shrugs with a smirk on her face.

31

The Lost One: Wrath of the Tyrant

"It's the second time you've caught up to me when I didn't think anyone would. You're good," I say.

"Are you going to come with us willingly this time, or do I have to sedate you again?" she asks.

"How about option number three? I escape, and you go home empty-handed," I suggest.

"I have a job to keep. Doesn't sound like a very good option for me," she says.

"Nalrai, go," I yell.

Nalrai spits a blue fireball at Ak'dech's dragon and takes off at top speed, heading back towards the abandoned island of Zir'gez. I believe this island will be safer because I know my way around it better than any of the Dragon Knights do, and there will be no civilians to worry about getting injured in the crossfire. Nalrai is flying well and manages to dodge the attacks while putting distance between us and our enemies. Normally, I'd be shooting my bow and arrows at any pursuers as Nalrai gets us to safety, but I have to settle for trusting him since they took my weapons when I was captured.

"Don't let them escape!" Ak'dech orders, frustration clear in her voice.

Her dragon gets a lucky shot in by blowing flames at me and Nalrai, but they'll have to be luckier than that. I duck past the flames as the fire rolls over my fireproof dragon suit.

"Nalrai, what's that?"

I stare ahead at several quickly approaching figures: glimmering armor, and the sun shining off swords. I'd say reinforcements for the Dragon Knights, but the color the knights wear is blue, and the first splash of color I see ahead is green.

"Rul Warriors! Prepare for battle!" the lead Dragon Knight warns.

"Use this as a distraction, and slip away while they're fighting," I tell Nalrai, but there's no such luck. The warriors are even less interested in letting me get away than the knights are. One of the Rul Warriors is staring me down, eyes locked on me, and there is something... something familiar about her.

"Take the girl alive! Understand?" she tells the other warriors.

"No, not today," I whisper.

The Rul Warriors are wearing armor, but like the knights, they are only wearing chest plates. My blade finds its way to a throat on my left side, followed by a dragon's wing on my other side, thanks to Nalrai's agility. Another warrior is too slow to avoid my dagger driving into his thigh. I know from experience that his leg will bleed out in minutes. I jump off Nalrai onto an enemy dragon, slitting the rider's throat and jamming my dagger into the beast's skull. Nalrai catches me as I dive through the air, and I take out one more warrior on the way down.

"Arid?"

I spin towards the voice behind me, sword swinging, but it's blocked with a shield.

"You're alive," the warrior who seemed familiar breathes.

"Who are you?" I ask.

"Our village survives... some of them, anyway, but I'm forced to fight for the monster that destroyed us," she says.

"How do you know who I am? I was a child," I ask.

"You look like your mother. She was my sister. Arid, you can help save us," she says.

"H-how?" I ask, forcing out the question, as my throat is suddenly dry.

She glances up briefly and says, "I'm sorry about this."

The Lost One: Wrath of the Tyrant

Then she swings her shield at me. The shield hits hard, knocking me off balance, and she flies away as the surviving warriors retreat. The world is spinning around me as I begin to fall off my dragon, and I barely manage to catch a hold to one of his saddle's straps. Dizzily, I say to Nalrai, "Surrender or run, my loyal friend. You choose," I say in a final gasp before I pass out.

Chapter Four: Negotiations

"You're alive," a sigh of relief comes from Ak'dech as she grabs my arms tightly around her waist to make sure I don't fall off her dragon.

"Tha-that's what the Rul warrior said, too," I say, as I limply hold on to her waist.

I squint my eyes open and see Nalrai flying close beside us with no rider, while Ak'dech navigates her dragon and I over the ocean.

"You blacked out for a few minutes, so we're taking you back to Clearhallow. My friend Norkuz should take a look at you. I... I've never seen anyone fight like you before, and that Rul warrior... she seemed to know you and wanted you alive. Why?"

It's so hard to focus, but I manage to say, "I don't... know. She... said she's my aunt. I have to save my people. She said they're alive."

"I don't know what she told you, but I'd take it with skepticism. Warriors aren't exactly known for their honesty, but they *do* like messing with people's heads," she says.

"And why do *you* care?" I ask.

"That's... an explanation for another time, okay? You should rest, at least until Norkuz takes a look at you," she says.

"No, I have to save my people... my village. She said they're still alive. I have to find them. Let me go," I say.

"I can't do that," she says.

The Lost One: Wrath of the Tyrant

"What about that village back there? Those warrior scouts might've been sent there to scout and prepare for an attack. Either that, or they were preparing for Clearhallow. There are only *two* inhab... inhabited islands near here, and I ... I have friends on that island. Innocen... innocent people... live there," I say.

My head is foggy. I can't concentrate. I can barely stay awake. I feel like I'm going to black out again.

"We'll take care of them. When we get back, I'll have Prince Brezmard send some knights to protect them. That boy back at the village who jumped in to protect you was right. Their village has no army. They're too small. Their entire population wouldn't be enough for an army, but they're our neighbors. We should help protect them. You're a hero to them, apparently, so I think, maybe, you're not such a bad person after all. Clearly, Brezmard's not half as skilled as you are in combat, so you could have totally killed him when you broke in. Therefore, I don't think you mean any harm, or Brezmard would be dead already. As for your own village, you'll have to wait awhile. What good is one soldier against the Rul Coilband? One *injured* soldier, at that. I'll talk to the prince about helping you look for your village," she says.

"I don't... believe you. Don't... trust you," I say.

"Oh, but you trust that warrior who said she was your aunt? You just *happened* to run into her? It's a big world, and I don't trust anything a Rul warrior says."

"But she was so... familiar, like I knew her," I say.

"We'll see."

"She... could be the only family I have left. It's been so... long... since... I've had... a family... a home," I say.

"Which makes you desire it so much more, and that makes it so much *easier* to get your hopes up and convince you it's true because you *want* it to be true so bad. All I can say is that you should be cautious. I know that doesn't mean much coming from me, but I promise I'm not trying to break your spirits. I don't believe we've properly met. I'm Ak'dech."

"Ak'dech... guess I should apologize for the arm."

"I should apologize for my brother. I heard what he did. He's a hotheaded kid. Smart, but not always thinking clearly."

"Yeah, well, can you hurry and get me back to that dungeon the prince had me in earlier? Where it's dark... and quiet," I say as I rub my forehead and side temple.

"Headache?" she guesses.

"It's worse than... the sedative you gave me," I murmur.

"Hmm. Well, I doubt Brezmard still wants you in a cell."

"Why's that?" I ask.

"Because I think he'll be more interested in *helping* you," she says.

"Help me? I don't need help," I say.

"Uhhh-huh," she says disbelievingly.

"I especially don't need help from *your* people," I say, remembering the story Lulvom the merchant told me about their people driving my ancestors away. However, I can't remember why. It's so hard to think—

"Hey, are you okay?" she asks suddenly, as we approach Clearhallow.

"I'm fi... fine," I barely whisper, as I pass out on Ak'dech's back.

The Lost One: Wrath of the Tyrant

"Arid? Hold on, okay? Prince Brezmard would kill me if I brought you back dead. Qombaryth, hurry!"

In between brief moments of consciousness, I dream of fire. It's a dream I've had a hundred times: My village is burning. An infant's cries haunt the streets. My mother is dead. Ma'roog, the untouchable one, killed her. He's destroyed countless lives. Father knew it was a battle he couldn't win, so he had his dragon carry me away while he kept the attention of his murderer. His sacrifice bought Nalrai and I just enough time to escape, and Nalrai faithfully follows his final command to take me away and keep me safe day by day. However, I had to watch the violent deaths of both my parents… and I watched as their bodies burned in the flames. I clearly remember the feel of the blaze around me: the heat, and the smoke that burned my throat and lungs. My face was covered in soot, and any tears I cried were gone before they reached my cheeks—quickly burned away by the fire. Everything is seared into my memory in vivid detail. The heat, the smoke, their dismembered corpses, the smell of burning flesh… some of it my own. I feel every awful sensation down to the wind in my singed eyes. I see wisps in the smoke-like shadows. I hear voices in the wind, in my head. They're getting louder, but I can't make sense of what they're saying. Layers of voices overlap, echoing in my brain… hurting my head.

"Who—"

"Can—"

"Save us—"

"Lost—"

"Elders—"

"Girl—"

"Save us—"

There is pain that doesn't belong in this memory. Chaos I've never dreamt before. There's pain in my arm. Wait, my arm is burning. This isn't right. Something is different. I try to fight a faceless, smoky shadow wisp as it reaches out to me, grabbing my arm. Its touch sends fire through the limb hurting worse than before. If I could chop my arm off, it might be a relief, but I can't find my dagger.

"No! Stop! You're not supposed to be here! Who are you? Go away! Leave me alone!" I shout at the smoky shadow and whispering voices while pressing my hands over my ears, "And what are you doing to my arm? Let go!" I yell, waking suddenly on a feather-filled bed covered in pillows and plush blankets.

"I'm not hurting you," Norkuz's deep voice says, "Are you okay?"

"I'm burning. Help me," I clutch at my arm desperately, trying to make the pain go away.

"Burning?" he inquires.

I force my nails under my sleeve above my elbow and tear away the black dragon scale glove that is covering my skin down to my hand.

"Make it stop," I plead.

"You're not burning. But your arm... the scars on your arm are inflamed... and warm to the touch," he says.

"Is she hallucinating, or is she still dreaming and sleep talking of that fire that razed her village?" asks Brezmard.

"No, she's awake, and these scars *aren't* from a fire," Norkuz says.

Remnants of the whispering voices from my dream linger in my mind. Between the voices and the burning, the pain is agonizing. I haven't had voices in my nightmares before, and I never dreamt my arm was burning. I never woke up in pain like this either.

The Lost One: Wrath of the Tyrant

"Make it stop!" I shout, gripping at the feather-stuffed mattress I'm lying on. Then I rip the silk covers and feel it tear, just like my dragon-scale sleeve.

"Pass me that bucket of water," Norkuz's deep voice says to the prince.

In a moment, cool water is running over my arm. It instantly starts to soothe the burning. As soon as the fire-burning pain in my arm dims, the voices in my head become fainter.

"If not from a fire, where *are* these scars from?" Brezmard asks.

"I'd guess a whip," Norkuz says.

I take a moment to recover before I look around.

"Oh, it's you," I unenthusiastically say to the prince.

"Good morning to you too, Arid," Brezmard says.

"The scars are not from a whip, at least I don't *think* they are. I've had them longer than I can remember," I comment.

"How does your head feel?" Norkuz asks.

"Better. Must've slept it off. How long have I been here?" I ask.

"About three hours, and that *shouldn't* be enough time to recover, especially since your sleep wasn't very restful. And with what Ak'dech told me: slurred words, passing out, symptoms of a *very* hard hit to the head, it should take weeks, if not months, for you to get better, if at all," he says.

"I heal fast," I dismiss.

"No one heals *that* fast," Norkuz says.

"Why am I not in a cell?" I ask.

"We'd rather not have you as a prisoner," Brezmard answers.

"Just the other day, you were telling me I was possibly facing the death sentence. I stole your map... and your family seal. Why am I not in a cell?" I repeat my question.

"Ak'dech and her brother looked at the map and found evidence that it's as incomplete as you say, and the name Dho'zogg sounded like something I'd heard before. I think I know why *your* family heirloom has *my* family seal on it. You see, on Clearhallow, it's tradition for an object, such as a dagger marked with the family seal, to be passed down from the chief to their first-born child. Do you think that could be why your father gave it to you?" he asks.

"No," I say sternly.

"Why not?" he asks.

"It's just a dagger. Besides, this far down the generational line, it's highly unlikely that my father was... that I am... so no," I say even more harshly, "It can't be! And since I am not your prisoner, am I free to go now?

Norkuz picks up part of the sleeve I tore off, then he examines it and says, "*I* have some questions for you."

"About the history of my people? You probably know more than I do," I say.

"Not what I was going to ask, but... you *did* say you visited the ruins of your village, correct? Where?" he says.

"At the foot of a dormant volcano. Mount Tiendys. That's all I know," I say.

"People don't just *live* at the bottom of a volcano," Brezmard doubts.

"It's dormant," I say, not seeing the problem.

"Volcanoes thought to be dormant have been known to erupt," he says, as he crosses his arms and glares at me suspiciously.

41

"There's something very strange about you. Things you do seemingly without a second thought that defy probability," Norkuz says.

"Like what?"

"Ripping chains out of a wall. Breaking Nokk's ribs while he was wearing armor. Then when you escaped, the way you grabbed your dragon as he flew past, that should've ripped your arm right out of its socket. Ak'dech says you killed probably half a dozen warriors by yourself. Then there's you tearing this dragonhide sleeve," he says.

"Not hide, just the scales, sewn onto fabric," I correct.

Norkuz attempts to tear the sleeve and only ends up with a scratch on his hand.

"I was in pain," I shrug.

"Either way, how do you do that? What else can you do?" he asks.

"I don't know what you're talking about. What do you want from me?" I ask, exasperated.

"Your cooperation," Brezmard says.

"Excuse me? My cooperation? Why would I help *you*?"

"Prince Brezmard sees value in asking if you would stay and train with our army. In exchange, we'll help you fight the Rul Coilband and search for your people, if there are indeed any survivors after all this time. It seems to be a mutually beneficial agreement," Norkuz says.

"Mutually beneficial? And what? I have to follow orders from people I don't respect, and have aspects of my freedom taken away until a war that was started generations ago is over? And who knows who else from your ranks might attack me?" I snarl, as I survey everyone in the room.

"Norkuz, handle this, would you? I need to go clear my head," Brezmard scowls and leaves abruptly.

"Pardon the prince. His temper has been a little toasty since you escaped," Norkuz says and frowns disapprovingly, "But we've talked to the knight who attacked you. It shouldn't happen again, and his sister will help keep him in check; although I admit, you may have to watch your back around him. I can't make you any promises about Prince Brezmard, either. Most of the time, he manages to keep his anger under control, but he has more work to do there. Obviously, I understand your concern about being attacked, and I can't say it's unwarranted. Outside of those two, though, I don't foresee any unprovoked assaults from a Dragon Knight. We have strict policies when it comes to fighting our allies," he says.

"Oh, is that what I am? What about all my charges being dropped? Do I get my map back?"

"Brezmard talked to the chief, who reluctantly agreed that if you help us, he'll forget anything ever happened. You work with us, and we'll study the map together to decipher any clues as to the potential whereabouts of any survivors from your village. You may find it difficult to work with some of us, but you stand a better chance with an army beside you than a single dragon. Besides, you may find more freedom here than you are expecting because I feel like you're the kind of person who wouldn't actually follow orders, yet you would probably get away with doing so," he says as he pulls a book from the shelf.

"Hm. Does not following orders actually happen here, or do you just read too many books with edgy heroes and happy endings?" I mock.

"I read books with tragic and sorrowful endings, too," he sneers, as he walks toward the window with the book.

"And who would that make you? The knight in shining armor who slays the dragon and rescues the lost princess? You know, the character without any flaws that said princess is destined to swoon over?"

43

The Lost One: Wrath of the Tyrant

"No, I'd be the prince's right-hand man. You know, the guy no one listens to who ultimately fades into the shadows of the background. Besides, the girl I have my eyes set on is no princess, at least not by the literal definition *or* by fairy tale standards," he says as he peers out the window.

"Ah, mushy. Well, I will admit that trying to fight the world's biggest army on my own isn't exactly the best plan. Just please tell me I don't have to pull 12 or 24-hour shifts guarding a specific area or roaming the palace because my time would be much better spent with other tasks," I plead.

"I don't think that'll be a problem."

Chapter Five: Conflict Resolution

7he sun is not quite beginning to set, but it hovers high above the ocean, as sweat drips from my face in the outdoor training arena of the Dragon Knights. I can feel how flushed my cheeks are from working hard in the heat. My breath comes out almost forcefully, but my sword doesn't quiver as I hold it above my defeated opponent, who's flat on his back after having his feet taken out from under him.

"Please tell me every day is not like this? We've been out here over twelve hours, and it's been nothing but knocking your knights around while they continuously fail to improve," I pant, lowering my sword and allowing the prince to get to his feet.

"I agree. This was a waste of time. You're a lousy teacher," he says.

"You dare insult me? I wanted nothing to do with training *your* troops. I wouldn't have to teach them *anything* if you were any good at your job! Or is it not *your* responsibility to prepare your army for battle?" I shout at him, ready for another fight, but it's not for some sort of safe-training brawl this time.

"Are you *yelling* at me?" Brezmard asks, shocked.

"Well, I'm certainly not yelling at the air!"

"Touch him, and I'll cut your hands off, thief," Nokk, the other hot-headed knight, steps up and says.

"You could try," I say.

Every dragon and every knight in the training arena are on edge. They are watching the situation with anticipation and ready to hop in and defend their prince if necessary. Ak'dech stands between Brezmard and I and says, "I think it's time to call it quits for today. What do you say, Sir Norkuz?"

The Lost One: Wrath of the Tyrant

"Yes. It's been a long and tiresome day for those of us who have been training since dawn. Sir Brezmard, perhaps you should reconsider my advice about not having Arid train four sessions in a day."

"He warned you this ridiculous schedule was idiotic!" I raise my voice louder.

"Norkuz, are you seriously *defending* this criminal?" Nokk says.

"Calm down, dumbass. I've told you. The attack on me wasn't personal. Don't make it so. Let it be in the past," Ak'dech says to her brother.

"Brezmard, let's go for a flight," Norkuz says.

"You, come with me. We should talk," Ak'dech tells me.

"No," I say, climbing onto my dragon's saddle.

"It's about that map of yours," she says.

I hesitate on my departure and tighten my grip on the reins. I clench my teeth, and then I tell her, "Lead the way."

The sun still burns bright as I follow Ak'dech's dragon into the sky. For a few minutes, we fly in silence, as she allows me a while to cool off and calm down.

"I tried to look over the map earlier," she starts, "But I couldn't make sense of it. Even if I were more of a linguist, it would take time for me to decipher the foreign language. However, Norkuz says you can read it."

"I've been studying it for five years. Despite knowing the definitions of the words, I fail to understand the meaning of the passage, but I could probably write a translation," I say.

"With the translation, I could ask our scholars. They have dedicated their lives to knowledge and understanding that which others find cryptic. Surely they could help us decipher the meaning," she says.

I nod and say, "Sure. It's worth a shot. Is that all you wanted to discuss?"

She smiles for a brief moment and says, "Norkuz is working to convince Brezmard to not push you to exhaustion every day. You must have patience with the prince. He is spoiled and quick to anger; however, I would caution restraint with your own frustration. If you manage not to annoy or offend him, he's only moderately agitating," she says.

"No promises. I have a lot to be angry about," I say.

"I'm just impressed all that anger didn't burn out after a full day of hitting people," she says.

"As I said… I have a lot to be angry about," I say.

"Hm," she looks me over.

"What?" I ask, irritated.

"You must be exhausted, but if you are, you hide it very well," she says.

"Exhaustion gets you killed," I say.

"Exhaustion is human," she says, sounding curious rather than scolding or argumentative.

"It's one of the many reasons why humans die so easily."

"So what does that make you if you're not human enough for exhaustion?" she asks, tilting her head in wonder.

"A survivor," I answer.

"Ah… yes, of course," she smiles, "Well, have a pleasant evening, *survivor*."

Her dragon dives away from Nalrai and I and flies off toward the little islet not far from Clearhallow that the knights use for their main training grounds.

"What a weirdo," I tell Nalrai, bemused.

It's the next morning, and I'm stuck in a conference room pacing back and forth. When Brezmard enters I shout, "I thought we were supposed to be looking for my people, but we haven't been. I'm not going to sit around all day not making any progress!"

"What do you propose? We go out and search every centimeter of the world until we find them? We have nowhere to start!" Brezmard says, veins bulging as he fumes.

"The *obvious* place to start is somewhere I suggested we pay a visit to *days* ago! My village. Let's go to Mount Tiendys and search through the ruins again," I say, lowering my voice away from shouting levels.

"What do you expect to find there?" he asks.

"Something. Anything is better than the nothing we have. Let me take a few knights to look for any clues that might still be there, or I swear, if you don't approve this mission, I will rip your arrogant head off!" I threaten.

"Do you think threatening me is going to help you?"

"Both of you settle down. The rest of us are fed up with your constant arguing," Ak'dech moans, rolling her eyes.

"It's a constant headache," Norkuz agrees.

"Can you two *not* be arguing and fighting like children *all* the time?" Ak'dech repeats her complaint, "Besides, I don't think looking through the ruins again is a bad idea because the scholars have yet to find any translation of the map's scribblings."

Brezmard glares at her for a moment before stomping off.

"I'm *not* sitting around any longer," I re-emphasize.

"Understood," Norkuz nods, "But it might benefit you to put together a plan of action to present while I talk to Brezmard and get him to calm down," he says, as he calls for his dragon and follows Brezmard out the door.

"Need help with that action plan?" Ak'dech asks.

"No," I say.

"If you say so," she says with a smug smile.

"What, you think I need your help?" I ask.

"Not necessarily, but I know how to present a plan to Brezmard. I can be a bit helpful in getting him to approve it," she says.

"Great. I will consider running it past you first," I say.

"Hey, listen… it's obvious you don't get along with Brezmard, and I can see why. He's arrogant and not used to his authority being challenged by anyone but his father. You have no experience working under someone because you manage yourself. This must be a difficult change, but you don't have to hate all of us just because you're pissed at the adjustment. If you ever decide that having a friend might not be the worst thing in the world, I'll be around," she says before walking out.

"Yeah, right. I already have a friend," I grumble to myself, "Nalrai! Let's get outta here. I have to think."

The Lost One: Wrath of the Tyrant

After my flight, I decide to meet the Dragon Knights in the conference room to brief them on my plan. I say to everyone listening, "I need enough knights to search the ruins thoroughly and quickly to minimize the risk of a surprise attack, but not so many that it's impossible to move without detection. Since it's a long flight, I want six well-trained knights with me, preferably with dragons that are strong fliers to minimize the time we spend waiting on the dragons to rest. It's going to take several days to get there, and I don't want the journey to be any longer than necessary due to excessive rest periods. Four days at the village should allow a sufficient amount of time to go over every centimeter and recover before we make the journey back. Of course, the ruins of a village at the foot of a volcano don't provide the best concealment. It leaves us wide open to attack. There is, however, another island about half an hour away that is heavily forested and doesn't have any known human inhabitants. It would provide a much better temporary base of operations while we scour the ruins. The total mission time should take no more than two weeks."

"I'll admit, that's not the worst plan I've heard, but I'm not going to give you six knights. I'll allow four, and I already have them selected," Brezmard says.

"Seriously?" I fume, "I need six."

"Apparently, you're a formidable warrior by yourself. The smaller the team, the easier it is to conceal. I've picked out a team leader, healer, navigator, and scientist for you to take along," he says.

"Team leader? I thought I would lead the team to *my* village," I say, "And why would I need a navigator and a scientist? I could give you the tour."

"I'm sure you know your way around, but I'd feel more comfortable with a navigator. As for the scientist, who better to search for answers? Especially one with acute attention to detail and a knack for spotting anything unusual. And the team leader? Well, did you really think I'd take any other position?"

"You? *You're* coming with us?" I scowl.

"Despite what you might think about me, I'm a decent fighter with years of experience in leading and conducting similar operations," he says.

"Doesn't mean you're *good* at leading," I murmur, displeased, "Besides, if you're not *here*, who's going to lead your mighty army?"

"My nation is not so reliant on me that I can't occasionally disappear for a couple of weeks. Between my father and the dozens of other commanders, the Dragon Knights are perfectly capable of defending the island while I'm away," he says.

"So, if this is what it takes to get the mission approved, who are the others you mentioned?"

"Norkuz as the healer, of course. The scientist is Ak'dech. The navigator... you're not going to appreciate this so much, but it is *not* negotiable. It is Ak'dech's brother, Nokk," he says.

"You mean the kid who tried to kill me in prison?"

"Yes. That one, but don't worry. I'm sure Ak'dech can make sure he behaves," he says.

"Prince Brezmard," Ak'dech says.

"What?" he raises an eyebrow.

Ak'dech hesitates as she considers protesting having her brother come along, but she decides it wasn't worth arguing about.

"Never mind," she mumbles.

"These are my top knights. We leave two days from now, at dusk. I'll adjust the guard schedule to accommodate our absences, and I suggest everyone rest up."

The Lost One: Wrath of the Tyrant

"You can't be serious. You're going to just take the lead? This is my mission! We're going to *my* home to find *my* people! You expect me to hand you the reins and let you do things any way you want?" I say with burning anger bubbling up my throat.

"This is *my* home. These are *my* soldiers. I'm not going to let you command my knights on a dangerous mission when all I know about you is that you're a thief, determined to find your people at any cost. I don't know that you care at all about the lives of my Dragon Knights. I can not allow you to take charge of my team as you rush into this war with your blind thirst for vengeance," he says.

"Vengeance? You think this is about vengeance? And you think I'd let my team die? I'm not the one who's unconcerned with the preservation of lives! Let me remind you there's a little island out there with people living on it that you just pursued me from, people that *you'd* be willing to let die if it didn't affect your island's interest. Meanwhile, I'm the only one who came to their rescue when rogue warriors attacked them. Look, I know I can't win this fight alone. As it is, the odds aren't looking so great with your *whole* army supposedly on my side because the Rul Coilband's army is much larger, but I'm not the one you should worry about letting down the team! You know what? I can't work with people I don't trust, and I don't trust you!" I yell, spitting on the ground in disgust, flustered.

I can feel my face reddening in rage. I take a step toward him with my fist half-raised.

"Wanna switch dance partners for this one?" Ak'dech asks Norkuz.

"Gladly," he says, stepping in front of me and putting his hands on my shoulders to keep me from taking a swing at Brezmard.

"Let's go chat," Ak'dech says to Brezmard, as she leads the runt away.

"Arid, take a breath," Norkuz says.

The sudden removal of the target of my anger is disorienting. I was fully invested in this argument, but once they separated us, I didn't know where to place that anger.

"Conflict resolution is a skill that has proven most useful in many negotiations between the prince and foreign nations. By now, Ak'dech and I are highly adept at keeping Brezmard out of any serious altercations with foreign ambassadors. We've also become exceptional at apologizing for his behavior as we get him to calm down," he says.

"Come to think of it, you've been doing a fair bit of separating us before it came to physical blows... for the most part. I see now. Brezmard doesn't keep Clearhallow prospering, does he? It's because of you two. This island would fall apart without you," I deduce.

"Most likely. I'll admit though, I'm doubtful we can change his mind about his plan for your mission, but to be honest, it's not actually a bad plan. Knowing what you know now, it's safe to say that Brezmard won't be doing as much leading as he thinks he will. Since Ak'dech and I are both coming, we can keep him out of your way for the most part. We'll be in control of the situation. As for Nokk, his reasoning for bringing him makes sense. His ability to find shelter and use nature and the terrain to our advantage to hide and gather food has saved the lives of dozens of Dragon Knights. For a stealth mission, we need a good navigator with stellar survival and map reading skills, and he's the best. Ak'dech knows how to handle him. She'll keep him out of your hair as much as she can. Besides, after your previous confrontation, I doubt he's eager for round two," he says.

"Isn't he still recovering from that? Taking a soldier into the field when they're not at their best isn't usually a very good idea," I say.

"He's recovered enough. He's tough, and his ribs are healing just fine with minimal pain. In a fight, he'll be ready, but hopefully, his talent in avoiding potential threats means we won't have to find that out for sure," he says.

The Lost One: Wrath of the Tyrant

"Okay, I might not trust Brezmard, but you at least seem reasonable. Do me a favor and tell the prince I accept his proposition."

Chapter Six: Living Nightmare

*I*t's the next day, and the Dragon Knights and I walk along the south side of Clearhallow beach to mount our dragons to begin our expedition.

"Here, I found these. Thought maybe you'd like them back," Ak'dech says, offering me my mask and hood.

"Oh, finally... thanks. There's nothing like the feeling that the wind is going to rip my face off every time I fly to remind me I'm no longer free to do as I please," I say.

Then she says, "I've seen your dragon outrace our fleet. Out of curiosity, how fast does he fly?"

"I've never been too good at math or speed or anything. I just know he's fast," I say.

"Well, the rest of us can only go about 475 kilometers an hour, and we might have to slow down even more than that due to the distance," she says, fitting her own flight mask over her mouth and nose before mounting her dragon.

"I'll try not to be too impatient," I say, tucking my braid into my hood before I climb onto Nalrai.

"Everyone ready?" Brezmard asks.

"And waiting," I confirm.

"Let's get this over with. I don't particularly appreciate working with a criminal," Nokk says as he glares at me.

"Nokk," Ak'dech warns.

"Fine. If you need me, I'll be keeping an eye on the ground to make sure we don't veer off course," he frowns.

"Good. Glad to hear that you're willing to focus on the *one* reason you're coming along," I say.

"I'll do my job. I just hope you can do yours... except, I can't seem to remember exactly what that would be again. Are we stealing something?" he says.

"Nokk!" Ak'dech repeats.

My hands clench the side of the saddle in frustration.

"To be fair, he makes a good poi—" Brezmard says but gets interrupted by Norkuz before he can finish.

"Arid is here because this is her mission. She's here because she's better at fighting than anyone you've ever met, and that could be the key to finally gaining an edge in this war we've been fighting for longer than any of us have been alive. If we can find her people and free them from whatever captivity they may be in, we could gain their support as well," Norkuz says.

"Do you really think her people are alive? In hiding somewhere? I'd believe imprisoned... maybe... because Ma'roog has been known to take slaves from the villages he raids, but he rarely goes to such lengths to destroy every trace of a village. Her people must've really irked him somehow to kill them all off," Nokk says.

"My aunt is alive and forced to fight for the Rul Coilband. She says some of them survived and are imprisoned. They need help," I say.

"Someone who *says* she's your aunt," Brezmard snarks.

"She's also someone who knew my name. She recognized me instantly and passed up an opportunity to kill me in battle. She's someone I've seen before, a long, long time ago... somewhere. Why would a Rul warrior know my name and spare my life if she didn't know me? I'm a nobody—a small-time thief who wanders from place to place without leaving a significant impact anywhere. It's not like I'm on Ma'roog's hit list. I doubt he cares about some kid who got away from a burning village once upon a time."

"Just… don't get your hopes up too high, okay? Finding them is still a long shot. I'm sure you're aware of what Ma'roog is capable of. He didn't become the most powerful tyrant in history by having a loose hold on his prisoners. He keeps all his assets safely tucked away in secure, unknown locations," Ak'dech says.

"So I've heard," I say quietly.

"Well, what are we waiting for? Let's get going," Norkuz says.

The past two days of flying and stopping on various islands to rest have been uneventful and quiet. However, I think a few members of the group are just about losing their minds from the silence, but because the Rul Coilband army controls the southern half of Vrarg, we must be quiet and steer clear of inhabited areas. Luckily, we have been successful in avoiding villagers while moving through enemy territory because it can be dangerous to make a lot of noise, as it may attract attention. Norkuz, in particular, has been tense, fidgety, and on edge since we landed on Zram, but his noise discipline is holding. The next day, we land on an island called Zorzim so our dragons can rest. This island is heavily forested with multiple streams of fresh water running through it, and like we did yesterday, we'll spend a few hours here during the brightest part of the day until we're ready to continue. As soon as we land, Nokk and his dragon, Nynnu, perform a quick search of the surrounding area, searching for the best site to rest while looking for signs of danger.

"All clear," he reports.

"I'll take lookout this time," Ak'dech volunteers.

"I'm going to see if there are any rabbits or anything around to catch and eat," I say, stepping over a cluster of tree roots protruding from the ground.

"Wait—" Ak'dech starts.

"I'll be fine," I say over my shoulder curtly.

The Lost One: Wrath of the Tyrant

No one follows behind me, and it only takes a few minutes before I stumble across the path of a scrawny, brown rabbit. My dagger is already in hand, and as an experienced hunter, it should be no problem to catch it. I take a silent step towards it, careful to avoid branches or crunchy leaves.

"Lost child of Tiendys," a voice whispers in my head.

Startled, I spin around and lose my footing, landing in an entanglement of roots on the ground. The voice comes with the memory of a face that's rough, scarred, and covered in soot. It's deep and gruff, sounding almost like the speaker is gargling rocks in his throat.

"Who's there?" I ask, wiping sweat out of my eyes and blinking rapidly to clear them.

My breaths come quickly, and my heart is racing with a feeling I don't experience often—terror. My eyes dart around quickly to every shadow in sight because the rabbit ran when I tripped, along with any other creatures nearby. The only movement is in the slight breeze as it blows through the trees, tickling the leaves and branches. I remain on the ground for a few seconds before scrambling to my feet with my senses burning on high alert. I hold my dagger defensively as I look around. There's no one. After a while, my heart rate begins to slow down. For some reason, this raspy voice has haunted my dreams lately, along with another pleasant voice, which is like the echo of a siren's song from ancient myths. It's enchanting and soothing, like a woman singing a lullaby to a giggling child, but that voice always fades, giving way to darkness and the gargling tones from the harsh voice—the voice with a terrifying scarred face, revealing firelight from a burning village flickering across it. It's the same voice that harmonizes with the dying screams of innocent families and the desperate plea of my mother as he turned from massacring my father. As the memories drift away, I slowly lower my dagger and lean against a tree trunk as I take deep breaths to clear my head to purge it from the nightmares I'm so desperately trying to avoid.

A shout from Norkuz draws my attention away from any lingering imagery in my mind, and I notice a thin pillar of smoke rising from the area we touched down on. I race toward the spot, ready to fight.

"Come on! Subdue it!" Norkuz yells.

I come upon a different battle than the one I was expecting. Instead of a mob of Rul Warriors, a single foe dragon stands tall, roaring and spreading its wings in an attempt to scare off the Dragon Knights. Smoke billows from between its sharp teeth. It bends down and screeches in Nokk's face, sending him tumbling backward as the dragon's hot breath makes contact with his skin. Nokk lets out a cry and grabs at his face in pain, rolling on the ground. Our dragons are wary and blasting at it from a distance. Even Nalrai hangs back, cautious of his opponent's might. I've seen some large dragons, but none of them compare to the vastness of this particular beast. The largest of our dragons is dwarfed by the span of *one* of its wings. It has thick, gray scales, and it likely lives in the cave we were going to take cover in for the next few hours. Nynnu, Nokk's dragon, darts in and drags him away from the fight just before the cave-dwelling dragon plants its ginormous front claws in the ground where Nokk was lying, which causes the island to shake, causing Brezmard to stumble, lose his balance, and almost fall to the ground.

"Whoa! Easy there, bud," I call out to the dragon, stopping a safe distance away.

Its head swivels in my direction, swaying, but not looking directly at me.

"Nalrai!" I call.

My friend flies around the mountainous dragon, weaving through the trees near the small grassy clearing by the cave where the battle takes place. I grab his saddle as he whizzes by. Not a second later, a molten ball of fire crashes into the exact spot I was standing. The beast roars in pain as Norkuz and his dragon manage to fly in close enough for Norkuz's sword to slice through part of its ankle. Before it can reach out to retaliate against Norkuz, Ak'dech distracts it by shooting an arrow into its belly.

The Lost One: Wrath of the Tyrant

Meanwhile, Nalrai has been using his incredible agility to dodge the flailing wingtip and tail of the beast, but his speed is greatly slowed by the effort to avoid and maneuver around the oversized creature's obstacles. I grip my dagger tighter as we get closer to its neck, and I pick a spot behind its skull to target. Somehow, we catch its attention. Its head swings towards us as its wings suddenly extend fully, smacking me right in the chest as it screams at me. I slam into the rocks on the edge of the cave, and all the air is forced painfully from my lungs before I fall to the ground. I will admit: this is the occasion where a metal set of armor would have been nice—because each forced, shaky breath comes with a sharp pain. There are splotches of black in my vision. My ears are ringing. I can taste blood as I cough it up. I grit my teeth and push myself off the ground slightly with my arms, grunting as a grating sound indicates my upper arm is snapped in half. I look around for my dragon. He lies next to a tree, wing bent at an awkward angle, and the only movement I see is his shaking and trembling. Brezmard takes a few steps back from the dragon, afraid, but at least he doesn't back down and run. Honestly, just laying here and passing out sounds like the most appealing option at the moment. I feel like I'm already almost there.

"You don't get to die today," I growl, as I look back at Nalrai.

I focus on my anger. It's the only thing left to fuel me in this fight, and it's the only thing powerful enough to distract me from the pain radiating through me. I force myself to my knees first, then I use the stone wall I smashed into to get to my feet while feeling around on the ground for my dagger before I rise. My vision is blurred, and the spot where my skull made impact with the stone throbs. My ribs feel like they shattered on impact, and they grind together with every motion I make. My legs, although uninjured, shake under me as I try to stand. I pull my mask down, unsheathe my sword, stick it into the ground, and lean on it. Fortunately, I'm too dizzy and angry to acknowledge my ability to be of any help in my condition, but doubt tries to bubble up to the surface of my mind. I have no idea how I'm going to aid the others like this, so doubt holding me back is the last thing I need right now.

"Arid, what are you doing? Lay down," Norkuz says sternly, as his firm hand grabs my arm.

Fortunately, it's my good arm.

"No," I say, wiping blood from my lips.

"You're injured—bad! You need to lay down," he insists.

I said no while twisting my arm away from him and walking forward toward the beast.

He grabs me again.

"Let go of me," I say, swinging my broken limb at him.

My arm hurts, but I complain silently as my palm strikes his chest plate, sending him backward a few steps.

He runs forward again and says, "Are you insane? You can't fight like this."

"You're barely holding it at bay. You need me," I say.

"Norkuz!" Brezmard yells for help.

Norkuz looks torn for a moment.

"Be careful," he tells me, as he runs off to help the prince.

"Not a chance," I mutter.

Nokk is back in the fight; although, with burns around his eyes, I'm not sure he can see so well because those burns look excruciating. However, admittedly, the knights work together well, even despite the situation. They're in sync with their dragons and have managed to put together an organized attack, but it isn't enough. They're barely holding it together. Let's see... how to beat it. *Think!* Cave dwellers aren't usually an aggressive species. Why did it attack? Maybe it's defending itself... or it feels threatened.

The Lost One: Wrath of the Tyrant

Maybe we could run, but with Nalrai down, I'm not sure we could get away fast enough. My head wound makes my thoughts hazy, but I must figure this out. How do you make a potentially territorial dragon defending itself feel less threatened? For all I know, it could have little whelps in that cave. Hmm, what else do I know about it? I've been observing it, and it looks in the general direction of a noise but rarely locks in on the source with its eyes. When it can't pinpoint what it's hearing, it'll flail around until it locates it. I think it's blind. Therefore, its other senses are likely heightened. Sound, touch, smell.... wait! Can it smell our fear? Does that agitate it more? Maybe I can use its functioning senses to make it feel safe somehow. I stare at it intently, watching its behavior closely. Scars. Why does it have so many scars? It isn't unheard of for wild dragons to get in fights with wolves, birds of prey, or other dragons, but I've yet to see a wild dragon with this number of scars, especially one so ferocious as this one. The scars are clustered on its back and face and across its eyes. This is not a natural blindness. This has been caused by trauma, definitely *human* intervention, as they are the only creatures that can cause so much damage to such a large dragon.

"Back up, and drop your weapons! Then hold still!" I shout, dropping my own weapons and running in front of the beast.

"Look what it did to my face! Are you crazy? It'll kill us!" Nokk says.

"That is a possibility, but do it," I say.

A single sword clatters on a pile of rocks. It's Ak'dech's. She backs away from the dragon slowly. Norkuz follows suit.

"Good... Good..." I say in a soft assuring voice, as I keep my eyes fixed on the dragon.

It roars in confusion as it hears the sound of weapons being thrown aside and discarded. The other dragons retreat to the tree line, wings spread in a defensive stance.

"Nokk, Brezmard," Ak'dech whispers, encouraging them to drop their weapons.

After another moment, Brezmard drops his sword and walks away. Nokk thinks for a few seconds longer before finally joining us, while the dragon is holding still, puffing and listening.

"There we go..." I shuffle towards it cautiously, allowing my heavy breaths to carry the sound of a soothing tone.

It huffs, drawing away slightly as I approach.

"No more fighting," I say, as I step all the way up to its claws, gently placing my hand on it.

The creature roars and spreads its wings again, baring its teeth and stepping back. I hold my breath as its defenses are activated again, but instead of fighting, it turns and disappears quickly back into its cave. My knees crack in the grass as I collapse onto them.

"That was... how did you do that?" Norkuz asks, as he kneels beside me, immediately looking at the wound on my head.

"I paid attention," I say, "Is Nalrai okay?"

"We'll take care of him, but promise me, you'll rest," he says.

"You should know better... I've never been good at following orders," I grin.

"I'm serious. Looks like we're going to be here longer than anticipated, so get some sleep," he says, as he stands and runs over to look at Nalrai's wounds.

"Not a chance," I say.

Chapter Seven: The Calm

*L*ater that day, while we sit in the tent under shade trees in the forest, Norkuz secures the make-shift splint around my arm and says to me, "This should help... and here's something for the pain: a slightly alcoholic syrup with feverfew, turmeric and ashwagandha, but I'll warn you... it doesn't taste good. However, Nalrai is sleeping more comfortably thanks to it," he says, proudly looking at Nalrai napping in the corner of the tent.

"I think I'll pass," I say.

Norkuz shrugs, stands, and says, "I should go look for herbs and anything else I can use to replace some of the medicines I've used. Ak'dech is looking for shelter, so Brezmard, if there's any danger, you're the first line of defense."

"Wait... you're leaving me with these two?" I panic and yell at the thought of being left with Brezmard and Nokk, "Norkuz, don't you dare leave me with them! I'll take that pain medicine now!"

"Sorry, we have to be prepared. The longer we go without equipment or real shelter, the higher our chances of running into something we can't handle," he says, as he hands the medicine to me.

I chug it desperately.

"Whoa, take it easy. It's not guaranteed to put you to sleep. It's just supposed to help take the edge off. Ever had fermented ale before?" he asks.

"Like alcohol? You have any? I'll take that, too," I say.

"Uh, no. I don't need any of you drunk at each other's throats, okay? I won't be gone long," he says.

"Norkuz, don't leave me with them... Norkuz!" I shout.

"Kemoss and I will keep watch from the air. We'll see anything approaching, but if we miss anything, holler," Brezmard says to Nokk and I as he leaves the tent and mounts his dragon.

At least there's one less jerk to worry about, I think to myself.

"So, uh…" Nokk starts.

"Don't talk," I say.

"No, I… I'm sorry," he says.

"What?" I ask after a moment.

"I haven't given you a chance. That's unfair. It was also… not a good idea to attack you in jail, but I would *die* for my sister. All I could think about that day was her being hurt, and you were the one who hurt her. Now that I think about it, attacking a restrained prisoner is kind of… *really* messed up," he says.

"Why apologize now?" I ask.

He shrugs, looks away, and says, "Back there when we were fighting the dragon, how… *why* did you get back up?"

"Nalrai," I say.

"I didn't realize you cared about anything other than yourself, but when I saw you still fighting that dragon even after the hit you took, I assumed it was for something you cared about. I was blinded by my anger until I saw that, but you're brave," he says.

"You know, I wasn't the only one injured who got back up to fight," I say.

"As I said, I'd die for my sister," he whispers.

"You really admire her," I acknowledge.

The Lost One: Wrath of the Tyrant

"She saved my life about eight years ago when we were boating with our parents. I was eight. She was eleven. We survived the accident, but our parents didn't. She has spent every moment since protecting me. I try to do the same for her," he says.

"You both chose a pretty dangerous job," I say.

"I know, " he says.

"You know, it was nothing personal," I say.

"As I said, I was wrong," he says.

"Thank you… for the apology. Truce?" I ask, as I hold out my hand.

He shakes it and says, "Don't mistake my apology for anything more. I'll agree to a truce, but I'm not going to be your friend."

"I wouldn't dream of being your friend. My alliance to Clearhallow is not for the sake of *friendship*. I don't trust Brezmard. Or you. Not sure about Ak'dech. Maybe Norkuz. But none of you are my *friends*," I say.

"Works for me," he says.

"Good," I say.

There's a part of his tone that's cold and dark. I search his eyes in an attempt to find it there, too, but all I see is the pain he's trying to hide.

"Ak'dech says you don't remember much about your village," he says, lying back against a rock.

"No, not really," I say.

"That sucks," he says.

I change the subject and say, "I didn't know the Dragon Knights allowed you to join their army at sixteen?"

"Sixteen is when you're legally an adult on Clearhallow, so it's the minimum age requirement to join the army. However, most can't join because you have to graduate from trade school first, then make it through the selection process and training. The normal age to graduate is seventeen, but I graduated early," he says.

"Was Brezmard guaranteed a position with the Dragon Knights?" I ask.

"As the prince? Yes. He's trained his whole life for this. When he turned sixteen, his father started testing him by slowly giving him more leadership opportunities. Over the past year, he's earned his father's trust centimeter by centimeter," he says.

"So Brezmard's father trusts him. How does his mother feel about him being out leading the army?" I ask.

"She died before he started his training, but him leading the army was always part of the plan. You know... tradition and such," he shrugs.

"I'm noticing a trend. We all have lost loved ones. So, let me guess. Norkuz has dead family, too? And that's why he dedicated his life to healing and protecting others?"

"I don't know. Norkuz has never mentioned his family. To be honest, I don't really know *anything* about Norkuz. It's as if being a Dragon Knight is the only thing he's ever done outside of training to be a healer," he says.

"That's... suspicious," I say, "Maybe Norkuz *shouldn't* be trusted. People who hide their past usually do so for a reason."

He smiles and says, "I'd trust Norkuz with my life any day of the week."

"And Ak'dech. How long has she been with the Dragon Knights?" I ask.

"Two years," he says, "About the same time as Norkuz, but I've only been in a few months. I joined to fight beside her and to keep her safe."

"You know, Ak'dech is strong; she doesn't need you to protect her."

"She plays tough, Arid Dho'zogg, but she's not as fearless as she pretends to be. She has nightmares, but sometimes she has them during the day when she's awake, too. She fears constantly, and that's why she tries so hard to prove herself to everyone else. She thinks if she can pretend she's unafraid, someday she'll believe it," he says.

"She's a good pretender," I say.

"Yes, she—" he sits up suddenly.

"What is it?" I ask.

"Why would I tell you that? It's none of your business! I've never told anyone. Why would I tell you?" he says, both angry and confused.

"I don't know, but if you're concerned that it'll make me see her as weak, you don't have to worry. I don't," I say.

"No, no, no," he mutters to himself as he stands up, agitated.

"No need to freak out," I say.

"You don't understand. I can't be your friend! I don't want to be your friend! Why would I tell you? It's none of your business!" he yells.

"Ohhhh kay…" I say cautiously.

"What am I doing?" he asks, running his fingers through his hair in distress.

"Are you okay?" I ask, uneasy at his reaction.

"I… I'm going on a flight with Nynnu. *Don't* talk to me," Nokk says, as he storms out the tent and mounts his dragon.

The island is now much quieter than I would've imagined. There are no birds or crickets chirping. No squirrels running through the trees. No breeze rustling the leaves. Even the voice tugging constantly at the back of my mind, threatening to break into my thoughts, is quiet for now. The only thing I hear is Nalrai's breathing as he sleeps. It's very calm and peaceful at the moment, but the island's serenity puts me on edge for some reason. Finally a quiet moment, but it feels like the calm before the storm.

Chapter Eight: Before

*B*ecause of Nalrai's broken wing, we've been unable to identify a suitable place to take shelter, so we've been on the same island for two weeks sleeping under the treetops—practically out in the open. We've been fortunate to not come across any more trouble so far, except now the storm clouds are blowing in. The bad weather hasn't hit yet, but as the sky turns dark, I agree with the assessment Ak'dech and Nokk gave: it's going to be a rough storm to sit through in the forest.

For the most part, my traveling companions have been civil, but with the coming storm, diminishing supplies, and constant proximity to each other, we've all been somewhat easier to annoy. I've tried not to talk to anyone, and I have been fairly successful because Nokk hasn't been as bothersome. In fact, I think he's avoiding me as much as I'm avoiding everyone else, which works for me. As we work to fix up the area we've been camping in, Brezmard and Nokk start bickering about some pointless argument they had during training back on Clearhallow. While they quarrel back and forth, we tie together rope and vines to build a wall, which is supposed to provide protection from the elements. After that, we lean it against a tree trunk. It hasn't been helpful at all because it isn't large enough. It leaks and provides very minimal protection from anything, but it was an attempt.

"Shouldn't you be resting that arm?" Ak'dech asks, as I tie rope around a branch that is still alive and attached to the tree.

"It's fine… barely even sore anymore," I say.

"That's odd," she comments.

"Yeah, I guess," I say, tightening the knot.

"Brezmard!" Norkuz yells, as his dragon wildly comes flying through the forest, almost crashing through the trees, breaking several branches on the way down.

"Trouble?" Brezmard asks Norkuz.

"Or an opportunity," Norkuz says, ecstatic, "There are pirates out there, and their ship is full of loot: food, money, all sorts of things. This could be a chance to get some much-needed supplies!"

"One problem with that. They're pirates. Pirates steal. Even if we had anything to trade with, I've never known a pirate to trade for something he can take," Nokk points out, raising an eyebrow, "They're dangerous. We should stay out of sight."

"I know what pirates do, Nokk. They're criminals, but what if we had something to offer them that they *can't* steal for themselves?" Norkuz asks, still excited.

"Like what?" Brezmard asks.

"I'm... still working on that," Norkuz says, as his energy diminishes a little, "But if we have a chance to gather resources, we need to take it."

Ak'dech smiles like she has a crazy idea.

"Why trade for something that we can take," Nokk says and grins as he catches on to her plot.

"Um, no. Do you know how difficult it would be to sneak aboard undetected and take what we need without being caught?" I ask.

"Arid, how good are you at conning people out of their money?" Ak'dech asks.

"Conning? You think I can talk a pirate out of his gold?" I ask, "That's ridiculous."

"Maybe, but we can't let that ship leave without you convincing them to do a few things for us, including getting supplies off that ship," Brezmard chips in.

I stare around at the four of them. They're all staring back at me expectantly.

The Lost One: Wrath of the Tyrant

I sigh and say, "You're all crazy, but let's see what a smile and a 'please' can get us, other than a dead thief," I mumble, sounding defeated as I walk toward my dragon.

"We'll hide just out of sight. If you're in trouble, we'll be right there," Ak'dech says.

"Fine. Watch out for Nalrai, too. He's in no condition to fight," I say.

"Neither are you, so let's hope it doesn't come to that," Norkuz says.

I tug at the splint on my arm and say, "I don't think this is helping anymore, and I'd rather go in *not* looking like I'm completely helpless."

Norkuz helps me take the splint off.

"How close is their ship?" I ask.

"They'll be passing the beach in probably twenty minutes."

"Alright, let's see if I can charm loot off the pirates who stole it."

Twenty minutes later, I'm waving down a pirate ship. Have I mentioned this is crazy? I'm pretty sure I mentioned it's crazy. What's worse is they seem to have spotted me and are changing course to greet me. I nervously run my fingers through my hair. I figure it's better to look like an unassuming, stranded kid than a mysterious traveler, so hood and mask off, hair down, smile up. I kept the dagger, but ditched the sword and left it with my teammates as they hide close by behind the rocks and trees.

"Ahoy," I say, as they toss their anchor overboard and one of them jumps off to talk to me.

The pirate glares at me suspiciously, trying to size me up.

"Morning," he grunts.

"Are you the captain?" I ask.

"No. What do you want?" he replies gruffly.

"I want to speak to your captain and request a trade because I was flying with my dragon, and we landed here for a break and were attacked by a local, very wild dragon. My beast broke his wing, and we've been stranded here while he recovers. I would very much appreciate if I could barter for some of your supplies?" I say, as innocently as I can.

"You out of your mind? This is a pirate ship. We don't barter. Besides, I don't see you having anything that'd be worth stealing," he says.

"Let me at least talk to your captain, please?" I ask.

He looks me over again and says, "I can arrange a talk with the first mate."

"Thank you," I smile.

"Not the words I'd use," he says, twisting my arms behind my back and pushing me toward the ship.

"Ow! Am I a prisoner now?" I ask, wincing at the harsh movement of my sore arm.

"That's up to the first mate," he growls, "Now call off your friends. We saw them setting up for an ambush a long way off."

"No, not an ambush... a safety net," I say.

"Come out and play, Dragon Knights!" he calls.

The Dragon Knights oblige and come out of their hiding spots to join me. I take a mental inventory of what we pass as we walk aboard the ship. There is lots of money!

The Lost One: Wrath of the Tyrant

"This went well," Brezmard mutters sarcastically.

"I don't know what your game plan is, knights, but if any of you, or your dragons, make a move, your friend here will be dead before you can complete it," the pirate says.

Many of the pirate's shipmates gather around while he holds a knife to my throat.

"Easy, we're not looking for a fight. We're looking for a trade," Brezmard says.

"Silence! The first mate will come and talk to you. Then he will decide what we'll do with you," the pirate says.

The doors to the cabin below deck open as Irbor, the first mate, walks out.

"Well, this should be interesting," I say, as I recognize the man.

He scowls instantly upon seeing me. Clearly, he remembers me too.

"Now, what are the good Dragon Knights of Clearhallow doing associating with a lying, cheating thief like this one?" he says, grimacing in my direction.

"Hey, I didn't cheat, nor did I steal anything that evening. Well, not from you. It was a misunderstanding," I say, smiling nervously.

"You know her?" the pirate holding me asks.

"Make sure you have a tight hold. You wouldn't expect her to hit so hard, but I've seen her in a brawl, " the first mate says.

"Look, I... uh... I apologize for that. It was nothing personal. It was a convenient distraction to escape. You were drunk. I was in trouble, and a fight breaking out definitely slowed down the bartender," I jokingly say with a shrug.

"Troublemaker," he says, then he spits at my feet as an insult.

"But trouble is not what I'm looking for today. I need help. We're stranded here while we recover from a fight with a wild dragon. We need something to make a shelter, and food would be nice too," I say.

"I don't trust you, and the Dragon Knights don't trade with pirates. It's one of the few places we've never been successful in raiding. So what do *you* have to offer?" the first mate asks.

"She doesn't. I do," Brezmard says.

"Who are you, knight?" he asks.

"Prince Brezmard of Clearhallow—one of the wealthiest nations on planet Vrarg. You give us supplies, and I'll give you a free pass to Clearhallow. You can talk to my father. He will compensate you for your assistance… generously," Brezmard offers.

"How generously?" the first mate asks, interested.

"You'll have to discuss that with him, but I promise, you will be satisfied with the trade," he says.

"A most appealing offer," another pirate who's been listening from the upper deck says as he walks down the stairs.

"Captain," the first mate says and nods to the newcomer while stepping back, allowing him to negotiate.

"The Prince of Clearhallow, huh? What is stopping us from taking you prisoner and holding you for ransom? Surely we could get a lot for that," the captain says.

"You sail into Clearhallow holding me prisoner, and my knights will kill you on sight," Brezmard says, "Trust me, my offer is worth more than the risk you run holding me for ransom."

"So you claim," the captain says, as he looks at me curiously.

"You look most familiar," he tells me.

The Lost One: Wrath of the Tyrant

"That's odd. I'm usually very good at remembering the faces of those I befriended, or those I steal from or rip off. I don't remember you," I say.

"And yet, I feel I've seen your face before... a very long time ago, perhaps," he says.

"Doubtful," I say.

He grabs my chin and tilts my head a couple different directions while examining me. I tug at the firm hands holding my arms behind me. Although Norkuz has kept Nalrai heavily sedated while he recovers, he growls as I struggle to get loose.

"Easy, child," the captain says, letting go of my face, "Do you have scars, by chance, on your arm?"

"Who are you?" I ask.

The captain ignores me while looking me up and down to find anything else to confirm my identity. He notices the dagger sheath around my waist and the handle marked with the seal.

"Ah, yes... the dagger. Let her go, Akrar," the captain says to the pirate holding my arms behind my back.

The knife disappears from beside my throat, and my arms are released. My hands instantly grab the captain's throat. He holds a hand up to halt his crew from attacking me. I slowly let go as he refuses to fight.

"Who are you?" I repeat my question.

"You first. Your name is Arid Dho'zogg?" he asks, coughing.

"Yes," I say.

"I knew the man who wielded that dagger before you. He was a good person—his wife too. You look very much like her. They were friends of mine... before I was a pirate. Last I saw you, you were barely old enough to walk. I'm sorry for your loss," he says.

"You knew my parents?" I ask.

"It's a small world, sweetheart. Prince Brezmard, your offer is acceptable. We will help you find what you need and head to Clearhallow for compensation. This is a one-time deal for a debt I thought I'd never get a chance to repay," he says.

"Captain, this girl is a thief," the first mate complains.

"Are we not also thieves? Don't think I'm going soft, Irbor. I owe my life to her father, and I never got the chance to thank him for it. Even pirates can carry an ounce of honor with them," the captain says, "Prince Brezmard, I would like your promise written down before you touch anything because the word of a pirate is no good to the chief of a village."

"I merely need parchment and a quill with ink," Brezmard says.

"To be included with our fee," the captain says.

"Of course."

"You knew my parents?" I repeat.

"Child, we will talk *after* business has been taken care of," he says.

As Brezmard starts writing, he tells the knights, "Start looking for what we need," then he warns the pirates, "Sail into the harbor flying a white flag. The patrol will be wary, but so long as you don't draw your weapons, they will not harm you or your crew. Insist upon seeing my father, Chief Firestride, and hand them this message. He will discuss payment with you. Arid, I need your dagger," he says, as he signs the bottom of the page.

"Why?" I ask.

"Only briefly," he says, rolling his eyes.

The Lost One: Wrath of the Tyrant

I hand the dagger to him. He slits his wrist and lets the blood drip onto the paper before he rolls the handle of the dagger in the blood, leaving an imprint of the seal.

"You forget your seal?" I ask.

"Shut up," he sneers, wiping the blood off my weapon before giving it back.

The captain carefully reads over the message before smiling in satisfaction.

"My parents... how did you know them?" I ask.

"I was a merchant and captain of a trade ship from Xymrar—an island not far from yours. I negotiated directly with your father on occasion. He was always very fair," he says.

"So my father was a merchant?" I ask.

"What? You don't... I suppose you *were* very young. No, he wasn't a merchant. Have you not wondered why your dagger has the same symbol that is so important to the family of Prince Brezmard?" he asks.

"My father wasn't chief," I say.

"So you *do* know, but you don't want to acknowledge it. After all, that would make *you* the rightful chief of a dead village. Very well, we can play the game where you pretend that isn't the case," he says.

"You're a liar," I say.

"You're not wrong about that. I am indeed a liar, but not everything that comes from my tongue is a lie. Your father was a good man: fair and courageous. I was a good, honest merchant once upon a time. As I said, he saved my life, and now that debt is repaid. So, Chief Arid of Likenhallow, my first mate will assist you and your friends with your purchase, and I shall bid you farewell," he says, then walks away abruptly.

"Wait! Do you know if anyone else survived? There was a warrior who claimed she was my aunt, and she said some of my people were alive," I call out.

He pauses then turns back toward me to issue a warning, "I know your mother *did* have a sister, and if that woman you speak of says she's your aunt, stay far away from her."

"Why?" I ask.

He gives his answer as he starts down the stairs, "Because once upon a time, I was a better person… and now… "

Then he disappears below deck.

"That's not an answer!" I yell.

"Told you I couldn't con some stupid pirates out of their treasure," I grumble to Ak'dech as the able dragons drag our new equipment through the trees back to camp.

"If it were any other set of pirates, I bet you could. Ones who didn't watch us hide in the rocks and trees… and ones you haven't picked bar fights with," she says, "It's okay though. It turned out alright."

"Wasn't because of me," I say.

"Kind of was."

"We got lucky, okay? The plan—which I protested to all along—fell apart. We were lucky Brezmard had something to offer, and lucky the captain felt that helping me could pay off a debt he *happened* to feel he owed to my father," I snap.

"Sourpuss," she says.

The Lost One: Wrath of the Tyrant

"That plan was reckless! We can't rely on luck or half-baked ideas! That's how people die! I can't believe I let you convince me to go along with it!" I explode at her.

"It was an opportunity we couldn't pass up, and it paid off," she says.

"The *only* part of the plan that worked was the outcome! Is that how you run things in Clearhallow? You come up with some kind of end goal and hope everything works out okay for you? Do you know what we're up against?" I yell, hands in fists.

"Yes, of course I know what we're up against! We're up against a tyrant who's destroyed most of the world's nations. We're up against the largest army to ever exist on this planet... against the man that murdered my family right in front of me and let my brother and I live for a reason I don't understand! He's the reason I have nightmares every night and haven't told anyone except my brother! Don't you think *I* might have a reason to hate him, too?" she shouts, with tears in her eyes.

Suddenly, everything is silent except the wind dragging the clouds ever closer.

"Nokk said your parents died in a boating accident," I say.

"We were out boating, but it was no accident. That's a lie we've been telling ourselves, and everyone around us, since the day it happened because it was easier than dealing with the fact they were murdered. Now, if you'll excuse me, I think I'd rather have somewhere *dry* to sleep than standing about doing nothing," she says, angrily wiping away her tears as she continues briskly toward camp.

"Ak'dech," Norkuz blurts out, reaching out to her.

"No," Nokk pushes his hand away, "She'll be okay."

"So, all of us watched at least one parent die in front of us?" Brezmard contemplatively says.

80

"No. I only walked in on their bodies," Norkuz says, as he heads toward camp without saying another word.

Chapter Nine: The Storm

Our shelter was rushed but sufficient. It's snug and cramped, but there are minimal openings for wind and rain to seep through. Everyone is being unusually quiet. Normally, I wouldn't complain, but it feels uneasy after the argument and everything that was said. I almost feel bad for some reason. As the wind blows past the tent, we sit in silence. Quldriag, Norkuz's dragon, shifts uncomfortably every few minutes. He's having a particularly difficult time with the limited space. Most of the other dragons are asleep, as is Brezmard. Ak'dech is meditating or something. Nokk is reading a book he brought with him, and Norkuz is going through his medicine pouch to see what he has after the trade with the pirates. I jump to my feet in alarm as lightning flashes outside. There was a shape in the flash, a voice in the thunder, a menacing laugh. I wonder if it's Ma'roog.

"What?" Nokk says to me, as he looks up from his book.

"Nothing… it's nothing," I say, although my heart still pounds rapidly.

"Okay, well, next time there's nothing, please don't alarm everyone else with it," Nokk says, as he rolls his eyes and gets back to reading.

I sit back down and try to relax, but a few minutes later, another flash of light brings back the shape of the imagined nightmare, clear as day, right in front of my face. I breathe in sharply, scrambling backward as Nalrai jumps up, growls, and takes a defensive stance.

"Still nothing?" Norkuz asks me, concerned.

"Jumpy… that's all," I say, voice dry and breathy.

"What about Nalrai?" he asks suspiciously.

"It's okay buddy," I say to Nalrai in a raspy voice while putting my hand on his wing, "He's overly protective is all."

Nalrai growls again, looking for any sort of threat.

"*Arid,*" the deep, raspy voice says in my head.

It always gets so hard to breathe every time I hear this voice, as though something were squeezing all the air out of my chest. The male voice brings me somewhere in my mind… to an island with another abandoned village. It's dark and storm clouds tumble in the air as they wrestle with each other in the sky. It hasn't started raining here; however, I can make out most of the details around me. I'm standing on a stone street with fine, swirling lines engraved with intricate patterns. This must be the town's center. A large fountain with a marble statue of an armed soldier ready for battle sits in the middle of the street. There's a sign sitting at the base of the fountain written in the same ancient hieroglyphics as the scribblings on the back of my map.

The Champion of Glul'gur, it reads.

"Arid!"

I snap back to the tent as Norkuz shouts my name.

"I'm fine!" I yell, startled.

"Arid, you're shaking," Ak'dech says.

"No, I'm fine. Please … just leave me alone," I say.

"Okay," she says, backing off.

The burns on Nokk's face are healing well, but the damaged skin has been starting to slough off. Nokk's dragon, Nynnu, whines, sticking her snout in Nokk's face as he scratches at it.

"I'm okay Nynnu. Norkuz, do you have anything for the itching?" he asks, looking greatly uncomfortable.

The Lost One: Wrath of the Tyrant

"Give me a moment to get it ready," Norkuz says.

All the dragons are getting antsy. They're not made to sit in confined spaces for long. Unfortunately, this storm could last a few days. Qombaryth, Ak'dech's dragon, is fast asleep, but the rest have woken up and are fidgety. Kemoss, Brezmard's dragon, is making an annoying clicking sound from deep in her throat, so the atmosphere is getting even more uncomfortable inside the tent with every breath she takes.

"Kemoss, you okay?" Brezmard yawns to his dragon, at last waking from the noise.

He scoots over to lean against her, stroking her wing. Norkuz holds a bowl up to his dragon's mouth and says, "Quldriag, I need some saliva to mix with these aloe leaves."

Quldriag is the largest dragon here and barely fits under the roof of the tent. Unhappy with the conditions, he roars softly in complaint and pushes the bowl away.

"I know you're cramped Quldriag, but the alternative is sleeping outside in the storm. Now, can I please get some saliva?" Norkuz asks, somewhat impatiently.

The dragon drools into the bowl.

"Thank you Quldriag," Nokk says.

I'm trying to convince myself there's no reason to be scared of the hallucinations. I've rarely been frightened by real enemies in combat, so why should I be terrified of an enemy that can't touch me? He's just dreams and nightmares, so why should that gurgling voice send shivers through me every time I hear it in my head?

"You have to refrain from touching your face while it sets into your skin," Norkuz says to Nokk while mixing the leaves together with Quldriag's spit.

"Gross," I gag.

"Whatever it takes," Nokk says, "Hey, Norkuz, you don't think my face will be all marred even after it heals, do you?"

"There might be some light scarring, but it wasn't as bad as it could have been. The dragon's breath was scalding, but it wasn't actively spitting fire. It's more like a bad sunburn that starts blistering," Norkuz assures.

"You're worried about your looks?" I ask.

"Oh sure, like you wouldn't be upset if *your* pretty face was all mangled and twisted suddenly," he sneers sarcastically.

"I'm just saying you shouldn't *worry* about it. I'm sure your pretty-boy image will only look more mature with a scar or two," I say, rolling my eyes.

"I happen to like my skin smooth and flawless, thank you very much," he pouts indignantly.

"Ouch!" Brezmard yelps, smacking himself on the neck.

"Mosquito?" Ak'dech asks, "I didn't think they'd be out in this kind of weather, even in a tent," she frowns.

"We've been here for two weeks, and this isn't the type of area mosquitoes are attracted to. There's been no sign of slow-moving or stagnant water... no swamp, nothing. There shouldn't be a bunch of mosquitoes on this island," Nokk says.

"Then what bit me?" Brezmard asks.

Norkuz looks at his neck and says, "That's not any bite mark I've seen before. It looks more like a burn. There's this one line here that looks deeper than the irritation around it," he continues, "Almost looks like someone took a scalding rod and pressed it into your skin."

"Wait, let me see," I say, alarmed by the description.

I rush over to Brezmard to look at the wound.

The Lost One: Wrath of the Tyrant

"That's… that's not a good sign," I breathe.

"I take it you've seen that before?" Norkuz says.

"Yes, and where there's one, there's a hundred more," I say.

"A hundred what?" Ak'dech asks.

"They're called lightning beasts—little gray dragons small enough to hold in your hand comfortably. They're fast, and they create what has been described as little bolts of lightning as they fly. They travel in packs of a few hundred and love to come out during thunderstorms," I say.

"Why is that so bad? Do they kill humans?" Brezmard asks.

"I wasn't dumb enough to stick around and find out, but I've heard stories which suggest that's the case," I say.

Norkuz slaps himself on the arm. I catch a glimpse of a spark.

"How do we get rid of them?" Nokk asks, wearily looking around for them.

"I don't know. As I said, I didn't stick around last time I encountered them."

I swat at a spark in front of me, somehow managing to catch the little dragon.

"Hello," I say to it while it squirms to get free.

As I examine it, it squeaks like a mouse, panting quickly as it tries its best to escape with its wings hopelessly trying to flap.

"How'd you catch that?" Brezmard asks.

"Fast reflexes, I guess."

"It's not stinging you?" Ak'dech asks.

"Their little shocks can't get through my gloves, but it's interesting… I don't see an ounce of lightning on it."

"Static electricity," she says.

"What?" I ask.

"That's all lightning is… static electricity," she repeats.

"Sure… whatever that means," I say, running a finger down the creature's belly. Then I say, "He's kind of cute, isn't he?"

"Might I remind you we're about to be eaten alive by his friends," Brezmard says, as hundreds of lightning beasts emerge from a hole beneath a tree root near the tent.

The tiny dragons gather in a small swarm with lightning sparking between them.

"Their wings keep rubbing together. That must be creating the static charge. That's why this guy stopped sparking," Ak'dech says.

"So what, we keep them from flapping their wings? Easier said than done," Nokk says.

"What do you want?" I ask the tiny dragon I'm holding as he chews at my finger, still insistent on escaping, "Survival… food?"

"That's a lot of dragons," Norkuz says, as more beasts add to the gray, sizzling cloud buzzing around in their swarm.

Nalrai roars at them, and they break off into groups scattering in different directions. I gently stroke the wing of the little dragon I'm holding, and its little bolts zap my glove. He finally starts to calm down and doesn't struggle as much.

"You're not so tough, are you, little guy? Is that why your friends are just flying around staring at us? What is it about thunderstorms that bring you out? And why are you in our tent?" I ask.

The Lost One: Wrath of the Tyrant

"They probably don't like the rain," Ak'dech says suddenly.

I hold the little dragon out towards a water leak that's slowly dripping through the roof, and it squirms. None of the other lightning beasts are going anywhere near the wet patches in the tent. As Ak'dech said, maybe they don't like the rain.

"Scared of a little storm? Hmmm, so rain flushes them out of hiding. They look for shelter, but they seem scared of us, too. Maybe they're trying to scare us off so they can have the shelter to themselves," I say, petting the dragon caged in my hand.

"What about those stories you heard?" Brezmard asks, swatting at a cluster of them and receiving several stings on the hand.

"Don't rile them," I say, "Stories aren't always reliable. You especially can't trust a story from a traveler. They exaggerate to make themselves seem more interesting. No one really knows *what* happened to those people I heard about in those stories."

The dragon in my hand allows his wings to hang limply, and he makes a high-pitched squealing sound as his head droops. I'm torn, for a moment, between being concerned for its well-being and having a cold fascination with its potential death. The notion of helping it die slowly crosses my mind. I release it and move it to the palm of my other hand. It lies in the middle of my palm, licks my glove, then rolls on its back, lying limply.

"No, don't die! I didn't mean to hurt you buddy," I say, petting his neck and stomach.

Thunder cracks through the forest again. The swarm scatters. Several of them seem to have accepted that I'm not going to hurt them, so they land on my neck and arms. The rest of the lightning beasts have found dry places in the tent to land on for the time being. Our dragons have been on edge since we've been in the tent, but most of them start to relax—except Nalrai, who bares his teeth and growls at the dragons that landed on me.

"I don't think he's dying," Norkuz notes.

The dragon in my palm stretches out, rubs his head against my hand and makes a sound similar to his previous screech, but this time, it has more of a calming purr to it.

"Okay, handsome," I say, continuing to stroke him, "Just don't squeal like you're in pain… like you did earlier."

"Don't get too attached. You're not keeping it as a pet," Brezmard says.

"What are you? My mother?" I say, sticking out my tongue like a child.

"How dare you—" he starts to get up, hands in fists, but Norkuz stops him with a hand on his shoulder.

"Easy, Brezmard. I don't think fighting in this flimsy structure is such a good idea," he says.

Nalrai growls at the little dragon, sticking his snout right up against my hand. The lightning beast, terrified, scurries up my arm and across my neck to my other shoulder, cowering and shivering against my neck.

"Don't be jealous, Nalrai. You know you'll always be my favorite dragon in the entire world," I say.

Nalrai growls once more, trots in a circle, plops down irately, and curls up, as if he were going to sleep, with the tip of his tail flicking back and forth in an annoyed manner.

"Okay, be jealous for a bit, but it's not worth it. As soon as this storm clears, we're out of here, and this little guy is staying behind," I say.

He huffs and moves his head grouchily, looking as far away from me as he can.

"Ignore me then. See if I care," I say, offended.

"Nynnu, mind if I sit here?" I ask Nokk's dragon.

The Lost One: Wrath of the Tyrant

Nynnu grunts and flexes her wings, which is a clear answer: no.

"Nynnu, I know you'd love to get out and go for a flight, but you can't be grumpy toward everyone the whole time we're in here, okay? Go ahead and sit," Nokk says to me.

I give Nokk a suspicious look and ask, "You sure?"

"You can sit here, but only if you let me examine these dragons that have warmed up to you," he says, trying to urge one to climb into his hand voluntarily.

"Don't hurt them," I say, taking a seat.

"Ow! I'm more concerned about *them* hurting *me*," Nokk says, shaking his hand and sucking his finger after a lightning beast bites him.

The little dragon starts flapping its wings and creating sparks as its wingtips brush against Nokk's suit trying to intimidate him.

"I guess they're still scared of you," I say.

"They *love* you," he grumbles.

I pick up the first dragon off my shoulder and try to calm him, stroking mainly his wings and neck until he stops trembling.

"Here, you can hold him. I'll see if I can get the rest of them used to you," I say, handing over the first dragon that fell asleep in my palm. I grab another one from my elbow, petting his wings until they start to droop and he stops squirming.

"What are you doing?" Nokk asks, as I hold the tiny creature above his head.

"Relax," I grin, while putting it in his hair.

"Arid, I do not appreciate that at all," he says, frozen in place as it rustles in his hair.

I watch the dragon panic for a moment as it tries to figure out what's going on, while Nokk is anxious and doesn't move a muscle.

"Relax, would you? It's not going to hurt you," I say.

"It's in my hair. I can't see it," he says.

"I can," I say, tickling the beast, who then rolls over onto his back.

"By the way, what's up with your hair?" I ask, "I can't tell if it's brown with blonde patches sprinkled through it, or blonde spotted with light brown. Ak'dech has the same thing to some extent, except her hair is most definitely brown with a few gray highlights."

"An unfortunate family trait," he says, sounding annoyed.

"What's so unfortunate about it? It's interesting," I say, pulling the dragon out of his hair and placing it on the back of his head, where his hair is cut much shorter.

"Arid... get it off my head," he says, petrified.

"Fine," I say, letting the dragon crawl back into my palm.

Nokk sighs in relief and starts petting the sleeping dragon I handed him earlier.

"Don't do that again," he warns.

"Or what?" I taunt.

"You wanna find out?" he smirks, trying to stifle his laughter.

"What's so funny?" I ask.

"Some of the dragons seem to think *your* hair might make a great nest," he says, still laughing.

"Oh, ha, ha," I sneer sarcastically, not amused.

The Lost One: Wrath of the Tyrant

Annoyed, I give Nokk a little shove before pulling a couple of dragons out of my hair and running my fingers through it to untangle any knots. I find my brush from Nalrai's satchel, brush my hair, and begin braiding it back into a single ponytail again. Nokk moves on from laughing at me and says, "Their wings are a strange texture, almost like cotton... thin and fragile. I can almost see through them."

He then spreads the wing of the sleeping dragon in his hand and says, "And he has little split wingtips. They're going to rub past the other layers of his wing and create friction. His wing probably creates a little bit of static just flying by himself, but that's why they fly so close to each other: to produce enough static for a spark."

"Fascinating... but you do realize that all that science stuff makes no sense to me, right? I wasn't educated at some school that teaches numbers and... static... and... sparks and stuff," I say.

"I was mostly talking aloud to myself," he says awkwardly, "Well, educate me on something that's *not* scientific. Why is it they snuggle up to you like you're covered in dragon nip, but I get bit?"

I shrug and say, "Maybe it's because I'm covered in dragon scales."

"Ah, that tickles!" Nokk flinches as the little dragon wakes up and scurries around on his palm and wrist, clearly panting hard again.

"Easily scared, huh?" I say, picking up the frightened creature.

"Well, I don't blame them. If I stepped on one of these guys, they wouldn't have a chance," Nokk says.

Nalrai suddenly sticks his snout against my side, whining.

"Oh, *sure*, you're all apologetic now that you're lonely, and I'm over here being laughed at," I snort.

As a particularly strong gust of wind blows past, one of the tent's walls caves in. Nalrai throws his wings out instinctively to protect me, but the worst thing that happens is a few leaves manage to find their way in through one of the leaks. I can't help laughing, but Nalrai whines and lies down, head pressed into the ground. He even ignores Nynnu when she nips at him.

"Nynnu!" Nokk scolds.

"Aw, come on you big baby. You think I could be mad at you?" I ask, as I scratch Nalrai's head, "You didn't hurt your wing again flailing like that, did you?"

He plops onto his side and lies there.

"Maybe he needs more sedatives," Nokk says.

"I don't think he needs to be sedated any more. I think he's healed," Norkuz says.

Nalrai hops up and trots over to the tent's door. He sits in front of it and digs his claws in the dirt.

"Here, take Quldriag with you. He needs to stretch his wings," Norkuz says, as he pulls open the door, shooing the two dragons out.

"So Arid and Nalrai can recover from broken bones in two weeks or less, but I'm still in pain over a lousy burn? That doesn't make sense! Nor is it fair," Nokk pouts.

"Dragons heal fast in general. Normally, a little slower than he did, but…" Norkuz pauses, staring off after Nalrai in confusion.

"And what about Arid?" Nokk asks.

"I don't have an explanation. I don't know how Arid can do half of what I've seen her do," Norkuz says, glancing at me.

"I haven't noticed anything out of the usual… well… okay, so maybe I've been healing a *little* faster than I used to," I say.

The Lost One: Wrath of the Tyrant

"We can try to figure it out after this war. For now, I'm just grateful that our best fighter can recover so fast," Norkuz says.

"Whatever," I say, lying back, careful not to squish any dragons before closing my eyes.

Chapter Ten: Ruins

*I*t's been a few days since the storm, and Nalrai is healed enough to fly and leave the island of Zorzim. We are now in Tiendys, where the black sands meet the gray sea. This island is a dead village at the foot of a dormant volcano, but splotches of blue break through a clouded sky as a warm breeze whistles through the crumbled ruins of my childhood. Despite the muggy warmth, the dreary island carries a haunted chill as I hop off Nalrai and my feet land in the ashy rubble. I'm instantly on edge. My heart pounds slowly but hard, and each breath I take sends a throbbing sound to my ears. However, the island is still and silent, except for the breeze, yet my imagination rebuilds the ruins, ablaze with orange and red fire that destroyed my village. As I recall the memory, the silent air is filled with ghostly screams bouncing off the sleeping mountain. My mouth is dry like cotton. I force a swallow, but it goes down like sand. For comfort, my hand clenches Nalrai's reins to remind me that he's close by my side as I stare at the ruins of dust and stones, which is all that remains on the island now.

"Where did you find the map?" Brezmard asks.

His voice is a light echo in my head, like a dream or distant memory.

"I-I can't remember," I airily mumble, numbly dragging my feet through the sand, paralyzed with fear as memories of my parents' death haunt my soul.

"Oh, great. *That's* helpful!" he shouts sarcastically, "There's nothing out here!"

"Brezmard!" Ak'dech says quickly to shut him up, then she says, "Arid, you okay?"

"Mm, I'm fine," I affirm, distracted by flashbacks of screams and flames.

The Lost One: Wrath of the Tyrant

"Let's start looking for any hint of what may have happened to the survivors," she says, pushing Brezmard into the ruins.

Nokk makes the mistake of putting his hand on my shoulder and says, "It's okay—"

"Don't touch me!" I yell, reactively throwing him to the ground.

"Ow," he huffs.

"Why would you think that was a good idea?" I yell.

"I-I'm sorry," he groans, climbing to his feet.

"You good, Nokk?" Norkuz asks.

"Yeah. I'll go catch up to Brezmard," he says, throwing a troubled glance at me before going with Nynnu to search for survivors.

Qombaryth sniffs the air.

"Okay, we'll go look too," Ak'dech tells her dragon.

No wonder they were so good at finding me in the eddies. Qombaryth is a natural-born tracker with keen senses, specifically smell.

"Need to talk?" Norkuz asks me, as everyone except our dragons leave the area.

"What if they really are just gone? Maybe we should give up. There was so much smoke and fire… so much screaming," I say.

"We'll do our best to find them," he says.

"What if that's not good enough?" I raise my voice.

"Take a seat," he says, sitting in front of me while looking through his healer's pouch.

"Why?" I ask, feeling concerned because Norkuz only goes through his pouch for wounds and ailments.

"Please sit," he requests calmly.

I hesitantly sit down, and Nalrai curls up beside me.

"Why are you looking through your pouch? I'm not sick or anything," I say.

"I know. You're stressed though," he says, as he sprays something near my face, leaving a flowery scent hanging in the air.

"What is that?" I ask.

"Lavender. Now take my hands and close your eyes," he says.

"What? No," I say.

Norkuz doesn't say anything, but he leaves his hands out in offer with his eyes closed. Reluctantly, I follow his instructions.

"Breathe slowly and deeply," he says.

His calm, deep voice is difficult to not trust. The lavender sits softly in the air.

"Keep your eyes closed, but pay attention to your surroundings. What do you hear? Smell? Feel? Describe it to me," he says.

"This is stupid," I say.

"Maybe so," he says.

"I hear waves on the sand from the ocean... and Nalrai's breaths. I can feel his heart beating beside me. I feel your hands and the wind. I smell the lavender and the ocean. I hear... footsteps," I say, opening my eyes.

"Sorry, not trying to interrupt," Ak'dech says, sitting down beside us.

The Lost One: Wrath of the Tyrant

She is alone, so Qombaryth must be searching the ruins without her. I notice an old piece of parchment on her lap.

"We will finish this later," Norkuz says to me.

I let go of his hands and take the parchment from her lap and ask, "Where did you get this?"

"Over there… from the ruins I was searching," she says, pointing north.

Finally, it's more of the map I stole back from Brezmard. It was incomplete ever since I found it in the treasure chest, and this appears to be another part of it.

"I was hoping you could translate it," Ak'dech says.

The paper is torn and stained worse than the other piece I originally had. It's still legible, for the most part, so I begin to read.

"This is a story about a lost island where magic was supposedly born. The people of my village were looking for it. They call it Glul'gur," I summarize, as I think about that eerie, abandoned village in my vision.

"Have you heard of it before?" Norkuz asks, noticing my frown.

"No," I claim.

"Well now it makes sense that the stories of magic and seers are scribbled on the back of map pieces since Glul'gur is what they were looking for," Ak'dech says.

"Maybe they found Glul'gur and are hiding there," I say, flipping it over to look at the map side.

"This still isn't the whole map," Ak'dech notes, as I desperately look over it several times.

"What if this map is all we get? There has to be clues to help us find this place. See here? There are markings on the parchment, but I don't know what they mean. Can you understand the numbers?" I ask.

"I'll have Nokk take a look at it. That's his area more than mine, but we're going to keep searching. Hopefully we can find something more," she says.

"I'm sorry. I should be looking too," I say, starting to get up.

"Are you feeling better?" Norkuz asks, standing with me.

"Much better," I say.

"Good. Let us know if you need anything," he says, as Nalrai and I walk away to search the ruins for more clues.

After several hours, the sun starts going down, so the Dragon Knights and I leave Tiendys and set up camp about half an hour away on the island of Roldraak. After pitching our tents, Nalrai and I leave the others to take a night flight so I can think. We glide gently over the treetops of the island, as their branches sway softly in the wind. An owl hoots from somewhere in the branches, while the moon shines brightly in the dark sky, surrounded by an infinite canopy of stars. The air carries the familiar scent of the ocean, yet it is cool and crisp without the warmth of the sun. We're now flying near the farthest beach from camp, which is only a few minutes away, but it's relaxing to be free from everyone. The peaceful flight and pleasant breeze help clear my head, temporarily erasing my troubles.

"No! No, keep breathing!" a desperate shout catches my attention, breaking the calm of our surroundings, as agony and panic fill the cry.

Anticipating what I was about to tell him, Nalrai changes course to investigate the disturbance. My eyes scan the beach, straining to see through the dark.

The Lost One: Wrath of the Tyrant

I spot a small, heavily damaged ship drifting by the shore. About twelve waterlogged survivors are still evacuating the devastating remains of the wooden vessel. My hand drifts to the hilt of my sword. Nalrai grunts in disapproval as I start to draw it.

"What? We don't take chances. They may look like innocents, but it could always be a trap," I say.

He whines as the wail of torment continues.

"Fine. I'll go in with my sword still sheathed… but always with caution. Be prepared to fire if it turns out to be a well-acted ruse," I say, rolling my eyes.

Nalrai lands near the group.

"Be wary!" an old man says, jumping to his feet, fumbling for a sword on his hip, as we proceed closer to them.

"Calm down. You don't appear to be Rul Warriors, and as long as that is really the case, I am not your enemy. It looks like you could use some assistance," I say, as I jump down from my saddle.

Two bloody hands grab my arm tightly, yet because of my dragon-scale material, the young man's hands slip down my sleeve regardless of how tight he tries to hold me.

"He needs help. Please, do you know how to heal? Save him!" the young man says with tears running down his face as despair wracks his expression.

He pulls me towards a gravely injured casualty lying nearly motionless with a few more survivors trying to assist him.

"I-I can't help. I'm not a healer," I say.

"Take a look, please!" the young man begs.

"O-okay," I stutter, "Nalrai, go get Norkuz. Hurry."

Nalrai flies off, and I kneel on the sand beside the limp man, observing the damage. I don't know where to begin. A large portion of his skin is charred from flames. The other young man who dragged me here clasps his hand, sobbing uncontrollably.

"You need to save him," he pleads.

"I don't know anything about medicine," I say.

"Please save him!" he croaks despairingly, "Heal him!" he shrieks hysterically.

"Come on, Nalrai, hurry back," I mutter under my breath, clueless on how to help.

"Kim'ir! Don't leave me," the young man yells, "Swear it! Don't leave me!"

Kim'ir's breaths are becoming more and more shallow, and his heartbeat feels weaker and weaker under my hand.

"Master Ezzut, you know not all loved ones can be saved," the old man says, while putting a hand on the young man's shoulder.

"Don't touch me! He's not going to die. He's *not* going to die!" Ezzut yells, while swiping his arm at the old man who tries to comfort him.

"Breathe... please," I say quietly, kneeling uselessly by the dying sailor as he continues to weaken, and then gradually, his breaths come to a complete halt.

"No... no, no, *no*!" Ezzut screams, throwing himself over Kim'ir, "You're... you're not dead," he denies, voice cracking.

"Sir, I—" I start.

"Leave him be, Miss," the old man says, gesturing for me to follow him.

The Lost One: Wrath of the Tyrant

Anyone who was near Kim'ir is moving away to give Ezzut space.

"I'm sorry I could be of no help to his friend," I say, with a sense of guilt nagging at me.

"Master Kim'ir's death is unfortunate, and I'm afraid it will take Ezzut a long time to recover from this tragedy. Poor boy feels too much," he says.

"The rest of you don't look to be in the best of situations, either," I note, looking around.

Some survivors are trying to stay warm because many of them are shivering from the cold and drenched from the ocean. Several others have injuries being tended to by their friends. I'd estimate a dozen of them are here trying to make sense of their new surroundings. Two of them are young girls, maybe between four and six years old, huddling together as everyone else tends to tasks of starting a fire and addressing wounds.

"My name is Ozarm. We're from the Isle of Xymrar—a village a ways to the west. Our people are sailors and merchants... innocent people. We fled for refuge when the Rul Coilband came to attack a few days ago. We had more on our ship, but they didn't survive their wounds long enough to make it here, so we buried them at sea. Kim'ir held on longer than expected," the old man says.

"I mean no disrespect, but judging by the state of your crew, none of you will last long alone. You're extremely fortunate I happened to come across you," I say.

"Indeed. I was under the impression this island was uninhabited," he says.

"It is. My group is only camping here a few nights, and since your people are having difficulty getting a fire started, I'm going to help before you all freeze to death," I say.

"Thank you, Miss," he sighs, exhaustion evident in his tone.

102

I walk over to the currently ignored little girls while everyone else focuses on other high-priority injuries and fire-starting duties. The young girls are both thin with long brown hair. They're soaked with water and wearing very oversized coats that the other survivors gave them. The older girl wears an empty expression, staring blankly off into the distance as tears drip off her chin. The younger girl gasps and sobs, clutching a doll tightly with one arm and the older girl with the other. Confusion taints her frantic tears, and her eyes dart around to each survivor. It's a bit chaotic as we see all the suffering of Ezzut and the injured people. Most of them are recovering from burns, and a few others recuperate from lacerations of swords. Once again, I remember the flames of my home. I was about the same age as the younger girl.

"Hello," I crouch in front of them, level to their line of sight, "I'm Arid. It's nice to meet you. I'm so sorry about what's going on. I know this all must be very scary, but I want you both to help me with something, okay?"

"I don't know you," the younger girl whimpers, sniffling and taking a step back while the older girl doesn't reply but continues to stare off into the dark without any acknowledgment of me.

"I know you don't know me, but I promise I won't hurt you. We need more wood for the fire, especially small sticks and dry plants. Can you come with me to help find some? It'll be okay. I'll keep you safe," I say, brushing hair behind her ear.

The younger girl holding the doll flinches, but then she slowly grabs my hand and stares at it.

"Why do you have scales? Are you a dragon?" she asks suspiciously.

"No, I'm not a dragon. It's a suit of dragon scales. Here," I say, as I take off my gloves, shove them in the pouch around my waist, and hold my hands out to her, palms up.

"I-I don't know where my mommy is," she snivels, "Or my daddy."

The Lost One: Wrath of the Tyrant

"What's your name sweetie?" I ask.

"Naissyt," she says.

"Is she your sister?" I ask, looking toward the older girl.

"Yes, but I don't know what's wrong with her. She won't speak to me!" Naissyt sobs.

"What's her name?" I ask.

"Yrserross," she says.

"Yrserross, can you hear me?" I ask, putting my hand on her shoulder.

No response.

"Since we got on the boat, she just stands and stares and doesn't talk or do anything," Naissyt says, while hugging her doll tighter.

"Okay, let's go get wood. Maybe the warm fire will help her feel better," I say, as I stand from a kneeling position.

I take them by the hands and lead them towards the trees, but I don't venture too deep into the woods in order to stay in sight of the others on the beach. Yrserross walks numbly, feet dragging hazardously over the plants and roots. Her hand is freezing, even more so than Naissyt's icy fingers. Once Nalrai gets back—which should be soon—we won't need the kindling, but I think giving the little girls something to do is better than sitting around waiting. I would rather keep them occupied for a bit. I remember the shock, pain, confusion, and numbness that followed the destruction of my village. Nalrai was familiar and kept me alive, but it would have been nice to have someone explain things to me. As we walk along the woodline, Naissyt picks up a very small handful of twigs and dry brush.

"Arid!" Norkuz says, sounding bewildered as Nalrai lands on the beach.

"Alright, that's enough. Thank you. It's time to go back now," I tell Naissyt.

I pause for a moment, pick Yrserross up, and carry her towards the beach so she doesn't trip on the way back.

"What's going on?" Norkuz says, as he looks around.

The other Dragon Knights finally catch up and land on the beach, quickly taking in the devastation of Ezzut wailing over Kim'ir's body, injured survivors, and a ship splintering against a shore.

"Refugees," I say to the Dragon Knights, "Ma'roog destroyed their village, and they have casualties," I sadly say.

While putting Yrserross down, Naissyt runs over to add her small contribution to the woodpile the refugees have been trying to light.

"They could use some help with the fire," I hint to the dragons.

"Stand back," Nokk warns the refugees.

Everyone clears away before Nynnu sparks the fire to life.

"Everyone, come to the fire," Brezmard orders, "I am Prince Brezmard of Clearhallow, leader of the mighty Dragon Knights. I understand the tragedy that has befallen upon you, and my condolences are with you. We will help you, and Clearhallow will offer you a place to sleep and food to fill your bellies. It will be a journey of several days, but we will protect you and keep you safe."

"Was all that necessary, mighty prince?" I mock, gagging at the speech.

"Shut up Arid," he sneers, "There was nothing wrong with it."

Norkuz walks around the circle of gathered refugees, summing up the wounds and injuries. I notice Ezzut isn't in the circle. He is still clinging to the body of his friend.

"Um, Brezmard... how are we going to get them back to Clearhallow? We only have so many dragons," Ak'dech points out.

"That is a, um... that's a good question. Keep in mind, we still have a mission to finish. It's just been... complicated some... but we have some time to figure it out," he says.

"We're still searching the ruins?" I ask, "I would have thought you'd given up."

"The deal was four days to thoroughly search the ruins, and we only searched about a quarter of the island due to the sunset. I keep my promises, Arid. The mission will continue," he says.

"Thank you," I say.

Norkuz reports, "The remaining injured are treatable, although I will need help addressing some of the wounds. Some of them *are* severe, and if they're not cared for, it could become life threatening. However, I believe everyone still alive will be fine."

"Prince Brezmard! We have questions to ask you," one of the women says.

"Of course," Brezmard says, finally dismounting Kemoss, "Ak'dech knows some medicine, right? Use who or whatever you need to help them," he tells Norkuz, before stepping away to talk to the people.

"Ak'dech, you know how to splint?" Norkuz asks.

"Absolutely. I remember everything you taught me," she says.

"There's a man over there with a leg injury that needs help. Quldriag has supplies in his saddlebag. Nokk, what do you know?" he asks.

"I'm not much help in these kinds of situations," Nokk admits.

"Take Nynnu and find some food," Norkuz says.

"Okay," Nokk obeys.

"Arid, what's the deal with the kids?" Norkuz asks.

"Sisters. Apparently, their parents didn't make it on the boat with them. They're cold, but otherwise I think they're uninjured. They're traumatized, though, and the older sister is unreactive to anything," I say.

"And the guy who didn't make it... how's his friend doing?" he asks.

"Distraught. I think he has a burn on his arm, but I'm not sure how bad it is. I don't know anything about medicine. I never even patched up my own wounds. I just let them heal on their own," I say.

Naissyt sits by the fire, sniffing as the heat dries her tears. Yrserross hasn't moved from where I set her and stands motionless beside me. I lightly stroke her hair in an attempt to comfort her.

"That's all I know Norkuz. If you have questions, the old man seems to know what's going on and doesn't have any visible injuries," I report.

"Thanks. Stay with these two. Make sure they get warmed up," he says.

Chapter Eleven: Sunburn

"*W*here are you going?" the old man, Ozarm, shrieks as we pack up our dragons the next morning.

"We have a mission to continue on Tiendys, but don't worry, our healer will stay here with you to make sure all is well," Brezmard says.

"Tiendys? What mission could you possibly have on Tiendys? There's nothing there but ashes of a village long dead," Ozarm scoffs.

"Maybe so, but I've made a promise to my ally that I intend to keep," says the prince.

Darkness falls over Ozarm's face, and he solemnly asks, "You seek the Isle of Glul'gur, don't you?"

"What do you know about it?" I ask.

"People go mad looking for that island, and yet, after all these generations, no one has located it. The island is a myth. It may have once existed, but if it did, it no longer does. Your search is a fruitless endeavor," he says.

"How can you know? If the people of Tiendys found it, they could have taken refuge there. They could be safe and hidden on that island," I say defiantly.

"You seek the people of the dead village?" he asks.

"Tiendys was my home. I wish to find my people and any who survived Ma'roog's brutal attack all that time ago," I say.

"Child, they did not find Glul'gur. That, I can guarantee," he says.

"How? How can you promise that?" I ask.

"My nephew… he had the same obsession with the island as you, and before the Rul Coilband raided your village all those years ago, he often traveled with the people of Tiendys as a hired hand to help search for the elusive Isle of Glul'gur. One day, his search party returned from a voyage to find the village of Likenhallow burned to the ground by Ma'roog. Some of the survivors took refuge on Xymrar, where we just escaped from, which means the last of your people are either prisoners of the Rul Coilband, or they are no more," he says.

"You lie," I say.

"Arid," Ak'dech says quietly.

"No, shut up!" I yell.

She puts her hand on my shoulder and says, "You knew from the beginning it was a long shot. No matter how much you wanted her claims to be true, I warned you not to believe the words of a Rul warrior saying that your people survived," she says.

"They are alive! They have to be… at least some… I haven't spent the last weeks fighting by your sides to give up on my family! I've seen Glul'gur in my dreams. I hear their voices in my head! They can not be gone," I say, pulling away sharply from Ak'dech's hand on my arm.

"Hm. Interesting. You were ready to give up yesterday after seeing the ruins," Norkuz accuses.

"And *you* talked me out of it!" I say, "His nephew was with *one* group, and Tiendys was vacant when they got back. There's no way for them to know if another group of survivors found the island or not."

"Miss, Glul'gur is gone. Whatever your dreams tell you are merely a desperate child's unconscious clinging to a spark of false hope," Ozarm says.

The Lost One: Wrath of the Tyrant

"I am *not* a child, and these are not dreams I have when I sleep! I saw Glul'gur in a vision before I heard its name, before I was even aware it existed. In my waking state, I could feel the stone beneath my feet and the wind on my face."

"You have gone mad, just as the others who searched," Ozarm says, waving his arm in exasperation.

"I believe you," says Ezzut, who has kept himself isolated from everyone else until now.

"Thank you," I say, nearly startled by his response.

"Ozarm, I doubt she was dreaming. Seers are known to have visions of the past, present, and future, but it is not unheard of for others who are not seers to have visions... of sorts. Of course, sorcerers are nothing like seers. Their power is more like magnets, and their magic likes to connect with other magic, so it would make sense for a sorcerer like her to bond with, and find, Glul'gur, since it is the source of all magic," he says.

"What do you mean, sorcerer?" Nokk asks.

"You're all... *shocked* by this?" Ezzut says, then he looks at me and shouts, "You didn't know you have magic? How can you not know?"

"I *don't* have magic!" I yell defensively.

"I feel it radiating off you like a sunburn. It's blatantly obvious and hard to ignore," he says.

"You're saying you can *sense* magic?" Norkuz asks.

"Ozarm said I feel too much. That isn't because I'm overly sensitive in the usual sense. I feel *everything*. I feel the sorrows and joys of the world, and believe me, this is not a curse I would wish upon anyone else. I feel her magic. I feel your prince's insecurity. I feel the pain in your left knee. I feel the agony of my village. I feel all of it," Ezzut says.

"You... watched your village burn," Ak'dech states, horrified.

"No, I *felt* my village burn, and I felt all the pain and fear of my people, my friends, and Kim'ir... my love. It's the downside of being an empath," he says.

"So, if Arid's a sorcerer, what does that make you?" Brezmard asks.

"As I said, I'm an empath. My magic's passive. It's like breathing. I don't have a choice, and I don't have much control over it. Arid's magic is active. It's like a muscle in a sense that she can strengthen it and learn to control it, but right now, I doubt she knows what she's doing," Ezzut says, then he turns to me and finishes, "You can choose to use it or not in a given situation, but until you control it, standing next to you is like sleeping at the lip of an active volcano that I hope desperately doesn't erupt."

"I'm not convinced about magic, but whatever is inside me—whatever has been messing with my head—it's not something I can control," I say.

"That's your fear talking. I believe you can control it," he says.

"Stop it," Nokk demands.

"Stop what?" Ezzut says, raising an eyebrow.

"Stop playing the wise sage. You're what? Like 20? You have but a few years on us, yet you act like you have it all together. No one should be so calm after their village was destroyed and their people enslaved by the greatest evil in living memory. Empaths, seers, witches... they don't exist. Magic is a fairy tale. It's not real, so stop pretending you're this great, all-knowing miracle we can get all our answers from," Nokk says, disgusted.

"I don't know it all, but I know more about magic than most because I've studied all I could find on it. I'm not wise. I'm not calm... not on the inside, at least. I do a lot of meditating and praying to the god and goddess just to tolerate the insufferable agony that is thrust upon me every day, but it's not always enough.

111

The Lost One: Wrath of the Tyrant

On occasion, I lash out at others or dwell in self-pity until I'm drowning in melancholy," Ezzut admits, "But trust me, I know magic better than almost anyone alive."

"Magic isn't real! There are no gods or goddesses!" Nokk's voice rises, fists clenched.

"Nokk," Ak'dech says, trying to calm him.

"I'll believe what I do, and you can believe purely in science," Ezzut says, "I'm not hurting anyone, so why do you care? Does it have something to do with that shame and guilt you carry around?" he says.

Nokk freezes and glares at Ezzut with an unnatural stillness.

"Why would he feel guilty?" Brezmard asks, confused.

"He's not the only one. In fact, you're the only one who doesn't seem to have some level of guilt haunting you, Prince Brezmard, but I'll let your friends have their confidentiality because I don't usually expose secrets I learn through others' emotions. It's not my place to tear apart friendships. However, your friend here was annoying me," Ezzut says.

"If I actually have magic, and you know so much about it, teach me," I challenge.

"Long ago, my grandfather upset a sorcerer, and the sorcerer put a curse on his entire bloodline to make him and his descendants empaths. Therefore, I studied the magic of empaths because I was trying to find a way to lift the curse off my family. I don't know a thing about active magic like yours," he says.

"You know more than I do," I counter.

"Um, Arid... if you want to continue the search on Tiendys, we should get going," Brezmard says.

"I've given up on the map. I'm reasonably convinced that nothing on that island could help us now. I'll just stay here and learn everything he knows about magic," I say.

"You're just going to learn here in this forest?" Ezzut asks.

"If I have to," I say.

"It takes a great deal of time and self-discovery to learn control. Besides, we are exposed to the dangers of the wild here. This island is not safe. There are limited resources, shelter, and a limited number of capable fighters to defend us. The young ones are especially vulnerable. I'd rather focus all our efforts on getting back to civilization," Ezzut expresses.

"There's an abundance of resources if you know what you're looking for," I disagree.

"I agree with Ezzut. We need to get you all back to Clearhallow. You should be safe there because we're the only island that has successfully fought off Ma'roog's attacks," Norkuz says.

"The dragons can't take everyone that far… at least not in one go. How are we going to get them all back?" Nokk asks.

"Their boat shouldn't be too difficult to repair," Ak'dech says.

"They can't ride in that thing. It's a several week journey by boat, and that small craft is not keeping them alive for that long. The sea is dangerous," Brezmard says.

"We'll attach a rope to the dragons and tow them, and the dragons can take turns pulling," she says.

"That actually sounds promising," Norkuz says.

"Arid, you start your *lessons* with Ezzut. The rest of us will repair the lifeboat," Brezmard says.

The Lost One: Wrath of the Tyrant

"I don't appreciate your skepticism, but I approve of this plan. Lady Arid, let us find a place where it'll be easier to focus," Ezzut says.

"By 'the rest of us,' you don't mean you'll be helping, do you?" Nokk asks Brezmard, sarcastically.

"Of course I'll be helping," Brezmard says, slightly offended.

Chapter Twelve: In Your Dreams

"I think you and Norkuz would get along very well," I comment casually to Ezzut after what feels like hours of me sitting still on the ground with my legs crossed, trying to connect with my supposed magic, "You both enjoy sitting still and not thinking for hours on end," I say.

"Norkuz is one of the most even-tempered people I have ever met. He is less difficult to be around than *some* people I've met," Ezzut says, slightly offending me.

"Well, he doesn't show much expression. Does he have emotions?" I ask.

"As I've said, I don't usually put forth private information freely. He keeps his head clear, but yes, he does feel. Now, focus," he says.

"It's pointless and silly," I say, frustrated.

"Meditation is not pointless. You weren't even aware of your magic because you've never bothered to find it. I wish I could've had the same luxury and be blissfully unaware of my magic. Instead, I can't escape it," he says.

"At this rate, they'll finish fixing the ship before I find a scrap of magic," I say.

"Perhaps, but you've used your magic before, subconsciously. All you have to do is reach out to it then *allow* it to exist," he says.

"What can I do with my magic?" I ask.

"I haven't the faintest idea. You'll have to learn, now shut up and concentrate," he says.

"Fine," I say, closing my eyes.

The Lost One: Wrath of the Tyrant

"You feel that tingling in your fingertips?" he asks.

"Sure, I guess," I say.

"Arid."

I hear Ma'roog's voice in my head, and my sword is in my hand faster than I can think. I find myself on my feet without meaning to, fearfully looking around while screaming *no* out loud to scare the voice away.

"What are you so afraid of? That fear is what's keeping you back. You have to get over it," Ezzut says.

"Is it the magic that puts Ma'roog's voice in my head?"

"Magic likes to connect with magic… like a magnet," he says, as enlightenment turns his tone darker, realizing that Ma'roog is telepathically communicating with me.

I don't think Ezzut can hear Ma'roog's voice like I can, but I think he senses my fear. I can tell he isn't happy that Ma'roog is speaking to me.

"Lady Arid, Ma'roog can sense your magic from a much greater distance than I could, no doubt, which means he knows your power is a threat to his throne. In fact, he's so powerful that it's incredibly difficult for entire armies to defeat him without magic, and you Miss, have similar powers, which makes you the best hope of ever defeating him."

"Does that mean he's a sorcerer too?" I ask.

"Yes, a very powerful one," he says.

"So, my choices are… either I destroy him, or he destroys me?" I ask.

"That is likely the case, yes," he concurs.

"But he has a massive army to shield him," I say.

"Lady Arid, I can sense your magic is stronger than his. The only issue is that you have no idea how to use it. I suspect he also seeks to find Glul'gur because it holds secrets about magic nobody has known for hundreds of years, and he would not pass up an opportunity to enhance his powers. Clearly, he hasn't found it yet, or we'd know. We wouldn't stand a chance, and there would be no more resistance. Lady Arid, you need to find Glul'gur before he does, but you need to connect to your own magic first," he says.

"But he's in my head," I say.

"Block him out," he says.

"How do I do that?" I cry in frustration.

"Calm down. You'll hear his voice for a while, but you'll learn how to defeat him. He'll try to keep you scared to prevent you from learning and controlling your magic. You can't be scared of him. He is not unbeatable. You are just as powerful," he consoles.

I sit back down, take a deep breath, and close my eyes to focus better.

"You're trying to learn magic. How quaint. I could teach you. You don't know what you are capable of, but I'll show you if you accept my help," Ma'roog says in my head.

"I'm good, thanks," I say aloud.

Ma'roog laughs and asks, *"Where's Glul'gur?"*

"I won't help you," I say.

The scars on my arm that I've had since birth start burning. No one on Vrarg has been able to tell me why I have these scars, but it feels like I strained a muscle.

Could it be from the magic? I think to myself.

The Lost One: Wrath of the Tyrant

"You don't understand. I could take you under my wing and give you everything. You'd have power—and knowledge—and you can have your people back if that is what you really wish," he says.

"My... my people?" I ask.

"I know where they are. I know how to set them free," he says.

"Wherever they are, you put them there," I say.

"Don't worry. They're safe where they are... unhappy, but very safe. Help me find Glul'gur and conquer Clearhallow, and you'll get your life back. I'll let you take your place as chief of Tiendys, and we could both rule as we're meant to," he exclaims.

"You're no ruler. You're a murderer," I say.

"So you won't side with me because I've taken lives? Haven't you done the same? Or have you forgotten the Rul Warriors you've slain in the past that bloodied your hands? Time does not remove stains from your conscience," he says.

"I was surviving! I had no choice. If they weren't trying to kill me, I would have let them be," I say.

"Would you?"

"I won't help you," I say.

"I recommend you reconsider your answer. You see, I know what's wrong with your memories, but do you? They are so inconsistent and unreliable," he claims.

"I don't know what you're talking about," I say.

"I've seen your dreams. You don't remember as clearly as you believe."

"What?" I ask.

"My offer won't last forever. Alone, you won't even learn to cast a simple illusion before I have the whole world at my command. You can't run anywhere I can't find you. Join me or die," he growls.

"I won't help you," I repeat.

"Then you choose destruction," he snarls, then he sinisterly whispers, *"Answer me this: Who did I kill first? Your mother? Or your father?"*

"Arid, can you hear me?" Ezzut asks, kneeling next to me.

"I've never... had a conversation with him before," I say.

"That was progress," he says.

"Was it?" I ask, as I snatch off my gloves, disturbed by my itching arms and Ma'roog's question about my parents.

"I can sense you're distressed... and your arm..." he says, as he examines the red, swollen scars.

"It burns with my visions and my nightmares too," I say.

"Magic does have consequences, but the burning will get better the more you exercise your power and learn to accept it," he says.

"He killed my parents, intrudes my thoughts, and now my arms are burning! I hate him," I say, holding my arms out in an effort to cool them.

"You have valid reasons," he says.

My rage motivates me to practice more magic, so I close my eyes to enter quiet stillness again.

"No, that's enough for today," he says.

"No, it's not," I say.

The Lost One: Wrath of the Tyrant

"Yes, it is. It's time to stop and take a rest. You don't become skilled at any one thing overnight. You work on it over time. Magic has to be done the same way, or you could kill yourself. It's not dangerous just to others, but if you don't know how to handle it, it's dangerous to you too," he says.

"I'm not done," I say.

"Yes, you are," he says, as he grabs my arm and yanks me to my feet.

"Okay, but I expect to continue very soon," I say.

"After you're rested," he promises.

"Sure," I say, unconvincingly.

"Arid, I'm warning you," he cautions.

"I really hate being told what to do," I say.

"If you continue with no rest, you're going to get yourself killed, and I can't let that happen because we need you to stop Ma'roog," he says.

"At least you're not *pretending* to care about me personally," I say.

"I just lost everything I had to that monster, including the love of my life, the one person who helped keep me sane, and I want revenge for his death," he says.

"Okay, I'm on board with the revenge thing. I get that," I say, "Guess I can't blame you for wanting the exact same thing as me. Hmm, I wonder... was Ma'roog with the Rul Warriors who invaded your island?"

"I felt his magic there, so yes. I doubt he's there for long, though. As soon as he's confident that his warriors have absolute control of the island the way he likes, he'll be back to his home base on Gler Island, I assume. Why?" Ezzut asks.

"I'm curious if he participates in the battles he sends his army to, or if he stays away until the battle has already been fought... just wondering how clean he likes to keep his own hands," I lie.

"Uh-huh," he says skeptically, obviously seeing right through the fib.

"Thanks for the lesson," I say, standing abruptly.

"What are you doing?" he asks.

"Since we're done here, I'm headed towards a different type of learning," I say.

He stares at me for a moment then says, "Whatever you're plotting, it's driven by your impulse and anger. I don't think it's a good idea."

"I think it is," I say defensively.

"Fine," he shrugs, "Do as you wish. Just don't get yourself killed. As I said, I want revenge, and you're—"

"The best you've got," I say, as I walk towards the others who are working on the ship.

"Arid! How'd your lesson go?" Ak'dech says, skipping over to me curiously.

"Splendid. We're all doomed," I say, looking around the group.

"What?" she asks.

"Never mind. Where's Nokk?" I ask.

"Nokk? He's searching for more food to stock onboard the boat," she says, mystified.

Nalrai is sleeping on the beach near the woodline. I almost feel bad waking him from his nap, but there's an opportunity I must seize.

"Nalrai, let's find Nokk and Nynnu," I instruct, while gently rubbing behind his ear as he stretches.

"What do you need Nokk for?" Ak'dech asks.

"A different kind of lesson," I say, mounting Nalrai and saddling up, "If I'm going to find Glul'gur, why not consult with the geography expert?" I ask.

"Right now? We're rather busy," she says.

"Clearhallow isn't going anywhere, and we're safe enough on this island for the time being. He can spare a few minutes of hunting," I dismiss, while loosening my grip on the reins, cueing Nalrai that it's time to go.

Ak'dech starts to say something else, but Nalrai takes off, gliding just above the tree line. It isn't difficult to find Nokk because he didn't travel far, and Nynnu makes a great deal of noise as she moves through the trees. Her species is native to ravines and canyons, so she's much better suited for rocky terrains and water instead of the heavy vegetation that's here.

"Nynnu, hold still. You're scaring all the wildlife," Nokk says.

"Indeed, she is," I say, as Nalrai lands.

"Don't worry, I've got this," he says, puffing out his chest.

"Sure you do," I skeptically dismiss his comment, "Do you have a map?"

"A map? Why wouldn't I?" he says.

"Let me see it," I say.

"Uh... sure. Why?" he asks.

"I'm looking for something."

"If this is about Glul'gur, I assure you, I've looked... repeatedly," he says.

"Well, supposedly, if there's someone who can find it, *you're* not the one. I'm the sorcerer, remember? Now where's Xymrar?" I ask, scanning the map as he opens it up.

"Xymrar? Why?" he asks.

"I'm checking out the refugees' story," I claim.

"You think they're deceiving us... warrior spies or something?" he asks.

"Not exactly," I say.

"Then what?" he asks, pointing to the Isle of Xymrar on the map.

"And we're here?" I confirm, tapping a nearby location.

"Yes, but what do you need this for?" he repeats.

"I don't like being this close to a recent warrior attack of that size, do you?"

"No, of course not. That's why we're trying to get their vessel fixed so we can get the hell out of here," he says, "But if they were followed, or even worth chasing after, don't you think we would've been attacked by now?"

"Ma'roog knows I'm here, and I just pissed him off. So, you need to work faster because we leave first thing tomorrow morning. I'll go warn Brezmard and get everyone else hurrying too," I say.

"I'm going to need help gathering food to make sure we don't run out on the trip," he says.

"Gather more plants than wildlife because we don't want them to go bad over the next few days. We'll fish on the way to Clearhallow if we don't gather enough now, but get a move on," I insist.

"Arid," he says, as I get ready to leave.

"What?" I ask.

Nokk doesn't answer immediately, but then he says, "Never mind."

"Whatever," I say impatiently, "Nalrai, I need to talk to Brezmard. Let's go."

Chapter Thirteen: Wings of Death

7he sun has gone down, and most of the sailors are already asleep on the beach around a small fire that burns at the center of camp as we finish the last rushed touches on repairing their escape ship.

"It's going to be fifty percent roaming patrol tonight, which means half of the knights will be on guard at all times keeping an eye out for danger, and the other knights will be sleeping and resting up for their next shift. *Any* sign of trouble, and we're getting the refugees out of here as fast as we can. Anyone not needed to evacuate the refugees will fight because we will need as many knights as possible to hold off the attack. We'll switch shifts every two hours. Ak'dech, Qombaryth, Norkuz, Quldriag, and I will take the first watch," Brezmard says.

"You're going without Kemoss?" Nokk asks.

"Fifty percent guard tonight, remember? I'll be grounded, and she'll take over for me in two hours. Dragons, watch the skies, but don't go much above the trees. Get back to your knight if anything happens. Check in with me every half hour. Arid, you'll check in with Nokk on your shift," he says.

"Fine," I say.

"Now get some sleep," he says, while shooing everyone away.

"In half an hour, we're leaving," I whisper to Nalrai.

It's been 30 minutes, and I'm leaning against a tree watching the dragons patrol. I silently get to my feet when they go check in with Brezmard. Nalrai's napping, but I nudge him awake, signaling that it's time to go. We fly out over the inlet of water where the sailors' ship is anchored. It's a warm, calm night. The ocean is as peaceful as I've seen it, with barely even a breeze to disturb the world.

The Lost One: Wrath of the Tyrant

I've managed to become a natural at melting into my surroundings like Nalrai because he's a nocturnal predator, so his anatomy is meant to blend in with the night sky. Darkness is his terrain, and years of practice allow us to work as a team. That's why it's not difficult to slip away without the knights realizing it, but if I could trust them, I wouldn't have to leave like this. For most of my life, I've tried to avoid trouble, and Ma'roog is the biggest trouble you can find. Therefore, I've kept tabs on him, stayed out of his sight, and identified his usual methods and patterns of attack in the process. Lately, Ma'roog has been busy taking over villages to expand his army, so he has no intention of tracking me down just yet. My magic—that I have no idea how to use yet—is my greatest threat to him. If he starts to really think I'm a problem, he'll come for me, but the Rul Coilband has been taking islands at an unprecedented rate. He's probably already getting ready for another raid, but with the Isle of Xymrar being such a new acquisition, there's bound to be quite a bit of important leadership overseeing the hostages' assimilation into the Rul Coilband's empire. It may sound cocky, but I can tell Ma'roog is threatened by me. Why else would he spend so much time trying to threaten me? However, I haven't done anything to pull his immediate focus, and it's time to change that. I need to fight him as soon as possible to end this war, even if I'm not ready. The more I can slow down his conquering, the more allies we'll have in the war because we're going to need all the help we can get. By now, the knights have probably noticed my disappearance, but they can't catch up, even if they were willing to spare Qombaryth to track me down. I'd normally enjoy a flight like this, but the solemn weight of my mission suppresses any bliss I might feel. As Nalrai glides under the stars, the sky gets even darker. If I weren't so tense, I'd be tempted to drift off to sleep. Eventually, I see lights glowing in the distance, and there's a vague smell of ashes, the remnants of the most recent Xymrar attack.

This island will be heavily guarded, I think to myself, as Nalrai and I approach Xymrar.

For just a moment, doubt races through my mind because there are innocents on this island, innocents who will undoubtedly be at risk no matter how cautiously I target the area, but my plan is to make precise attacks to minimize civilian casualties.

In fact, the survivors of this island are probably all slaves by now, so they should all be grouped together in as few buildings as humanly possible. I bet the sections of town that are damaged from the invasion will be worked upon by prisoners to rebuild, fortify, and turn the areas into a proper military base. With the warriors wanting the cushy areas for themselves, town hall would be a good place as any to have briefs and meetings among their troops.

"Nalrai, go straight through the city. Try to only hit buildings in the town's center, which should be used as a rally point for the Rul Warriors," I command.

As we approach the town's center, we fly right over a guard, but he doesn't seem to notice. The thought that we may kill civilians tonight crosses my mind, but it can't be helped.

"Ready?" I ask Nalrai.

Nalrai rains hellfire on the city's center, and flames envelop entire buildings in an instant. Panic breaks through the air as everyone starts running and shouting, but their screams are drowned out by the sounds of crackling fire. In mere seconds, the whole street burns.

"That row of buildings would be an ideal place for Rul Warriors to set up their barracks and chow hall," I say, as I guide my dragon towards that area.

Nalrai flies low through the street. He expertly navigates around enslaved civilians, buildings, and warriors, barely slowing down for them. The Rul Warriors will take too sizable a hit to ignore tonight, and even if it means a few sacrifices along the way, this island will be free from warrior rule.

"The guards are trying to find us," I say to Nalrai, reaffirming a grip on both my sword and dagger as I notice them on the ground pointing at us.

The Lost One: Wrath of the Tyrant

Nalrai stalls in the sky, roaring and letting off a jet of blue flame to draw the warriors in. He then becomes a whirlwind of death, finally able to let loose his destructive capabilities without fear of damaging what's around him. I sit almost useless on his back, ready to attack anyone who happens to get close enough for me to reach. He dives into the streets, chasing down a couple of warriors' dragons that's trying to fall back. I'm finally close enough to slice a wing, but I don't allow myself to feel bad, even as the blood of a tortured beast spurts over my dragon armor. Suddenly, one of the buildings in front of us catches fire and explodes. I can't hold on as the blast hits me, but I manage to roll when I hit the ground. It hurts, but I'm able to quickly get to my feet and start running through the city. Nalrai is now more focused on getting to me than his opponents, and he takes several unnecessary hits from warriors' swords and their dragons' flames. As he approaches, I reach up to grab his outstretched claw, but something hits me in the shoulder. I go from running forward to falling back, and an arrow sticks out of my arm. The archer hops off his dragon, approaching me slowly in a manner I'm sure he thinks is intimidating. I assess him, and my shoulder, deciding if I'm going to rush him or flee. He draws a sword, intentionally dragging it across the stone road.

"Cocky weirdo," I say under my breath.

When he gets closer, I sprint at him, knock his sword out of the way with my own, and slit his throat with my dagger.

"What an idiot. Should have stuck with the bow and arrow," I scoff.

His dragon roars at me, and his spit covers my suit. I ready myself to fight, raising my weapons.

"No! Arid, this way," a woman runs at me, grabbing my wrist.

I twist away and point my sword at her neck, pausing to take a better look at her.

"You again," I say surprisingly.

"Get out of here. It was foolish of you to come here alone," my supposed aunt says, as I sheath my weapons and follow her through an alleyway.

"I'm freeing Xymrar, whether I live to brag about it or not," I say.

"If you free this island, they'll just come back to conquer it again! You aren't saving any lives being here. In fact, you're doing the opposite. Do you hear those screams? Those are children! You're murdering innocents in a misguided attempt to save them. You should leave this island at once. When Ma'roog is dead, and if the Rul Warriors are ever disbanded, then Xymrar will be free. Until then, you're doing more harm than good," she yells in my face.

The archer's dragon catches up with us and roars.

"Nalrai!" I call, running through the alley, while reaching for my aunt's hand.

"Arid, I can't come with you yet. I'll try and get to Clearhallow when I have the chance, but I need more time to—"

A fireball smashes into the road right beside us, and I black out for a moment.

"H-hey," I hysterically yell, as I begin to crawl over to my aunt, but Nalrai scoops me up in a quick attempt to get away.

"We can't leave her," I shout, trying to squirm out of Nalrai's claws, but he grips tighter, roaring in disagreement as he weaves between a couple more attacks. My struggle to release Nalrai's grip distracts him, and he doesn't notice another dragon coming toward him. He crashes into the dragon, but both beasts manage to stay airborne. Nalrai's blinding blue fire hits the other dragon squarely in the face. It screeches in agony, tumbling toward the ground, and just like my aunt said, I can hear children screaming from all the smoke, fire, and further destruction of their village —children who didn't have to be in danger again.

The Lost One: Wrath of the Tyrant

This was a mistake. What was I thinking? I should have listened to Ezzut. He tried to warn me. At this point, am I any better than the warriors? Or was Ma'roog right about us being the same? Does the blood on my hands count as much as the blood on his? Surely I'm not in the right tonight. No, this wasn't right. How can I help end tyranny when I myself am a murderer? I think to myself.

Nalrai flees full speed from the burning village, and I watch the flames dully, depleted of hope and filled with shame. It's like watching my own village burn, but this time, I'm the one who destroyed it. After this failed attempt to defeat Rul Warriors, I hope magic isn't the only answer to win this war... it better not be... because if we have to rely on me, then all is lost.

Chapter Fourteen: The Horror of War

"*A*rid?" Nokk calls out, as Nalrai and I land at the campsite.

"Nalrai, stay here," I mumble, while numbly jumping to the ground, stumbling over the roots of overgrown trees.

"Norkuz!" Nokk hollers, racing over to me.

"I need to be alone," I say, unsure if the words are intelligible or not because I can barely feel my lips moving.

"What were you thinking? Where were you?" Nokk asks, agitated, as he tries to pull my arm around his shoulders to help me walk.

I push him away and keep staggering in a direction headed far away from everyone.

"Go away," I say.

Nokk walks beside me, animatedly trying to get answers from me. I don't mean to tune out what he's asking, but my mind is racing too fast. I'm in a daze, overwhelmed by guilt for the first time in my life, and I'm having a hard time processing my thoughts. I'm not even entirely sure I'm actually back at camp. I take a few more steps and sit heavily against a tree. I feel lightheaded. My breaths are deep and shaky. I feel sweaty and nauseous.

"Arid, you're covered in blood," Norkuz's deep, calm voice breaks through my daze.

"It's not mine," I choke.

"You sure? You have an arrow in your arm," he berates.

"It's not mine. I killed them," my voice cracks.

The Lost One: Wrath of the Tyrant

I start to rock back and forth with my head in my hands. I want to forget everything. I cannot get a full breath in, but then I mutter, "I'm a monster."

"Hey, take a deep breath," Norkuz says.

"Stop screaming at me! Stop it," I sob.

"You're the only one screaming," Nokk says.

I lean to the side and vomit.

"Leave me alone," I croak, wiping my mouth with my hand.

"No, there's something seriously wrong going on. We need you to tell us what happened," Nokk says.

Dried blood covers my gloves, and the sight makes me even more lightheaded. It's a fierce reminder of my crimes, so I blurt out, "I'm no better than Ma'roog. I've killed dozens of warriors who were more than likely forced into that role, and I've caused suffering to innocents. I wanted to help, but I made it worse," I say, as I force back more vomit and continue vehemently ruminating, "I went to free Xymrar but realized that Ma'roog would conquer it again, and now the only thing I've accomplished is driving up the death toll of this war even more. I could hear children and civilians screaming. I hurt them, and maybe even killed some."

Nokk and Norkuz remain silent for a long time.

"No one's perfect," Norkuz whispers gravely.

Outraged and shocked at his comment I say, "This is beyond human imperfection, Norkuz! I'm a murderer, just like the person we're trying to destroy! I can't pretend to be a hero and save the world when I'm no better!"

"Life isn't about good guys and bad guys, Arid! It's much more complicated than that. War is ugly. All victors shed blood. The people history portrays as heroes weren't always so flawless. Mistakes can be tragically devastating, but sometimes morals aren't the most important thing at the time. Yes, you were in the wrong. You made a mistake that cost lives unnecessarily. That's the horror of messing up in war. Maybe you're not a hero, but you can still help end this nightmare, and right now, that's the most important thing in the world. If we survive this war, then we can address the egregious crime you've committed, but we have to do *anything* necessary to win," he says forcefully.

I can't remember if I've seen Norkuz angry before, but he's certainly fuming now. He presses a bandage into my wound using more pressure than usual.

"Easy for you to say! You didn't just murder a bunch of people. You don't have the blood of innocents on your hands," I lament.

"You think we're so pure and clean of sin?" Nokk asks, "We've killed enemy troops without proof they individually were guilty of any crime. Our hands are stained with the blood of those bested in battle by a monster. We aren't glorious heroes. We're soldiers trying to protect our home."

"And we're willing to do anything it takes to prevent Ma'roog from taking it, even if that means damning our souls to hell," Norkuz says.

"Take a deep breath and soldier up. You can't dwell on your mistake. Focus on moving forward and ending the violence, even if it's through more violence," Nokk says firmly.

My hands are numb, but I can tell they're sweaty. My stomach keeps twisting in knots. My lungs insist I can't fill them fast enough as I hyperventilate. Thoughts still race around my head with dizzying speed. Nokk and Norkuz's words don't matter. They bounce off a shield of disgust and repulsion I have for my actions. I lie down and bring my knees to my chest while letting the vertigo drown out most of my surroundings.

"Will you be okay?" Norkuz asks.

"I'm going to lie here for a while," I say.

"I'll keep an eye on her," Nokk offers.

"No, Nalrai will do that. Give her some space," Norkuz says, as he notices Nalrai anxiously standing nearby.

After a brief hesitation, Nokk sighs and says, "Roger."

I wake with Nalrai's wing draped over me. I slide from under his blanketing embrace and walk to the ocean's inlet on the other side of camp. The dim moonlight is hardly enough for me to see properly, but I've learned how to navigate through the dark over the years. I scoop up a handful of ash from an abandoned fire pit, and then I ease into the water fully dressed, boots and all, until I'm waist-high in it. I wash my hair with the ash then proceed to scrub the blood and vomit off my scales. Afterward, I stand still, closing my eyes and allowing myself to feel the gentle waves sweeping through my fingertips. Despite only half the moon showing, I imagine I can feel her full light shining on my face. I relish the scents of the night, such as the salty sea and the clean smell of blossoms throughout the forest wafting in a barely moving breeze. After a moment, I wander out of the water and sit by the dead fire and stare at the doused pit.

"Mind if I sit here?" Ak'dech asks.

I shrug and ask, "Aren't you on watch?"

"Actually, I've been relieved for the next few hours," she says, while sitting beside me.

"Did they tell you where I went?" I ask.

"It doesn't matter, but whew... your hair's a mess! You have a comb on you?" she asks.

"Nah," I say.

She pulls an ivory comb from her satchel and starts running it through my hair. Then she says, "You know, I'm insanely jealous. Women pay good money to have naturally thick and blonde hair like yours. Of course, with my hair being so dark, I don't have the time or wealth to keep my hair thick and dyed blonde."

She then pulls out a graver, sections my hair, and weaves a pastel blue ribbon into the braid she started.

"You're gorgeous," she says, using the excess ribbon to tie off the end of the braid so it doesn't come loose.

She waits for some sort of response, but I can't bring myself to speak.

"You know, my parents were scientists, but they believed in magic," she says.

"I doubt people who believe so strongly in science actually believe in magic," I say skeptically.

"When I was little, my father would take me out to a stream that runs to the edge of Clearhallow, and he'd tell me about legends and myths. He said Planet Vrarg is alive, and it's a great source of energy. He told me if I tried hard enough, I'd be able to feel the magic flowing through the ground, the water... everything," she says, while digging her palm into the sand.

I have my doubts about magic—and about Vrarg being alive— but I bury my hands in the sand too.

"I don't feel anything," I say.

She takes my hand and pulls my glove off.

"Sit still," she says, as she puts my bare hand back in the sand, "You probably won't believe me Arid, but sometimes, I feel like Vrarg is trying to connect with me... like it's trying to show me something or tell me secrets that only the planet knows."

"Do you ever actually feel something?" I ask.

The Lost One: Wrath of the Tyrant

"Peace," she answers, with her eyes closed.

"So am I the only one who hasn't been doing the meditation thing my whole life?"

She smirks and says, "I don't, usually. Only when I'm feeling nostalgic or intensely stressed, and I doubt Nokk and Brezmard have even considered an attempt at it."

"I feel... something, but I'm unsure how to describe the warm, tingly feeling traveling through me," I say, as my hand rests in the soil.

She lies back, staring up at the stars and yawns, "Yeah, I know."

The world isn't screaming like my memories. It isn't burning like the Isle of Xymrar. It doesn't preach the horrors of war like everyone else around me. In fact, during all the time I've spent traveling the world, the recent meditations I've been forced into made me finally realize that the world is breathing.

Chapter Fifteen: Pub

*I*t's the next morning, and no one has mentioned my venture away from camp last night. Ezzut gave me a funny look while boarding the boat and mumbled something about guilt, but he's carrying on as if nothing happened. He's been attempting to continue our lessons en route. However, I can't focus while on the ship, and apparently he gets airsick. Otherwise, I'd be training on Nalrai's back comfortably in the sky.

The Dragon Knights, Nalrai and I, and all the refugee survivors have now been traveling for several days by sea. We are all on one ship while two flying dragons and their riders take turns towing the boat. It's been a difficult journey, especially for the dragons because they're doing all the work of pulling the rope that's attached to the battered ship. Before reaching Clearhallow, we decide to stop at another island so the dragons can rest. This also gives us a chance to resupply and take a break from being on the cramped ship. As we approach the Isle of Laig, Nalrai leaves my side and helps the other dragons drag the patched-up vessel into the harbor, while workers from the shore rush over to help guide us onto the dock.

"Are you sure this is a good place to stay?" I ask Brezmard.

"Relax," he says.

"Something doesn't feel right," I say.

The Lost One: Wrath of the Tyrant

"We have nothing to fear. It's a traveler's stop. These residents are mostly merchants looking to make profit off voyagers," he says.

"I know. I've been here before, but something doesn't feel right," I say uneasily, looking over my shoulder.

"Don't question my judgment," he says.

"Ha, never thought I'd see you back so soon, Arid Dho'zogg," the innkeeper of the island says, as he walks right up to me with no hesitation.

"For a loner, you know a *lot* of people," Nokk mutters under his breath.

"I've been to almost every northern island that's still free of Rul warrior control," I point out.

"First time I've seen ya bring friends," my acquaintance mentions.

"Aw, J'zren, you know I don't have friends," I say.

"Uh-huh," he says, giving a slight tug at the ribbon I never bothered to remove from my hair.

"No touching," I remind him, stepping back.

"Sure, sure. Well, you're lucky we have space for all of ya. How many guests do you have?" he asks, while silently counting the group, "And are you paying upfront, orrr… are you repaying me at the end of your stay like previous encounters?"

"We're not staying long," I say to J'zren.

"Arid, if he's the innkeeper, I'm sure we can make a deal of some kind to rest up for the night," Brezmard loudly whispers.

"Well, actually, there has been some... trouble on the island lately. A few rowdy warriors have been bullying the travelers and barkeepers. You clear that up for us, and you can all stay free for one night," J'zren offers.

"Deal," Brezmard says.

I thrust my elbow into Brezmard's side.

"What?" Brezmard snaps at me.

"Well, it's so many of us. I'd hate to take up so much space at your inn. What if we all double up in a room?" I propose to J'zren.

"What?" Brezmard objects.

"I count fifteen, so who's the lucky one left without a roommate that's getting their own room?" J'zren snickers in my direction.

"There will be three to a room for the odd number. I volunteer myself and the two young ones to share," I insist.

He smiles sourly and says, "Of course... I'll have your rooms prepared immediately. Oh, and that issue I was talking about... I wager you'll find it in the pub," he says, while walking off with his head held high to direct his employees.

The Lost One: Wrath of the Tyrant

Ezzut's empathic senses must have detected that J'zren is a creep and pervert because he blurts out, "Dreg galtersack," quite disgusted, as J'zren leaves earshot.

"Pardon?" Norkuz blinks in surprise at Ezzut's foul language.

"As you can probably sense, J'zren's not exactly the most upstanding guy. He has to be kept in check... a lot," I say to Ezzut.

"Yet you contribute to keeping him in business," Ozarm accuses coldly.

"You can thank the *prince* for that," I snap.

"I see a fair! They're playing horseshoes!" Naissyt interrupts, as she tugs at my hand and pulls me toward the live band.

"Let's go to the stables first so the dragons can get settled in for the night," I suggest instead.

"Anything wrong with the fair?" Norkuz asks me.

"Not in particular, but it's crowded," I say.

"A distraction might do them some good," he says.

"Stay where I can see you," I say sternly, making sure I get a hold on both Naissyt's and Yrserross's wrists as they try to pull me toward the jousting games.

"They've been stuck on a cramped boat for days, and after everything they've been through, they deserve some amusement," Norkuz says.

"I'll keep a close eye on them," Ak'dech volunteers.

"I'll go too. It'd be nice to stretch my legs," Brezmard says.

"Okay, fine. J'zren's inn is down the street. It's the largest building in town. You can't miss it, and make sure *no one* walks alone," I say.

"Yeah, whatever. Who's going with me to crack a few skulls in the pub?" Nokk asks.

"Let's get the dragons set first," Norkuz says.

"Eh, you can do that if you want. I'm going to find some ale," Nokk says.

"Don't do anything stupid," Ak'dech nags, but Nokk waves her off.

"Someone go with him," she says.

"Fine, I could use a drink," Ezzut murmurs, while running after Nokk.

The other refugees head to the island fair to explore with the girls, and Norkuz goes with me to the stables. I notice he is struggling to get his dragon to enter.

The Lost One: Wrath of the Tyrant

"Quldriag, I know you don't like being confined, but it's just for a night. You survived that big storm in worse conditions. Look, it has plenty of room," Norkuz pleads.

Nalrai, familiar with the stable, makes himself at home instantly by sprinting around the building, scurrying up the wall, and gnawing on a log beam that's part of the inner structure of the stable.

"Nalrai, don't cause too much trouble. I don't want you to break anything and get us banned," I call up to him.

"Speaking of trouble, how much trouble do you think your *friend* was talking about?" Norkuz asks, as he finally gets Quldriag settled into the stables.

"Enough trouble worth paying for seven rooms," I say, as we head back toward the pub.

"I don't trust him, and I don't like the sound of his problem," he says.

"I don't trust him either, but hopefully, Nokk knows not to stir up any trouble before we get there. However, I have zero confidence in that hope. To make matters worse, he's walking around with a bright blue surcoat bearing Clearhallow's insignia, clearly ready for a fight," I say.

"I don't think he's actually looking for a fight for once, just booze, but you're right, we don't exactly blend in with the other travelers and merchants with our armor on," he says.

"I don't like drawing unnecessary attention, and the Dragon Knights aren't exactly... well-liked outside Clearhallow. Don't get me wrong. You're well respected and preferred over the warriors. However, there are certain... biases against you," I say.

"Like what?" he asks, surprised.

"The general consensus is you're all arrogant, self-righteous, and ruthless. You know how the Rul Coilband started off as a self-designated police force? Well, while they evolved into tyrants, your nation started to take their place as global law-enforcement, so other islands are wary the Dragon Knights will head down a similar path as the warriors and end up just as bad as Ma'roog's troops trying to take over the world," I say.

"But we don't often travel away from Clearhallow," he says, baffled.

"That's not what I've heard," I say.

"Why would we? We have enough on our plate. We maintain our trade routes and political relations, nothing more," he insists.

"Sure, which is why I couldn't find a safe-haven on a neighboring island after fleeing yours," I snort.

"You violated our law on *our* island... serious crimes, might I add. We were trying to protect our land," he defends.

"And *I* was trying to find mine. See, in my eyes, I was taking back what belongs to me, but then I was followed to a place where you have no jurisdiction, arrested, and—"

The Lost One: Wrath of the Tyrant

I stop the conversation immediately as we reach the pub, and we stand in shock as Nokk is thrown through the timber planks of the pub's door, which breaks immediately upon forceful contact. He falls backwards on the ground and shrugs off the impact, climbing to his feet dizzily, as the men who threw him out walk back inside, laughing.

"You're dead!" Nokk yells toward the pub, charging back toward the broken door.

"Whoa! Hold on," Norkuz catches him and holds him back.

"Warrior scum!" Nokk spits, face red with rage.

"Well, what have we here?" a warrior says, stepping out of the pub and smiling, as he sizes up the scene, happy to see so few knights unguarded.

Norkuz's attitude changes in an instant. He lets go of Nokk and steps up to the lanky warrior, who's standing tall as though to intimidate him.

"You're dead," Norkuz growls, while grabbing the warrior's green surcoat and lifting him off the ground.

"You're ter-ri-fying now," Ezzut remarks to Norkuz, as he stumbles out of the bar with his face swollen and bruised.

"What's going on?" I ask, completely lost.

"Fight now, talk later," Nokk says to me while barreling into the chest of a second warrior coming out of the tavern's door.

"Let go of him, man-beast," a third warrior yells, while rushing out of the pub and into Norkuz, which makes him lose his balance and causes the first tall warrior to be freed from Norkuz's grasp to finally catch his breath.

Then the first tall warrior gasps and says, "Is that any way to treat your bro—"

"You're nobody," Norkuz interrupts coldly, while effortlessly throwing the third warrior out of the way to finish his attack on the first warrior.

"I'd guess he's *definitely* somebody," I say, leaning against the wall of the pub, just watching, not bothering to join the fight.

Ezzut, clearly full of rage, immediately goes after the discarded warrior Norkuz threw out of the way, and he allows his sorrow and frustrations to release through his fists. He is clearly out of his element and not as great a fighter as the trained soldiers, but he is managing his own well enough for now. Nokk, as scrawny as he may be, fights savagely with what seems like pure rage fueling his attacks. However, Norkuz's brawl is very one-sided. It's like the warrior isn't even trying to fight back.

"You're a traitor and murderer," Norkuz says, pinning the warrior under his foot.

"Pardon, Madam," the warrior wheezes to me, "My brother is slow to let go of a grudge."

"Brother?" I chortle in surprise, "Do tell... if you have the breath."

The Lost One: Wrath of the Tyrant

"He's no brother of mine. He's a murderer!" Norkuz shouts, flustered.

"Since when has that stopped you from allowing someone in your ranks?" I ask pointedly, with a chilly edge to my tone.

"He's a traitor. He murdered my parents because they favored me over him," Norkuz sneers.

"So murder is okay, so long as you don't know the victim personally?" I ask.

If looks could kill, the glare Norkuz forces toward me is one I wouldn't survive.

"This is different. His crime had no good intentions behind it, and he pledged allegiance to our enemies. He's nothing more than scum," he says.

"And you're a hypocrite! You were willing to accept my mistake but won't forgive your brother?" I probe.

"Fight now, morality later—"

Norkuz's words turn into a cry of pain as the warrior stabs a dagger into his thigh. He knocks his brother out with a punch to the face, while Ezzut is busy vomiting after taking a strong hit to the stomach. I throw down the warrior he had been fighting, crouch beside him, find a gap in his armor, and hold the point of my dagger into his shoulder so he can't get up without driving it further into his skin and through his back.

"Hey hotshot, I've never seen Rul Warriors travel, except for a battle, and it's only three of you. Y'all here on vacation or something?" I ask.

"Pathetic bitch," he spits at me.

"Norkuz, you're right. Morals can come *after* the war," I say, forcing my dagger fully into his shoulder as he screams.

"Does… does this island have a prison or something we can stick these warriors in?" Ezzut pants to me, trying to catch his breath.

"A prison? I didn't realize we were leaving them alive. Besides, there's no law enforcement here. It's a place for travelers to rest… nothing more," I say.

"Well, if we can keep them alive, then why shouldn't we? I don't have the stomach for killing and war, especially after all the pain I've felt through my abilities," Ezzut says.

"I'd rather throw them to a horde of hungry dragons," Norkuz growls.

Nokk successfully knocks his opponent unconscious and says, "By Clearhallow law, they'd be hanged as enemies."

"What *won't* get you hanged on Clearhallow?" I mumble sarcastically, leaving my dagger in the warrior's shoulder as I stand.

The warrior then reaches for my foot, and I kick the knife through his shoulder and into his back, causing another screech of agony.

147

The Lost One: Wrath of the Tyrant

"Nokk and I will take care of these scumbags," Norkuz decides.

"How?" Ezzut asks.

"Don't worry about it," Nokk says, "You look queasy from pain or the idea of killing warriors, so I'd suggest you go back in the pub for another drink."

"But Norkuz, you're bleeding out," I mention.

"I'm well aware, but we can handle it," he says confidently, slinging his unconscious brother over his shoulder.

"Fine, I could use a drink anyway," I say, while grabbing my dagger out of the warrior's shoulder.

Between being stabbed and the beating he took from Ezzut, the warrior is unresponsive, but he is still conscious. However, it doesn't look like he'll be much trouble to anyone else tonight.

"I hope they have strong mead in that tavern so I can get drunk as fast as I can to quickly forget about that fight," Ezzut says to me, as he and I walk toward the pub.

"Ezzut, you look very pale," I note.

"I don't fight much because it's difficult when you feel *every* hit *anyone* takes," he says.

"So why fight now?" I ask.

"I wasn't going to let Nokk take on all three of them by himself when I was sitting right there and could help. This is my team now, and I should act like it," he says, as he pushes broken pieces of the pub door open for me to walk through.

Chapter Sixteen: Lies

*A*fter a few drinks, Ezzut and I meander back to the inn and wish each other well as we stumble to our separate rooms. I decide to sleep on the floor so the girls could have the bed, but I wake up in the night hour with Naissyt cuddled up against me. I resist my initial instinct to react violently. Instead, I pry her fingers apart, scoot away, and walk toward the open window. I don't know what woke me, but there's something nagging at the edge of my consciousness. I vaguely remember a dream filled with senseless chattering, a long hallway and prison bars. It was a foggy dream, much less vivid than my nightmares have been as of late. As the girls sleep peacefully, I look out the window, noticing that the moon is high in the sky, approaching fullness. The stars are clear and glimmering, and the breeze seems to carry a faint whisper I can't quite make out. Since I'm bare feet, the dirt floor of the room brings me into direct contact with Vrarg. I can feel its energy... its breaths, so I sprawl out on my back and breathe with it. I don't know how to describe it, but I can feel so much more than my own senses. I can feel the whole world at once: the emptiness of Tiendys, the prisoners moving around being worked to the bone on Xymrar and many other islands, a destructive outburst on Ma'roog's home island, Gler, as he receives an update from his warriors about my attack, and I can dimly sense a concentration of magic that far surpasses the strength of Ma'roog or anything else. Perhaps, it's Glul'gur. I can't pinpoint a specific location, but I'm drawn to it nonetheless. However, something darker pulls my attention—something on Tiendys. It's a black void that brings a feeling of discomfort and twists my stomach into knots. Screeching voices of banshees emanate from the void, and I feel a sudden internal spinning sensation as their dark energy twirls in spirals, trying to suck me in closer to them. I've never believed in a hell, but I have no other word to describe the darkness and emptiness on Tiendys that I'm sensing and feeling drawn to right now. I snap out of the experience, gasping. Covered in sweat, I suddenly want to throw up, but I have the impression I'm being watched.

"J'zren?" I say, while squinting my eyes and looking around the room because it wouldn't be the first time I found him trying to creep in to watch me, hence my reluctance to stay at this inn and why I volunteered to stay with the girls to make sure nothing happened to them.

As I scan the room, I notice our room door is closed, and as I prop up on my knees to get a better view, I see a shadowy figure in the distance out the open window holding remarkably still and apparently staring in at us. I bolt to my feet and jump out the first-floor window, running at them. They scamper off, but whoever it is, it's not J'zren. This person has long hair that flows quickly behind them as they vanish from my sight. I could chase them to see who they are, but if I leave, I'd be leaving Naissyt and Yrserross unsupervised and unprotected. Instead, I watch the spot the figure disappeared from for a few seconds before climbing back into the room and moving Naissyt back onto the bed next to her sister.

It's the next morning, and we all leave the inn and stable to steer towards Clearhallow. I'm used to Norkuz's quiet, professional demeanor. However, his silence since the pub incident has been tainted with a nearly tangible darkness. Ak'dech tries to talk to him, but he is unresponsive to her genuine concern. It's a good thing he doesn't have to stand or walk much because he keeps shifting uncomfortably on his dragon because of his thigh wound, thanks to his brother stabbing him, and he needs to redress it every few hours because blood keeps oozing through the bandages. As we finally approach Clearhallow, we notice that everything on the island is the way we left it.

"Prince Brezmard!" other Dragon Knights yell with relief.

They immediately rush over to escort us in as they spot us.

The Lost One: Wrath of the Tyrant

"Anything happen while I was gone?" Brezmard asks immediately.

"Your father has been worried sick. I doubt he'll let you out of the palace for a year. Also, a group of pirates came by," one of the knights responds.

"You rewarded them?" Brezmard asks.

"Yes," the knight says.

"See to it that these refugees get situated with food and shelter. They will be my honored guests in the castle until more permanent arrangements can be made," Brezmard says authoritatively.

"Yes, sir," a couple of knights say as they fly off to complete the assignment while our dragons pull the boat onto the beach.

Meanwhile, more Dragon Knights come with enough dragons to fly the refugees inland with us, and our dragons are relieved and taken elsewhere. All of us are immediately escorted to the palace and taken to a large, empty ballroom that clearly hasn't been used for a long time because it has spiderwebs on the furniture and in the corners of the ceiling. The doors eerily shut and lock behind us as soon as the last Dragon Knight and refugee enter.

"What's going on?" I ask, looking around warily.

"I don't know," Brezmard admits uneasily.

Everyone is tense and looking around the room wondering what might happen next. Eventually, the doors swing open, and a large man, standing nearly as tall as Norkuz but twice as burly, storms in.

His posture indicates he holds more power and importance than anyone in the room.

"Where the hell have you been?" Chief Firestride yells, marching over to Brezmard and pointing his royal staff in his son's face.

"Father, we had setbacks," Brezmard recoils, flinching, expecting to be hit.

"I feared you to be dead! How dare you allow me to think that," he says.

"There wasn't anything I could've done about it," Brezmard retorts.

"Norkuz!" the chief snaps.

"Yes, sir?" Norkuz replies.

"Why is there a scratch on his face, and why did you allow a setback?" he demands.

"Sir, as Prince Brezmard said, there was nothing to be done about the setback. As for the scratch, I believe he nicked himself shaving, sir," he says.

I smirk, and the chief turns toward me as my barely suppressed laugh captures his attention.

"You! You are the thief I heard about."

The Lost One: Wrath of the Tyrant

"Eh, probably," I shrug.

"I should have you hanged! You're the whole reason my son embarked on this mission in the first place! You have broken our laws and put my heir in danger! You will stand trial at dawn!" he booms, as spittle splashes on my face.

"With all due respect, sir, I don't think that's best—" Norkuz starts.

"Insubordination? From *you*, Norkuz? You're usually so good at knowing your place," the chief says.

"I am *not* your subject, and my fate is *not* in your hands," I say.

"Silence, whelp," he shouts while backhanding me with enough force to send me back a few steps.

"Guards, arrest this thief," he demands.

"Father, stop," Brezmard says.

"I'm not catering to your games this time, Brezmard. You convinced me the first time she had a lead worth following up on, but allowing you to go was a mistake. I have lost my faith in your judgment," the chief says.

"She saved my life," Brezmard cajoles.

"She intruded your sleeping chamber, stole from your desk, caused you physical harm, and dragged you into danger! I should *not* have permitted this foolish expedition!" his father reiterates as guards grab my arms.

"Dammit, listen to me, for once! She is *not* our enemy!" Brezmard raises his voice.

"Don't yell at me, boy!" the chief says while smacking him across the face.

"Where are you taking Lady Arid?" Naissyt cries, visibly upset.

"Who are these people?" the chief asks, finally acknowledging the others for the first time as his son shies away, tenderly touching his face.

"Refugees from the Isle of Xymrar, sir. Ma'roog now controls their homeland," Nokk says while giving a brief glance of pity toward Brezmard.

"Fine. Do with them as you must," the chief tells the guards, "As for *these* Dragon Knights, they are to be punished. Extra duty for those three, and the prince is not to leave his room for a week without my explicit permission."

"We were attacked by a dragon. It's not anyone's fault," Brezmard protests.

The chief ignores Brezmard's complaints and says to the guards, "Make sure the prisoner is well bound, and don't bother to offer her food or water."

The Lost One: Wrath of the Tyrant

"You can't be serious?" I shout, yanking my arms free from the guards, "How has Clearhallow survived so long with *you* in charge? You're just as barbaric as Ma'roog!"

"Prepare the gallows. The prisoner will forgo her trial and be hanged at dawn," he says cruelly.

"Father!" Brezmard yelps.

"To your room!" the chief retorts.

The palace starts shaking, and a large blast causes the ground to tremble. The warning bell I heard during my first visit here follows the ear-splitting sound of an explosion.

"An attack now, of all times?" the chief bellows.

"Where did you take my dragon?" I ask the guards.

"*You* are a prisoner! You two, take her to the dungeon then join the fight," the chief says, appointing Ak'dech and Nokk to be my escorts, "The refugees can stay here for the time being. This isn't their fight. Norkuz, escort Brezmard somewhere safe. Everyone else, to battle!"

"Let's go, and don't talk," Ak'dech says, while guiding me by the elbow as she walks quickly toward the door.

Nokk walks on my other side, just as hurriedly.

"Of all the guards, I can't believe the chief chose you two to escort me to the dungeon," I say, frustrated.

156

"Of course. We follow orders," Ak'dech says.

"Usually," Nokk whispers with a wink in my direction.

"Walk, thief!" Ak'dech says while tugging on my arm.

"Where are we going?" I ask, hushed.

"Where do you think?" she says.

As soon as we get outside, they start running towards the dragon stable, and I follow. Any guards that heard the chief's commands must've gone off to join the fight. Nokk rushes into the stable without hesitation, and Ak'dech glances back to make sure no guards are coming as he unlocks metal doors and starts releasing all five dragons one-by-one. Meanwhile, all shades and colors of fire from dragons' breath light up the darkening, smoky sky over the beach of Clearhallow during the attack. Nalrai immediately snatches me off the ground as he is released and heads towards the battle, only slowing down to allow Qombaryth and Nynnu to catch up as Kemoss and Quldriag rush off to find their partners.

"Rul Warriors have never made it past the shoreline before," Ak'dech says.

"As long as we keep them from the village, it's fine," Nokk says.

There's chaos on the beach when we arrive. The knights are vastly outnumbered, and the warriors are clearly not here to take prisoners. A mist of blood and smoke fills the air, and it sticks to any inch of skin I don't have covered. My mask does well to protect my lungs from the contaminants, but it can't block out the reek of death carried by the mist.

The Lost One: Wrath of the Tyrant

"Arid! Head to that cave," Ak'dech points urgently.

"Why?" I ask.

"It's Ma'roog!" she yells, while navigating Qombaryth towards a hole in a nearby cliff leaving Nalrai and I behind.

"Nalrai, go," I waste no time saying.

Nalrai lands at the mouth of the cave with Nynnu and Nokk right behind us. I hop off, holding out my sword.

"Show yourself, coward!" I say, walking into the cave until it's almost too dim to see anything.

Nalrai walks ahead of me, gurgling a ball of fire in his throat to light the way.

"Arid, watch out!" Norkuz's unexpected voice warns behind me.

I spin around in time to see an arrow scrape my arm. Time almost seems to sit still as I identify my attacker. It's Nokk... holding a bow, and it's aimed directly at me. Surprisingly, Norkuz tackles Ak'dech before she has a chance to swing her sword at me, and I rush at Nokk, wrestling him to the ground as Norkuz pins Ak'dech to the ground.

"What the hell, Ak'dech?" Norkuz hollers, furious.

She gasps in pain as he twists her arm.

"You lied to me," I snarl in Nokk's ear.

"Arid," Nokk pleads, "Please let me ex—"

I shove him into the ground harder, hitting his face against a rock. He yelps in pain then clenches his jaw to silence himself from crying out loud.

"What explanation could possibly make this okay?" I ask.

Nokk and Ak'dech's dragons are squealing in confusion, and Nalrai's growling, fire still waiting in his throat.

"I-I'm sorry," Ak'dech says, sounding as though she's about to burst into tears.

"You're *sorry?* You just tried to murder an ally, and you're *sorry?*" Norkuz yells at her, "Speak fast. You have one chance to gain *any* sympathy, traitor."

"We didn't want to hurt any of you! We were following orders. Ma'roog let us live on the condition that we spied for him. We were kids when they killed our parents and took over our ship. We were scared, so we agreed. He had his best spy train us and tutor us in our studies to make sure we could join the knights. I swear, we didn't want to, but Ma'roog has a way of getting in your head. I was just trying to protect my brother!" she claims.

"I trusted you… with my life! And all this time, you were *never* on our side!" Norkuz's voice cracks as he screams, tears in his eyes.

I can't deny that despite my countless claims that I'd never trust anyone, this betrayal feels like a sharp knife to the gut.

The Lost One: Wrath of the Tyrant

"And why were *you* here?" I ask Norkuz, distrustfully.

"Ezzut said something was off with these two as you left the castle. I promised I'd keep an eye on them," he says.

"Where are Brezmard and the refugees?" I ask suspiciously.

"Brezmard is taking them somewhere safe. He'll sneak back to fight when he can," he says.

"I was going to be hanged at dawn anyway. Why help me now?" I barrage.

"You think we were going to let you be hanged?" he asks incredulously.

His reaction stuns me. Despite the time we've spent together, I hadn't even considered them rescuing me as a possibility. I might have believed him if I heard him say it before Nokk and Ak'dech revealed their treachery, and I certainly can't trust the Dragon Knights after what just happened. However, Norkuz does seem genuinely upset by their betrayal, and he did step in to warn me before Nokk could shoot.

"What are you going to do with these two?" I ask, less harshly.

"They'll be tried for treason. Then they'll be hanged. You can't trust a traitor," he says, voice breaking again.

"Good," I say icily, "I'll trust you to handle them. The innocent people here didn't betray me, so I'm going to see what I can do to save them. Then I'm leaving. Tell your prince our deal is broken. I don't want to see any of you again."

I quickly climb back in my saddle, and Nalrai flies me out into the fight. I take all my frustration out on the attacking warriors and mercilessly slice away at any warrior I can reach. I occasionally feel new scratches on my body, but I focus only on where my sword swings. I don't know how long the fight lasts, but eventually, the warriors retreat. I stare after them, filled with rage and the sting of betrayal. Scores of dead dragons and soldiers are piled on the beach, and countless injured troops sprawl about among the bodies. I spot Brezmard kneeling mournfully in the sand as he looks at the village's catastrophe, and his dragon waits patiently by his side. I glance at the cave, hoping to see Ak'dech and Nokk so the pain of betrayal is more fresh on my mind than the tragedy around me, but I can't see anything inside it. Nor do I spot anyone I left there. I continue to scan the devastated armies, and an injured soldier by the waterline catches my eye. It's a female warrior crawling closer to the body of the dragon I assume she rode.

"Nalrai," I urge him toward the warrior.

"Hello, Arid," she sniffs, tears staining her face as she forces a chuckle and says in slow breaths, "I said I'd make it to Clearhallow, aye? I hoped it would be under much different circumstances though."

"You're really my aunt?" I ask, climbing off Nalrai and kneeling beside her.

She nods and says, "I was traveling when Ma'roog razed your mother and I's village. When I returned, I was taken prisoner by a crew of warriors who were clearing out the ruins."

Then she forces a smile and says, "You look much like my sister. I'm sure she'd be proud of how strong you've become."

"What's your name?" I ask, offering her a hand up.

The Lost One: Wrath of the Tyrant

"Mazokah, and this is... was... my dragon, Ere'vay," she says, as her fingers trail along the dead dragon's scales.

I help her to her feet and notice she has a deep cut above her knee, and it causes her to nearly collapse the second she stands.

"I'm no healer, but I've watched Norkuz bandage enough wounds to help you with that," I say, helping her onto my dragon.

"Why not use one of Clearhallow's healers?" she asks.

"The Dragon Knights betrayed me. We're leaving," I say.

"Ah, that's most unfortunate. It's been too long since I've had family by my side. At least we finally have each other," she says.

"I concur. Nalrai, get us away from here... far, far away."

Chapter Seventeen: Catching Up

*M*azokah is sleeping as we land on the island of Zir'gez, and Nalrai flies us to the old library where the bookshelves are wooden and rotting away from age and neglect. Some of the shelves have collapsed, leaving books scattered across the ground in messy piles, however, I make myself at home on the overgrown grass that has long covered the floor of the ruins.

"Where are we? What is this?" Mazokah asks, waking up in the half-standing decayed remnants of the library.

"This is where I lived most of my life with Nalrai, and a few hundred books. This is also where I was staying when the Dragon Knights took my map," I say, while looking at the mid-day sky through a hole in the ancient roof that collapsed a long time ago.

"Cozy," she says, but she seems uncomfortable, "Is it not haunted?"

"Haunted? No, I don't believe in ghosts or spirits," I say, as I stretch out in the soft, overgrown grass.

"Hmm... tell me about your magic," she says, sitting beside me.

"My magic? How'd you know I have magic?" I ask.

The Lost One: Wrath of the Tyrant

"My sister insisted you were magical while she was carrying you in the womb, but it was confirmed the day you were born. Our people spent a lot of time studying magic, so these scars on your arm that look like you've been cut or whipped were instantly recognized. Every powerful sorcerer has them," she says.

"Why is that?" I ask.

"Something to do with being entwined with the magic, but no one really knows," she shrugs, "So, what can you do?"

"What can I do? I guess… I can see and feel things," I say.

"My dear, your magic is far too powerful to be an empath or a seer," she scoffs.

"Maybe you are right… because… I don't *feel* like empaths can feel. I *feel* like Vrarg can feel. It's like I'm connected to the planet. I can feel it breathe, and sometimes I can feel things happening far away. I also have nightmares that I think are linked to the magic, and I have this recurring dream where I'm in a large prison with faceless people shouting from their cells."

"That's interesting," she says.

"That's it really," I say.

"That's *it* for now, but we'll work on that," she says.

"Do you have magic?" I ask.

"No, not at all," she says, "But it seems I've heard more about it than you have. When I was growing up, the people of Likenhallow were shunned for our belief in magic. All our myths and legends revolved around it, but no one believed us. Frankly, there are probably many more islands with magical people, but we were one of the few to not dismiss our seers and empaths as crazy. We actually listened to ours. Most times, empaths are told they're too sensitive and that they're only imagining their pain, but I saw your mother up close. She was cursed with the gifts of an empath, and she did not *imagine* her suffering," she says.

"My mother was an empath?" I ask, sitting up, "So she felt…"

"All the joys and woes of the village, yes. In fact, her abilities made her a good and kind hand to the chief, but I never envied the agony and suffering she endured from feeling everyone's pain. I hope, for her sake, she died soon after Ma'roog's attack began," she says.

My head hurts as two conflicting memories shoot through my head. In one, I can see my mother crying over the body of my father. In the other, my father sends me off on Nalrai as my mother's body lay motionless on the ground.

"Arid, are you okay?" she asks, as I rest my head in my hands, squeeze my eyes shut for a moment, and try to sort out the conflicting memories.

"I'm fine. I just… wish I could remember them," I say, "It seems that everyone has a story about my parents. In fact, a pirate told me that my father was a chief, but I don't know whether or not I believe him."

"The pirate spoke truth," she says.

The Lost One: Wrath of the Tyrant

"So what does that make me?" I ask.

"Well, seeing as you had no elder siblings, you are the undisputed heir to the chieftain chair. Congratulations," she says.

"When I was fleeing from the Dragon Knights and ran into you with the Rul Warriors, you said some of our people are alive somewhere. Do you know where?" I ask.

"Not exactly. I heard they were taken to a place called Draug. I don't know much about it, but I've heard whispers that it's like limbo, a world between life and death. They say it's a prison you can't escape from," she says.

"How do we get them out?" I ask.

"I haven't the faintest idea," she says.

"None of your seers predicted or warned about this?" I ask.

"It's not as simple as that. They can see all of time: the past, present, and future—all at once—which is why they're often written off as insane. Therefore, the future is never set in stone because they see infinite possibilities, and any prophecies they make are based on the most probable course of events they can figure out. There's a lot of room for error in their predictions," she says.

"Then what good is a seer?" I ask.

"A seer's guess is better than no idea at all, and the further down a road of possibility you travel, the clearer the answers. It seems the most accurate predictions are of the near future, but the further in time you try to foretell, the more flawed the prediction," she says.

"So… we're winging it… with no clear rule book of how to control my magic," I say perplexed.

"Practice," she says.

"Not the response I was looking for."

"No, I imagine not," she chuckles, "But if you want a shortcut, it's said that the birthplace of magic is where the power is the strongest, and they say there is plenty of knowledge flowing through the island. According to the legends, it would certainly be the easiest place to learn anything about magic."

"Is the island called Glul'gur?" I ask.

"Yes. I'm glad you've at least heard of *that*. The trouble is, no one's been able to find it despite the passing of many generations. It's been said that it was once an inhabited village. They traded and compromised with other villages just like any other island. Then one day, some unknown disaster erased it from the map," she says.

"Maybe I can find it. I think I've *felt* it before."

"Well, lead the way," she gestures toward the dragon and the sky.

"But I don't know *where* it is… yet," I say.

"Then I guess you're learning how to control your magic without it," she says.

The Lost One: Wrath of the Tyrant

"I guess so. What were my parents like?" I say, quickly changing the subject.

"Aren't bedtime stories supposed to be *before* bed?" she jokes then continues, "They were kind. Your father was a fair chief who spent most of his time figuring out how to better the lives of the people of his village, but he was a very busy man. Your mother helped him with his duties and kept up the morale of the people by listening to their life stories at the marketplace when she was out shopping. She would share their concerns with your father so he could incorporate the changes and make the island better. One day, a house was torn apart by a dragon gone mad. The next day, your mother went with a group of soldiers to help clean, and she made sure carpenters were sent to perform repairs. Both of your parents were always very busy helping the villagers. The people loved them, and they always made plenty of time for you once you were born. Likenhallow was thriving under your father's reign. Our trade relations were growing, food was plentiful, and our army was strong and ready with defenses that always held strong when the Rul Warriors came to attack. The whole village started to think we were invincible. We had crews out exploring the world, looking for Glul'gur. Meanwhile, they were bringing back knowledge from other people and villages too. One day, I traveled to a nearby village to find out whether they'd be interested in trade opportunities or not. When I got back, our village was nothing but a smoldering pile of ash with warriors rummaging through the ruins checking for survivors. They spotted me when I was trying to flee, and I was forced to join their army. I didn't see any one I knew from our village, so I thought all our people were gone. Of course, I later learned they took many people from Likenhallow and made them prisoners. I just don't know exactly where they are or how to get there."

"I wish I could've grown up with them," I lament.

"It's a cruel world caught in an even crueler war. You've done well though, considering your situation. I'm sure they'd both be very proud of you," she says.

"I'm not so sure," I say, remembering the screams on Xymrar.

"You were trying to save those people. Your attempt was misguided, but well-meaning," she says, like she knows what I'm thinking, "Besides, there were only a few civilian casualties. I don't recall the exact number, but it was shockingly small."

"There shouldn't have been *any* casualties, and I shouldn't have been there," I say, shaking my head.

"You have to move on… at least until the end of this war. When we have our people back and we've defeated Ma'roog, then you can have a proper funeral for them, give a formal apology, or whatever it is you need to do to feel better. Until then, you can only look forward," she says.

Nalrai prances over and lays down right next to me and pushes his head into my lap forcefully, nearly knocking the wind out of me. He's covered in grass from rolling around in the fields.

"Hello there," I chortle, scratching his chin.

He rolls over on his back and starts licking the cuts on my arm that are showing through the slashed glove.

"Incredible how those slashes you took have healed so much already. They stopped bleeding on their own after what, a few minutes? Those cuts were pretty deep. You should have died without treatment," Mazokah says.

"I've always healed fast. Norkuz, the Dragon Knight healer I traveled with recently, was constantly saying how I heal *too* fast," I say.

169

The Lost One: Wrath of the Tyrant

"Want to hear my guess?" she asks.

"What?"

"Magic. I've heard of sorcerers having the ability to heal wounds. I wouldn't be surprised if you heal yourself subconsciously," she says, "Anyways, what happened with you and the Dragon Knights?"

"They're liars… can't be trusted," I say.

"Ah, so they betrayed you. Typical Dragon Knights. Their people have a history of stabbing ours in the back. It figures they haven't changed," she says.

"What exactly… happened all those years ago? I've heard there was a divide, which led to us settling on Tiendys instead of Clearhallow… something about Clearhallow didn't believe in magic, but we did. Is that all there is to it?" I ask.

"Magic *was* the main motivator, yes, but there were divisions before then—sibling rivalry, specifically—that festered and built over time. Many years ago, we lived on Clearhallow, and technologies were less advanced. We hadn't really learned how to make peace with dragons, and we were like uncivilized barbarians, one step up from beating people over the head with sticks. Of course, we still slaughter each other like animals now, but we've started to form a sense of morality over time and progress. Our scientists started to make breakthroughs. Blacksmiths were learning how to make steel, and with the advancement of knowledge came the disbelief of our ancient stories and traditions. That's when seers were first deemed insane, and more and more people began to believe it. Eventually, it came to a point where those who still held to their belief of magic were mocked and shunned. Now, another thing to note is the state of the royal family.

Elok Dho'zogg, your 4th great-grandfather, was chief. He didn't much believe in magic, but he tolerated those who did. However, he was old, and his two sons knew that he'd pass soon enough. The elder son, Alruz, didn't believe in magic and thought those who did, including his younger brother, were fools. They bickered and fought, and this drove them apart. Alruz planned to ban the traditional practices of his ancestors when he became chief. His brother, Miyan, was obviously upset at the declaration. They ended up dueling for the throne. Miyan lost. After his defeat, he was more bitter than before. He stated that he would leave Clearhallow to find a new land where he could believe in peace, and he invited anyone who wished to join him. He also promised freedoms his brother wouldn't permit and vowed to build a strong community culture that wouldn't shun the old ways. He had a fair amount of followers who packed up and sailed with him to the new island of Tiendys," she says.

"So Miyan ruled over Likenhallow, and his brother Alruz was chief of Clearhallow? Which means, I'm a direct descendant of Miyan, and... I imagine the current chief of Clearhallow is a direct line from Alruz?" I decipher.

"Yes, his bloodline managed to keep the throne," she says.

"So Brezmard's my cousin?" I ask, gagging over the thought.

"Prince Brezmard? Yes, I suppose he's your... fourth cousin," she confirms, "Listen, I've heard blood runs thicker than water, but it isn't always true. Family *does* stab each other in the back sometimes, so don't feel obligated to consider him kin," she says.

"Believe it or not, he's the one who did the least damage during my brief alliance with the Dragon Knights," I realize aloud, "It's his father who wanted me dead. Brezmard did his best to keep me alive."

171

"Really? I've heard he's kind of an ass," she says.

"He definitely can be."

"So, what's the plan for us? How do we go about finding Glul'gur so you can learn more about your magic and become stronger?" she asks.

"First, that's a deep cut above your knee. You need to heal and rest. From there, I have no idea."

Chapter Eighteen: Lokk

7he next day, Mazokah stands close by watching intently as I stand outside the ruins of the library pointing a long stick at Nalrai like a sword. He stands ready to pounce with his tail swishing back and forth as though he's nothing more than a playful kitten. I lunge at him, jabbing the stick forward. He hops to the side to avoid the hit. Expecting his reaction, I spin and bonk him on the nose lightly just as his full weight lands on the ground. He recoils and sneezes before pouncing forward, tackling me to the ground, and grabbing the stick between his teeth. Slobber runs down his chin as he gnaws on it, and the branch breaks almost instantly. He makes a noise somewhere between a purr and a whine, disappointed that the branch is broken.

"What did you *think* was going to happen?" I laugh, pushing him off of me.

"Watching him hop around innocently like that, no one would guess how truly terrifying an opal salamander can be," Mazokah says.

"He's a good dragon; although, I've heard they're nearly impossible to train," I say.

"Yes, they are. Those who were able to tame one used to be treated as if they were a god."

"How did my family end up with him?" I ask.

"Nalrai in particular has a tragic story. A dragon hunter fell upon his nest when he was a fledgling. The hunter slayed the mother dragon and sold anything he could from her body, except her hide, which he proudly wore as a cloak. He captured her three fledglings from the nest and took them on his ship. They became ill being away from their home without their mother, and sadly, the other two didn't survive the journey. He took Nalrai to a market to sell to the highest bidder. As you can imagine, a dragon so rare and dangerous can make you a fortune. Fortunately, your grandfather was negotiating potential trades with the village. He saw Nalrai and purchased him from the hunter. Nalrai was wild and wasn't easy to take care of. He kept biting people around him and destroying things. It took a lot of training to get him used to domestic life, but he clearly turned out alright," she says, reaching out to pet him, but he snarls and takes a step back.

"Nalrai," I say sternly.

"It's alright. He's never cared for me much," she says, "I'm glad he's protected you all this time."

"Best friend I could've ever asked for," I say.

"So, I have an idea," she says, clapping her hands together.

"An idea about what?" I ask.

"A few years ago, I heard rumors about an island called Lokk. Ma'roog hasn't shown any interest in it yet, and the people there aren't really much of a threat to him because they're not fighters. They treasure knowledge above all else. I've heard that their scientists and mathematicians at one point claimed a theory that our world is connected to another by a magical passage. So, I was thinking, *maybe* they were talking about Glul'gur.

If we can find their research, it may have clues as to how we can get there," she says.

"What if we can't find it?" I ask.

"What have we got to lose by trying?" she says.

"Good point. How far is Lokk from here?" I ask.

"Navigation was never my strong point, but considering how far north we are, I wouldn't think more than a day or two. Do you have a map?" she asks.

I spread my arms wide open and say, "We're standing next to an old library. I'm sure there's one in there *somewhere*."

We split up and start sifting through books. I think I remember the general area one of the maps was in. I start there and read titles as I peruse the shelves. The people of Zir'gez obviously valued creative literature over other genres because there are only a couple of texts related to history or geography in the whole library. As I walk past the dilapidated bookshelves, the ribbon in my hair gets snagged on a splinter. I stare at the ribbon for a second before snatching it from the rotten wood, then I loosen the ribbon from my hair and finally untie the braid.

"Nalrai," I say calmly, staring at the reminder of betrayal, "Burn this."

He blows a little puff of fire at the ribbon I'm holding, and I watch it burn in my gloved fingers until the final ashes blow away in the breeze. I slowly sink to my knees as I watch the ashes scatter. I don't even react to the hand I feel on my shoulder.

The Lost One: Wrath of the Tyrant

"Are you okay?" Mazokah asks.

"I thought they were my friends," I say, pain hitting me as I finally let it sink in, "They were my friends, and they betrayed me. I didn't even mean to trust them. I knew I shouldn't trust them, but I did."

"Are you talking about the Dragon Knights?"

"Yes," I say, as silent tears drip from my face.

"I'm sorry," she says while hugging me.

"It's fine," I say gruffly, gritting my teeth and pushing back my emotions, "Let's get back to it. We have work to do."

"You're right. The faster we find this map, the sooner we find the knowledge to locate Glul'gur," she agrees.

After finding the map strewn amongst a pile of books on the floor, we immediately head to Lokk Island. Dragons aren't welcome here, except as experiments, and Mazokah's leg is too much of an impairment to risk going on this mission. Therefore, Nalrai and Mazokah are staying out of sight, flying well overhead in the clouds while we are here.

"Excuse me," I say, stopping a villager in the street.

"Can I help you?" an annoyed scrawny man asks, carrying a bag bulging with books.

"I hope so. You look like a scholar. I'm a traveler, and I've heard about a theory developed here about a passage to another world. Do you know anything about that?" I ask.

"Ha! Those theories have been debunked. All the research that went into them is in the museum," he says, pointing to the other side of town.

"Great. Is there an admission fee?" I ask.

He rolls his eyes impatiently and says, "Yes, obviously there's a fee. You think you can just walk in and see our treasures for free?"

"No, of course not. Thank you," I say.

"Ugh, foreigners," he mutters under his breath as he moves along.

As I stroll down a side street on my way to the museum, I discreetly pick the pocket from a man strutting around dressed in velvet and gather a handful of silver and bronze coins. I'm unfamiliar with the currency, but surely, it should be more than enough, unless they charge a ridiculous entrance fee. I'd rather not have to steal the research, but I might not have an option because I doubt there will be a clear answer of Glul'gur or Draug's whereabouts outlined on the first page in the display case, especially after what that arrogant prick I talked to said about the magical passage theories being debunked. I'll probably have to dig through pages of research for a while to find anything related to a portal between worlds, but now that I'm here, it's time to scout out the building. I notice there are guards with spears standing still by the entrance. They let me pass without so much as a look in my direction. I walk inside to the first room. It has a sturdy desk made of dark wood.

The Lost One: Wrath of the Tyrant

There are lots of parchment piled on top of it along with some quills, an inkwell, and a bag on the edge of the desk for fee collections. There are a couple of guards standing behind the man that's standing behind the desk waiting to take my coins.

They must take this museum very seriously because Clearhallow didn't have as many knights guarding their prisons as this place does, I think to myself.

"One admission?" the man behind the admission stand asks.

"Yes," I say.

"Six fellings," he says.

I hold up the handful of change in my hand and poke through it for a moment, plainly clueless.

"Uh... six fellings?" I say, scrambling to grab six silver coins.

"Correct. What brings you to town?" he asks.

"The pursuit of knowledge," I say, handing over the coins.

"Looks like you need it. Where's the sixth felling?"

"Oh, apologies," I say, handing over another coin, legitimately embarrassed by the mistake.

"Where did you get this money from, anyway?" he asks, holding it up to examine it.

"Sold a book to a fellow on the street," I say.

"You read?" he asks, surprised.

"Am I good to go in or not?" I ask, irritated.

"Sure," he says suspiciously.

"Have a nice day," I say over my shoulder as I walk into the museum.

"Keep an eye on her," I hear him whisper to the guards.

Don't panic, and don't look suspicious, I remind myself.

I walk around the museum looking for displays that mention ancient stories of Glul'gur, Draug, or other worlds my family may be hidden in. As I peruse, I notice these people are seriously obsessed with their knowledge. The whole building is filled with papers and books about theories and scientific studies. The amount of research projects I see, all of which are secured behind guarded glass, are greater than the number of books I've seen in most libraries, and the building itself is very secure. It's going to be hard to get what I need without being noticed. I evaluate my surroundings and look at all the potential entry and exit points, just in case I need to escape in a hurry, but the only option is the front door. As I browse the aisles, I finally locate an exhibit that interests me. The description reads: Alternate Realms and the Tunnels Between, and the glass display has a book opened to a page with a complex diagram that I can't make heads or tails of. I don't know how much Mazokah knows about math or science, but I doubt she knows as much as the experts who came up with this theory I'm looking at right now. I doubt even the scholars on Clearhallow would know where to begin.

The Lost One: Wrath of the Tyrant

I've been in the museum for probably half an hour, which is more than enough time to look over every centimeter of it. It'll be difficult, but I'm confident in my ability to succeed in getting the information I came for, with a little help, of course.

"I'm still not sure about this plan," Mazokah says, as we fly high in the sky on top of Nalrai's back to avoid being seen by the villagers of Lokk.

"I need a distraction big enough to draw attention away from the exhibit for a few minutes. Nalrai is fast and agile. They won't be prepared to fight him, so the risk of you getting hit while you're on his back is low," I assure her.

"What do you know about probability? Aren't you bad at math?" she asks, recalling the story I told her about counting the coins at the museum.

I blush and say, "I know my dragon. You'll be okay."

"If you say so," she says.

"Drop me on the roof of the museum," I tell Nalrai.

Nalrai flies to the back of the museum where we're less likely to be spotted and hovers above the roof. I climb cautiously onto it, certain to avoid landing noisily. I stay out of sight, crouch low toward the roof, and wait until a horrendous cry shatters the air and a pillar of blue fire dances over the rooftops of other buildings in the city. Four museum guards stumble over each other as they tumble out the front doors.

Earlier, there were an even dozen, so I'm hesitant to enter because I know there could be eight more guards inside. The least amount of guards I have to sneak around, the easier it will be to pull off this mission without anyone being hurt. Nalrai instinctively feels my hesitation and flies through the air aggressively flapping his wings to deter the guards further away from the museum, but then a watchman spots Mazokah on his back.

"Warriors! Dragons! We need backup!" a soldier shouts after observing Mazokah's Rul armor.

Two more soldiers run out the museum door, but I wait for another moment to be sure the guards are focused entirely on Mazokah and Nalrai before I make my move. Since the roof of the museum isn't much higher than the top of the door, I lie on my stomach and bend over the side of the roof to peek through the museum's front door. I'm relieved to see there's no one in the front admission area, so I mentally prepare for the jump by estimating the distance of the launch, making sure to account for any uneven ground before I hop down and roll to avoid blowing my knees out— a trick I quickly learned jumping out of trees and off rocks as a child. Another thing my childhood taught me is how to walk in nearly flawless silence, which is definitely coming in handy now. I step into the admission room and move swiftly to the hall entrance, peering around the corner to check for guards. The museum isn't as dimly lit as I would like, but I'll make do. I look through all the nooks and crannies of the structure I noted while scouting it out earlier and notice two more guards. I can hear their footsteps getting closer, so I hide in an alcove next to one of the displays as they pass down the hall.

"Why do *we* have to sit in here? Whatever is going on outside seems like it would be more important than guarding some dusty, old parchments," a young soldier's voice carries down the hall.

The Lost One: Wrath of the Tyrant

"You looking to die tonight? I'd rather be here. Actually, I'd rather be anywhere *but* here or out fighting some dragons. So, I guess it's going to be stand here and look pretty until I retire," another guard responds with little enthusiasm.

"You make enough to retire?" his young partner asks.

"You make a good point. Guess I'm here until I'm dead," he amends.

"Probably after," the other guard jokes as both of them laugh.

I watch the guards stroll toward the exhibit I need to get to. I wait patiently until they pass by the book I need and turn down the next hall, then I head to the section I came for. I glance around the corner to make sure no one else is there. Then I wait a minute or two longer by the glass before breaking through it with my fist and grabbing the book. I turn back down the hall and sprint toward the exit as fast as I can—right into a guard.

"I told you it was a distraction!" one guard yells to his fellow soldier while unsheathing his sword as they enter the front door from outside.

Without hesitation, I jab the first soldier in the throat with my fist before swiping a kick at the other's knees, but he jumps out of the way and threatens me with his sword. Instead of fighting, I reaffirm my grip on the book and bolt out of the door.

"Get back here, thief!" he yelps, while quickly running after me.

"Nalrai!" I yell into the air to catch my dragon's attention.

Nalrai stops toying with the soldiers to come get me. As he and Mazokah get close, I hold my arm up and grab his claw with my free hand, and I hold on as the distance between the guard, my feet, and the ground grows swiftly, making sure to clutch the book tightly with the other arm.

Chapter Nineteen: The Book

*N*alrai lands roughly back at the ruins of our deserted island.

"Are you okay bud?" I ask, jumping to the ground.

He snorts as I run my hand down his neck, and I spot a scratch on his leg. It's oozing blood, but it doesn't look too serious.

"You too huh?" Mazokah asks him, looking closely at the scratch.

"I'll see to his wound. See if you can understand what this says about the hidden passage," I say, handing her the book I stole from the museum.

"I'll see. Check with me in a few hours," she says, while leaning against a tree to read.

I'm running low on bandages, but I wrap what I have around Nalrai's leg, even though he squirms while I put it on.

"Stop acting like a baby and let me help," I scold lightly.

He complains by pushing his snout against my chest, then with his mouth, he proceeds to grab the end of the wrap I'm holding, knocking loose what progress I've made.

"Nalrai!" I chide.

He spreads his wings and hops away.

"Fine. I won't help," I call out to him.

He pins the other end of the wrap that fell off his leg under his claw and shreds the fabric apart.

"I got it. No bandages," I say.

Mazokah laughs at me and Nalrai's interaction as she walks over to me.

"This isn't going to help us," she says, flipping through the book, "They're using signs and symbols I've never seen before."

"Then what do we do?" I yell as frustration shoots through me.

"We beat Ma'roog. Even if he won't tell us where our family is, surely someone else knows, or it's written down somewhere. And once we destroy him, we'll either make him tell us, or we'll find whoever else knows where they are and make them tell us," she says.

"How? How are we supposed to stand a chance against the largest army to have existed in history? We're alone. Even if I knew how to use my magic, I can't take down Ma'roog *and* his warriors! We don't know where Glul'gur is. We don't know where Draug is, so how can we win?" I shout frustratedly, as I walk towards the ruins of the library.

The Lost One: Wrath of the Tyrant

"Arid, our people have always defied the odds. A handful of travelers sailed across the oceans and settled onto a new land. We've survived natural disasters and attacks from other islands, yet we prevailed despite the risk. All we need is hope," she says.

"Our village was destroyed!" I retaliate.

"We'll figure it out. We can build an army and unite what nations remain freed from Ma'roog's control while you learn to use your magic, and we'll find Glul'gur and Draug too. You can't give up," she says, grabbing my arms forcefully.

"Why should I even trust you? The last people I trusted tried to shoot me in the back!" I say.

Her grip softens on my arms, and she says, "I know, dear, but we're family. I used to babysit you and sing you to sleep. I would never betray you."

"And I'm supposed to take your word for it? Nalrai doesn't like you, and I'm sure he remembers you well enough," I say.

"Nalrai never liked me. Admittedly, I was always jealous of your mother. I used to always wonder why did *she* get to marry the chief while I never so much as found my place in the village? Why did *she* get to have a beautiful child and the life I always dreamed of while I was alone? Nalrai didn't like me because of those resentments I used to carry, but I never meant any harm to you or anyone else," she says, "Besides, what else are you going to do? Go back to living here and stealing supplies, perfectly aware that your people are alive somewhere?"

"You say they're alive, but I have yet to see any proof," I say.

"You're willing to give up all hope? And for what? Ma'roog will still come after you. You'd be living on the run as he takes over the world, knowing you passed over any possibility of preventing his global domination. You can run all you want, but you would have no chance of winning if you do. So why not give yourself a chance, no matter how slim?"

I brush her hands off of me, step away, and run my hands through my hair, stressed.

"Dammit!" I yell, punching the side of a dilapidated bookcase.

My fist goes right through it, knocking books off the shelf as splinters catch onto my sleeve. I violently rip my arm free, and the shelf breaks even more.

"Give up, or keep fighting despite the odds. Not great options, I know," Mazokah says, "But we have nothing to lose and everything to gain."

"Yeah. I'm going to meditate," I say, walking toward a hill.

Nalrai starts to follow me.

"Stay here Nalrai. I need to be alone for a while."

I climb up the side of the hill to a natural outcrop. Although I didn't bring a book with me this time, it makes a cozy place to read with a nice view, and it has just enough cover that I'm not sitting out in plain sight. As the sun sets, the peaceful solitude keeps me here for hours. Before I know it, I'm listening to birds chirp as the sun rises over the horizon with streaks of orange chasing away the dark night.

The Lost One: Wrath of the Tyrant

As the first beams of light reach the hill, the rays of the sun glow warmly on my face. I breathe in the scent of the ocean drifting slowly up from the shore.

Where is Glul'gur? I ask myself, trying to remember and search for the island on the edges of my mind.

Where is Glul'gur? I ask, while burying my hands in the dirt as I try to let go of my fear and anger.

Please... where do I go? I beg the question, hoping Vrarg will listen.

I concentrate with all my might, but I feel no spark of life to answer my question.

<<<>>>

Hours later after meditating, Mazokah, Nalrai, and I work on an exercise in hopes of sparking my magic.

"Try harder," Mazokah says.

"I'm trying as hard as I can!" I say, sweat dripping from my face.

She signals Nalrai to swipe at me again. I block his tail with a stick, and she unexpectedly throws a rock at me as I do. It hits me in the stomach, and I double over, trying to catch my breath.

"Wha-what was that for?" I grunt.

"This tail-and-stick exercise with Nalrai clearly isn't doing anything to help spark your magic, so I tried something else to stimulate it. I figure I might as well try something new to get some reflexes going... but yours seem to be much slower than I expected," she says.

"What is this magic supposed to do? What do you *expect* to happen?" I ask, frustrated.

"You're supposed to have active magic, yet you've never once used it intentionally. How can you learn to use *a lot* of magic if you can't consciously use a little bit of it? It's like starting a fire. You need a spark first," she says.

"I need a break," I say, trying to swallow my frustration.

"You don't get one," she says.

"I'm well-conditioned for strenuous activities, but even I have my limits. I need a break," I say, gritting my teeth.

"Fine. We'll do this again tomorrow," she says.

"You know, I didn't ask you to train me. This was your idea, and it's not working. We'll come up with another method to access my magic tomorrow," I insist.

"Fine, okay. Have it your way," she huffs.

"Where is that book I stole from Lokk?" I ask.

The Lost One: Wrath of the Tyrant

"On top of one of the bookcases. Why? Are you hoping to understand their 'debunked' scribblings?" she asks.

"I'm going to look for *anything* in there that I might understand even a little bit. If not, I'll just stare at it until there's a hole through the pages," I say, walking over to the deteriorating bookshelves.

"Good luck," she says.

I flip through the book for several minutes before pausing on one particular page. It has a single word on it written in the ancient language of Vrarg. It's the same language as the back of my map, and it reads, *Birth*. The other side of the page contains a complete map of Vrarg covered with numbers and equations. My fingers tingle as I stare at it. The drawings seem to move around, and the numbers brush to the side. I set the open book down as magic brings the map to life around me. I forget to breathe for a moment as I witness a globe floating in the air in front of me. The islands on the globe are clearly outlined with glowing blue lines; except, there's one island I haven't seen on any map before.

"What are you doing?" Mazokah gives me a funny look as she approaches, "And why are your eyes glowing?"

Standing in a trance I say, "I think I know where Glul'gur is."

Chapter Twenty: Glul'gur

*A*re you sure you're ready to go to Glul'gur?" Mazokah asks.

"There's… a pull that draws me to it. I've seen it in my dreams. It's been reaching out to me. Vrarg wanted me to find it, and that's the only reason I did," I say.

"Okay, sure, but are you ready?" she asks.

"Why wouldn't I be? This is my chance to learn how I can defeat Ma'roog," I say.

"Okay. Drop me off on the island closest to Glul'gur," she says.

"What? Why?" I ask.

"People have searched for Glul'gur for so long, yet no one has ever found it. Surely there must be a reason why Vrarg showed you and kept it from others. I don't think I'm supposed to go with you," she says.

"Okay, fine. Zram is about halfway between here and where the magic globe says Glul'gur is located. I'll drop you off there. First thing you should do is find different clothes. I've only visited Zram once during my travels. They seemed friendly enough to a traveler, but I don't know if they'd be as welcoming to someone dressed as a warrior. Blend in, and you should be safe there," I say.

The Lost One: Wrath of the Tyrant

"Arid, I need you to promise me that you'll be safe going to Glul'gur. We don't actually know anything about it for sure," she says.

"I'll be fine," I promise.

From the air, Glul'gur appears as a mere shimmer on the ocean until I move closer, then it slowly comes into focus as a physical island. It takes a while to locate the precise spot the map indicated, but I finally find it! Upon my command, Nalrai tenderly touches down on Glul'gur, unsure if the street is actually solid or not because it looked like a mirage from the air. Surprisingly, it looks like a normal island, except it appears deserted. I must admit, I've been in many abandoned villages and lived in ruins, but I never got a chill down my spine when I landed on them... Glul'gur is different.

I hop off of Nalrai and examine the area. It doesn't appear this village was destroyed by anything. It doesn't look like it's seen any attack. The buildings stand tall and proud, and the shop signs creak in the wind. I might not believe in ghosts, but I can't deny the island feels as though it's filled with the presence of unknown beings. It puts me on edge. I find myself naturally breathing lighter and stepping more carefully, as though moving more quietly will prevent whatever might be here from sensing me. I walk through the eerily empty streets, which are smooth and clean, toward the town's center. All along, I keep my hand on Nalrai's shoulder as he walks almost silently beside me. Runes are engraved into the stone street around a fountain that still has water flowing through it. I don't know what the ancient symbols mean, but I can feel more magic here than I've ever felt before. I kneel on the street, tracing the runes with my hand. Nalrai growls, and I look up.

"I would like to thank you, child, for leading me to the one place I've been unable to find on my own. Glul'gur's magic will strengthen me so I can finally finish my conquest. I have offered you a chance to join me before, and I will extend the same invitation one last time," Ma'roog says, standing in front of me.

"So what you're saying is, despite your massive army, the reason you haven't conquered the remaining islands is because you're too weak to do so? And you must resort to magic? How pathetic! Why would I join you? Only a weak bastard resorts to controlling others through fear," I mock, forcing down the fright that fills me at the sight of him towering before me.

"Weak?" he laughs.

Then he raises his hand, and I'm thrown backward without him touching me. Nalrai pounces forward but has a similar fate.

"No, dragon. This isn't your fight," Ma'roog says, holding my dragon down with magic.

"How about a fair fight? No magic," I say, feigning more courage than I feel.

"You fool. Cheating is the most effective way to win a fight," he says.

"Do you have *any* good in you?" I ask, running forward and swinging my sword at him.

The Lost One: Wrath of the Tyrant

"Most likely not. Why would I choose good over power? What does goodness get me? Not peasants bowing at my feet. Not scores of warriors to follow my every command. The only thing goodness brings is misery," he says, throwing me back again with another wave of his hand, "Child, don't you think they call me untouchable for a reason? You have no hope in this fight."

I spit blood from my mouth, get to my feet again, and say, "You may be untouchable, but I have nothing to lose."

An invisible blow hits me in the back like the blunt end of an axe swung by a giant, which sends me to my knees. Ma'roog's magic doesn't seem to move in one particular direction. He can send hits from any angle. He barrages me with a series of unseeable blows. I try to protect myself from the hits, but in addition to the invisible attacks, he keeps me on the ground by sending rocks, shop signs, and whatever tangible objects he can find on the street to attack me.

"By the way, your aunt has been lying to you. She's the informant who gave me vital information I needed to gain an edge over your pesky island all those years ago. She also kept an eye on you while you figured out where Glul'gur was, and she sent word to me when you found it. So, you're right. You have nothing else to lose. You've already lost everything: your home, your family, and those you thought were your friends. Hell, at this point, you've even lost yourself," he says while laughing.

I curl up on the ground, arms covering my head as the attack continues. I can feel my ribs crack as blow after blow assaults me.

"As I said, nothing to lose," I whisper, forcing myself to my feet, but I fall to the ground yet again as a magical blow hits the back of my knees.

"Maybe there is *one* thing you still have," he says.

Then he turns to Nalrai and sends him flying through the fountain in the middle of the square. The stone crumbles around him, and he's hit hard enough that he's knocked unconscious.

"Nalrai!" I shout, "Leave him out of this! You said this isn't his fight, so leave him be!"

"I also said I cheat," he says, finally drawing his own sword and stepping closer to me.

I scream and leap at him. I don't make contact with my sword, but the runes in the road knocks Ma'roog off his feet. The street starts glowing a bright, magical blue, and I can feel the power infecting my whole body. I thought I felt powerful magic before, but I haven't... not until today. The magic gives me enough strength to climb to my feet, and I drag my sword across the stone as I walk closer to him. As I stand over Ma'roog, he looks to be in significant pain.

"We'll meet again, lost one," he laughs, as a cloud of magical smoke surrounds him.

By the time it dissipates enough to see, he's already gone.

"Coward," I spit, blood trickling from my lips.

I limp over to Nalrai, trying to wake him up. He doesn't wake, but at least he still breathes. I sit next to him, and I can feel the magic is fading away from my body. It served its purpose when I needed it, and it taught me what it needed to. I've been trying too hard. Magic shouldn't be forced. It should be as natural as breathing, but there are drawbacks to using it in great amounts. It's exhausting, painful, and I've got a glimpse of the magic to realize that it can be dangerous and potentially injure me.

The Lost One: Wrath of the Tyrant

I stand shakily when I see ships planting the Rul Coilband flag on the shore they were never meant to touch.

"Arid, I didn't think you'd still be alive by the time we got here. What a surprise," Mazokah says while walking over to me.

I point my sword at her and say, "You're a monster."

"Is that any way to speak to your family?" she asks.

"You're no family of mine. You're a traitor," I say.

"Yes, yes, so sad. Anyway, were you planning on fighting your way out of this? I have a fleet of ships at my command, and you appear to be... unprepared for a battle," she says.

"You helped Ma'roog murder your sister," I accuse.

"Ah, yes... my sister," she sneers in disgust, "I worked my whole life to earn power. My perfect, goody-goody sister never wanted power, and yet, she's the one that ended up with it when she wedded the chief. But enough chat. Bring her to the brig, and take the dragon too. We'll use him as leverage if she starts to get a little rowdy," Mazokah orders.

Dozens of warriors move forward at her command. I attempt to fight, but with my injuries and exhaustion, I last mere seconds against the vast hoard of warriors.

We have left Glul'gur, and the warriors have me in heavy chains on their ship. My arms are strung up above me, and I can't move more than a few centimeters. Nalrai is strapped down with sturdy, metal cuffs planted firmly into a large, metal platform. He's awake but just as unable to move as I am. I don't know where Mazokah went, but she has her subordinates trying to interrogate me.

"You've seen the secrets of the Dragon Knights. How do we defeat them?" a short, burly, warrior with an unkempt appearance asks.

"Your spies didn't tell you? They were there *much* longer than I was," I say.

"Their information was… *insufficient* in our attempts to gain an advantage over Clearhallow," he says.

"Why would I know anything more than them? And why would I tell you?" I ask.

"Do you not hate the Dragon Knights for betraying you?" he asks.

"I do know that the more islands survive, the better chance we have to fight off your cult, regardless of whether two of *your* spies almost killed me or not," I say, "Besides, haven't I already mentioned you know more than I do?"

"Okay. What about Glul'gur? You went there to learn its secrets. What did it teach you?" he asks.

"Stop trying to get information out of me. I have no interest in helping you, nor do I know anything that would benefit your army."

The Lost One: Wrath of the Tyrant

"You sure about that? You don't know anything about magic?" he questions.

"Enough with the nice guy routine," growls a heavily scarred warrior in the corner, "Beat it out of her."

"Looks like Ma'roog already tried," the short burly warrior says, laughing to himself.

"With all the rumors, I thought she would have put up more of a struggle when we captured her, but I think her fight, or judging by the blood on her face, her *annihilation* from Ma'roog has something to do with the ease at which we captured her. She's not scared of us, and she's not going to talk because we cause her a little discomfort," the warrior in front of me speculates.

"Then we follow Lady Mazokah's suggestion," the warrior in the corner says while pulling out a dagger and walking over to Nalrai.

"Don't hurt him," I say.

"Tell us something useful," he bargains.

"I don't know anything," I say.

He holds the blade close to Nalrai's snout, and Nalrai tries to get away but barely rattles the cuffs holding him to the metal platform because he's tied so tightly. Each limb is pinned down, and he can barely move enough to breathe. He manages a muffled growl, but only smoke snorts from his nostrils.

"You can't hurt anybody here, dragon. If you don't think we know how to handle a wild beast such as yourself, you are sadly mistaken," the warrior chuckles.

"Don't touch him," I demand.

"Give us some info," he responds.

"I told you, I don't have any," I say, yanking at my chains trying to get loose.

"That's not the right answer," he says, slicing a deep gash into Nalrai's flesh.

Nalrai squirms, trying desperately to break free.

"Stop it!" I yell.

"Give me a reason to stop," the warrior taunts.

I was previously having a hard time using my magic, but Glul'gur may have forged a stronger connection between me and my sorcery because I can feel it working now. It's flowing through my limbs, but I don't know how to control it.

"Don't you dare touch him again!" I shout as anger and magic well up inside me like an explosion ready to tear me apart in order to escape.

The Lost One: Wrath of the Tyrant

The warrior presses the blade into Nalrai's snout again. My frustration escapes with a scream, accompanied with a flash of brilliant blue light breaking free from inside my entire body that causes an explosion.

Chapter Twenty-One: Fugitives

I don't know what happened, but I wake on a piece of wooden debris with one of my feet dangling in the ocean. My other ankle is still imprisoned by the tightly clasped metal cuff, and it is attached to a chain that is balanced perfectly at the edge of the debris to keep me from falling into the water. Nalrai floats lifelessly beside me, freed from his shackles, and there is no one else in sight. The night is cold and empty… no ships, no warriors. My whole body hurts, and I'm not sure I have the energy to check and see if Nalrai's moving. I feel defeated, helpless, and more alone than ever as the ocean carries me wherever it feels.

"Na-Nalrai?" I shiver weakly.

A small wave unbalances the chain lying on the debris and drags the loose end of it deeper into the ocean.

"No, stay there," I groan, trying to grab the rest of the chain.

It's out of reach, and I don't have the strength to drag myself closer to it. With each wave that hits, I desperately try to reach the chain to avoid being pulled in by the bumpy ocean.

"No!" I yell, as the entire chain slides into the water, yanking on my ankle.

I try with all my might to hold on to the wood and keep my head out of the water, but I'm plunged into the black, icy sea. Many times, I've pondered my eventual death. I imagined how it might come to be. It's always been some glorious fantasy of battle, but I never considered the possibility I'd drown.

The Lost One: Wrath of the Tyrant

As my hand descends beneath the surface, another arm shoots down into the water, and fingers wrap tightly around my wrist, enough to bruise my arm. I didn't see anyone nearby, but I grasp at my only chance of survival.

"What are you doing? Don't touch me!" I splutter, pushing away my traitorous rescuer as we float on debris in the middle of the ocean.

"You're welcome," Nokk says uncertainly, "Would you rather have died?"

I spend a moment in flustered silence looking at all the faces surrounding me as they hover nearby on their dragons.

"Wha-what's going on? What are all of you doing here, and how did you find me? Why aren't you dead? And why isn't *she* dead?" I ask, glaring at Ak'dech.

"Take a deep breath and calm down, then we'll explain," Norkuz says, as Quldriag hovers above me.

"It better be one hell of an explanation," I say, glaring at Nokk as he lets go of my wrist.

"Well, it's not *that* spectacular, but we should probably get you out of the water," Brezmard says.

"Is Nalrai breathing?" I ask, allowing my anger to subdue for the time being to focus on my *real* comrade.

Nokk puts his hand on the dragon and waits for a moment.

"Yes, he's breathing," he determines softly while avoiding eye contact with me.

"Are you lying?" I ask.

"No. He's alive. Norkuz can treat his wounds once we get somewhere safe," he says.

"Nokk is right. Let's get going. We're not sure if there are any more survivors from whatever destroyed their fleet," Norkuz says.

"I hope there *aren't* any more survivors. I'll accept their deaths on my hands if it means that traitor from Likenhallow is dead," I say.

"This was *your* doing?" Brezmard asks.

"It was my *magic's* doing," I say.

"Ak'dech, do you think Qombaryth and Kemoss can carry Nalrai?" Norkuz asks.

"I believe so," she says.

"Where's the nearest island to take refuge on that's safe?" Brezmard asks Nokk.

"Zram. It's just south of here. Clearhallow doesn't have any current relations with them, but they may be open to a deal," Nokk says.

"Perfect," Brezmard says.

The Lost One: Wrath of the Tyrant

"So, what's your explanation for all this?" I ask Norkuz, accepting help from him while climbing onto Quldriag.

"You know we weren't going to let you be hanged, right?" Norkuz asks.

"That's what I thought at first, but then *some* of you tried to kill me yourselves," I say sourly, glaring in Nokk and Ak'dech's direction.

"Calm down and take it easy for a moment," he says.

"No! I just found Glul'gur, got my ass whooped by Ma'roog, been taken captive by a fleet of warriors, and I have no idea what happened after that! Then the people I least expect to see, who I didn't *want* to see ever again, show up and start telling me what to do. I don't know what's happening!" I exclaim.

"Breathe," Norkuz says.

"Don't tell me what to do!" I yell.

"Arid, it would be best if you calm down," he says.

"You want an explanation? Then shut up and listen!" Brezmard snaps, "You're not the *only* one with problems. Ak'dech and Nokk have been two of the closest friends I've ever had. You don't think their actions hurt us too? I trusted them with my life, only to find out they've been lying to me this whole time! You're not the only one they hurt, so stop acting like it's all about you!"

Brezmard's face is red, and his veins pop in his neck. Obviously, Brezmard has a short temper, so I've seen him get mad before... but I've never seen him angry like this.

"We weren't going to let you hang, and we weren't going to let them die either," Norkuz says.

"You broke them out?" I ask.

"Yes, we broke them out... and ran," he says.

"I hope they were worth it, for your sake," I say, glaring at the two as they listen to the conversation in complete silence, "How did you end up in the exact place I needed help?"

"We followed you from a distance," he says.

"Fantastic," I say sarcastically.

Speaking much calmer than before, Brezmard says, "This war needs to end now... no more waiting around. We're trying to unite as many islands as we can to take the fight to Ma'roog... no more being passive and playing on his terms."

"Do you think this is a wise idea now that you're a fugitive running from the island you're one day supposed to rule?" I ask.

"The warriors got closer to reaching the village in this last attack than they ever have before. I watched dozens of friends be carried off to a mass grave. There's no evidence that Clearhallow will survive another attack, and I'm not waiting around for another one," Brezmard says.

The Lost One: Wrath of the Tyrant

"Is your magic strong enough to beat Ma'roog?" Norkuz asks.

"No. I could barely scare him off... had to get a massive boost from the island's magic just to pin him down," I say.

"Did you hurt him?" Brezmard asks.

"Yes, well, sort of. Me... or the magic... we were able to knock him off his feet," I say.

"That's more than anyone else has done," he says.

"I'm not looking to join your team, *Prince Brezmard*. I don't care about your problems. Turns out, I'm best on my own after all," I say.

"Arid, I swear on my bloodline, I'm not here to cause you any distress. We need your help to kill Ma'roog," he says.

"Sometimes, cousin, words from *blood* aren't actually worth that much," I say grimly.

"Cousin?" he pauses to think for a moment.

"Sounds like you found out the truth about your lineage," Ak'dech says to me.

"Of course you knew, didn't you? I bet you knew my aunt betrayed my village, but did you know my parents are dead because of her?" I ask angrily.

"I tried to warn you about her. She was our overseer, Ma'roog's second in command," she affirms in a shamed whisper.

"Yeah, you did try to warn me. Then when you betrayed me, I dismissed anything you ever said. After all, why should I believe a liar?" I shout in frustration.

"I didn't want to lie to anyone!" she yells in distress.

"Congratulations, that makes it *all* better," I growl.

Tears cloud her eyes, and fear is audible in her far too quick breaths. With wide eyes, she stares aimlessly in the ocean and says, "We were *kids*! And if either one of us didn't cooperate, Ma'roog said he'd kill us both! He... has this way of getting in your head, and he won't leave!"

"Ak'dech," Nokk says, trying to calm her down.

Brezmard stares at his friend in concern. Nynnu and Nokk hover above Ak'dech and Qombaryth, then Nokk jumps from his dragon to Qombaryth's back to comfort his sister.

"Don't paint her as the victim," I say, watching Nokk try to snap Ak'dech out of whatever anxiety spell she's having.

"No, victim is *your* job, isn't it? No one else gets to be taken advantage of? No one else gets to feel pain or sadness? No one else gets to be angry at their traumas? No, it's all about *you* and *your* pain, huh, but Arid, you are not the only victim," Brezmard says, face twisted with disgust, "They were kids," he continues, "And Ma'roog used fear to manipulate them into doing what he wanted them to. Does that clear them of all blame? No, of course not. It just means it's not so simple.

The Lost One: Wrath of the Tyrant

You judged them based off of one action without taking into consideration the years of abuse they've gone through, but they have suffered with their guilt and fear for years. I understand you grew up alone, so you're probably not used to considering other people's motivations or problems, but you're not the only one who's trying to survive another day, and you're not the only one who gets to feel. The fact that they made a mistake doesn't mean their pain and guilt doesn't matter. They're my friends, and they didn't deserve to be molded into spies they didn't want to become. But noooo, you're the only one who gets to be scared that Ma'roog is whispering things in your head, aren't you?"

His tone remains tainted with bitterness, but his anger is controlled in the calm accusation.

"I... I'm just trying to do what I need to... survive," I say pathetically, at a loss for words.

"So were they," he says.

Once we reach Zram, the Dragon Knights pay for an inn, and we all retreat to our own rooms. It seems pretty safe. However, I'm having trouble sleeping, so I take a walk and see Brezmard sitting outside the inn on the steps staring emptily into the streets. I sit down on the same steps as him, about an arm's length away.

"Norkuz told you to get lots of rest," he comments dully.

"I've never been particularly good at following instructions," I reply, "Besides, your words keep spinning through my head. Brezmard, I want to apologize to you. I haven't carried a very favorable opinion of you.

I thought you to be arrogant and immature, but today, you acted like a leader and a good friend to people who hurt you, probably more than they hurt me. That takes more humility than I have."

With a heavy sigh and a mournful tone he says, "Admittedly, I've learned a lot lately. People I've known my whole life… friends, mentors… are suddenly gone. They are dead, missing, or sustained permanent injuries from the Coilband's attack on Clearhallow… and two of my closest friends in the world, who I thought I could trust with anything, lied to me and were helping the enemy."

"But you stuck up for them earlier," I say, confused.

"I understand what they went through, but that doesn't mean the truth didn't hurt. Even if I forgive their actions, part of me resents them for betraying my trust, and part of me will always be angry with them. Trust is impossible at current, but maybe one day it'll heal," he says.

"You forgave them enough to free them from prison at your own expense," I note.

"Yes. I don't know if I'll be able to return home. I was supposed to rule Clearhallow… uphold the law. And now… I, myself, am a traitor. I've tried my whole life to make my father proud of me. How am I ever supposed to face him now? My mother died when I was young. I have no siblings. He's the only family I have left," he laments.

"You're not a traitor. You're trying to follow what you believe is right," I say.

"How many times is that used as an excuse for the most inexcusable crimes?" he argues.

The Lost One: Wrath of the Tyrant

"Maybe one day, I'll have the same bravery to follow my conscience rather than focusing solely on myself," I say.

"Don't worry too much. You're not so bad. Compared to Ma'roog, you're the lesser of two evils," he says.

"Ha! He wishes! When I get my powers under control, I'll be the greatest," I grin.

"So, greatest evil in the world, what do you say to an alliance?" he asks.

Brezmard holds his hand out for a handshake, and I accept his comradeship by shaking his hand.

Chapter Twenty-Two: The Prince of Zram

7he next day, the Dragon Knights and I stroll through the town of Zram. If I'd spent more time this far south, I would have certainly spent more time here. It's a beautiful, bustling island, and there aren't many villages with valuables like they have here because a lot of places are struggling to ensure they have enough basic supplies to keep their citizens fed and alive. On the down side, the merchants, who can clearly tell we are visitors, are trying to push us to buy their goods at an increased price as we walk by.

"Arid, you know anything about the chief here?" Brezmard asks.

I tear my eyes away from the valuables that stand so easily within reach and say, "No, I've never met Zram's chief."

My attention involuntarily strays back to the expensive products beside me.

"No stealing," Brezmard frowns, noticing my temptation.

"I know... but do you realize how much any of this would sell for elsewhere?" I complain.

"We're not here to make money. Focus," he says.

"Says the man who carries more money in his pocket than I've had in my entire life," I pout.

The Lost One: Wrath of the Tyrant

"You're fully aware of our reason for being here," he says, annoyed.

"That doesn't mean I can't find a side mission," I say.

"We're not going to steal from the people we're trying to make a deal with. It'll be a difficult enough sell as it is, being that I have no army to fight alongside us, and I haven't recruited any other islands yet," he says.

"Yeaaaah, but how would they know that?" I ask.

"You're suggesting I lie?" he says incredulously.

"Why not?" I ask.

"We don't wish to make enemies out of them. They may feel betrayed by a lie," he says pointedly.

"Well, between Arid's experience with *livening* up a tale and our experience negotiating, surely we can come to some sort of agreement. After all, these people clearly love to make a profit. As long as we can convince them there's more reward than risk, I see no problem getting them to agree," Norkuz says.

"You say that like it's easy," Brezmard says.

"It's hard to tell without any prior meetings with the chief, but we don't have anything to gain by dawdling. It'll either work out or not, and I doubt we'll make progress standing here fretting," Norkuz answers.

"Shouldn't we at least bring a gift? We're uninvited guests trying to talk to the chief," Ak'dech says.

"Worst-case scenario, we'll offer *you* up," Nokk laughs, slapping her shoulder.

"Haha, very funny," she says, making an annoyed face.

We approach an elaborate palace with guards out front.

"Come no closer," a guard orders calmly, holding out his hand.

"Sir, I am Prince Brezmard of Clearhallow. I wish to make a proposition to your chief," Brezmard says, standing tall.

After a short moment of silence and no immediate answer from the guards, Brezmard gets nervous and adds, "I have gold."

"We will ask if this is permissible," the guard says while his partner slips through one of the wooden double doors.

A few minutes later, the guard returns with two more armed soldiers.

"They will escort you," he says.

The two guards lead us to a room filled with well-lit candles, velvet chairs, and red drapery. A heavy wooden table with delicate carved designs sits in the middle of the room. A gently crackling fireplace sits on the far wall with marble statues on either side. I feel out of place in this room.

The Lost One: Wrath of the Tyrant

I've never seen furnishings this expensive anywhere, and we're all blown away by the extravagant decorations about the room. As we wait, Brezmard doesn't say anything, but he glances nervously around the room while the two guards stand stationed at the door. Finally, it swings open.

"Greetings, travelers," a young man walks in, voice warm and welcoming.

The young man is clad in silk clothes and shimmering jewelry, and his whole body is laced with valuables. He exudes authority and is adorned with an inviting aura of friendliness. I bow a second later than the knights.

"Chief, it is an honor," Brezmard says.

"Oh, no, I am not the chief. That would be my father. I apologize for the confusion. Unfortunately, you may not speak to him. He is not well but sends his best wishes. I am Prince I'gur, and I will be handling you instead. I hear you have a proposition for us. Please, sit, and we will discuss it."

"I've brought an offering to indicate our good will," says Brezmard.

"That will not be necessary. Take a seat," the prince says again, sitting back comfortably in one of the lush, red chairs.

"Prince I'gur," Brezmard starts.

"Let's begin with an introduction, shouldn't we? It's only fair I know your name as well, don't you think?" the prince accosts while he stares at Brezmard with piercing inquisitiveness.

"Rrr-right, sorry," Brezmard stutters nervously, cheeks turning pink.

"I'm Prince Brezmard of Clearhallow," Brezmard spits out edgily, taking a quick breath to find his composure, "This is my personal guard, Sir Norkuz, and two elite members of my Dragon Knights, Lady Ak'dech and Sir Nokk. Lady Arid is my distant cousin from the dead village of Likenhallow."

"A pleasure to meet you, Prince Brezmard, as well as your friends. What brings you to my home?" Prince I'gur asks.

"Ma'roog and the Rul Coilband," Brezmard says, as the nervous edge to his voice dies down.

Prince I'gur's smile hardens.

"What about them?" he asks stiffly.

"They have wreaked havoc on Vrarg for far too long. We're trying to build an alliance with as many villages as possible in an attempt to finally defeat them," Brezmard says.

"How many others have joined you?" Prince I'gur asks, with a more relaxing tone.

"You are the first we've talked to," Brezmard says.

"Why me? We're a ways from Clearhallow, and surely you have other islands you have established connections with?" Prince I'gur asks skeptically.

The Lost One: Wrath of the Tyrant

"Circumstance brought us to your island first," Brezmard summarizes briefly.

"This is a tremendous endeavor you've set out on... ambitious and risky," Prince I'gur says, leaning forward with a ponderous expression.

"If the remaining armies don't band together, what chance remains at stopping Ma'roog?" Brezmard inquires.

"An interesting claim... something to consider, surely. How big is your own army?" Prince I'gur asks.

"Well, I... I'm... to be honest, I'm at odds with my father right now. He dismisses everything I say. I'm here against orders," Brezmard says, blushing even brighter.

"Ha! A bold move to tell me that," Prince I'gur grins, "Is there anything else to your proposition?"

"No," Brezmard says.

"Very well," Prince I'gur says, then he taps his fingers on his chin thoughtfully, and his polished rings click against each other as he does. Then he says, "I require time to mull over your request and discuss it with my father. I will provide my answer tomorrow. Sih'vir, see to it they have rooms and hot meals prepared for them."

Then Prince I'gur stands and strolls over to the door.

"Thank you for your time and consideration," Brezmard says.

Prince I'gur looks over his shoulder, pauses and says, "The pleasure is mine, Prince Brezmard. I am impressed by your boldness. Consider yourselves esteemed guests while you're here. Even if the final decision is unfavorable to your quest, I hope to have a relationship with Clearhallow in the future."

Prince I'gur allowed us to bring our dragons inside with us as his guards showed us around his palace. His generosity, general charm, and sense of openness makes him hard to dislike and very easy to trust. Due to that, he's definitely someone to keep an eye on. After the palace tour, we are all shown to our individual rooms and disperse in different directions. As I wander around, I notice there is a small, but well-stocked library in the palace. It's not lit as brightly as some of the other rooms, but a comfortable glow from the fireplace provides enough lighting to read. A plain red rug covers the floor, and Nalrai is already curled up by the fire, snoring lightly. A chilly draft blows in through a small window above the bookshelves, but the hearth is warm enough to drive away the cold. I peruse the shelves looking for a book of tales to pass the time and to get my mind off of life. The one I finally decide on is bound in leather, and the parchment is crisp and in good condition.

"Can't sleep?" a voice startles me as I return to the fireplace.

I nearly drop the book as I react to defend myself, but then I breathe out, "Oh," when I determine there's no threat.

"Pardon me, I didn't mean to give you a startle," Prince I'gur apologizes, sinking into a seat in the corner.

"It's difficult to sneak up on me," I mention.

The Lost One: Wrath of the Tyrant

"These rugs absorb footsteps better than other floors," he says, "Are you usually up so late, or was there an issue with your rooming?"

"No issues with the room. I don't sleep much," I say.

"Prince Brezmard mentioned you're from a dead village," he says to invite conversation while crossing his legs in his chair.

"Yeah, Likenhallow," I say.

"Yes, that's what he said. I dimly remember my father being furious upon finding out about its destruction. He'd been hopeful about an alliance with your chief," he recalls.

"Ma'roog holds the survivors of my village prisoner, and I want them back," I say.

"I'm personally eager to help you, Lady Arid, but first, I must receive my father's approval," he says.

"Why are you interested in helping?" I ask.

"I am no fan of the Rul Coilband. I've stayed silent as island after island became attacked and overrun by them, and I'm tired of sitting here waiting for them to take our village next. Other than some trading, we have mostly kept to ourselves to ensure we don't draw too much attention, and at my father's request, we have shown no sign of aggression to anyone in order to stay out of the war. However, I know he is unhappy with the Rul Coilband's attacks on other islands. At the rate Ma'roog is taking over, we won't be able to maintain our economy without new trade opportunities, and I no longer want to sit back and wait for the rest of our trade routes to be abolished because they've been taken over," he says.

218

"You don't seem to be hurting for wealth," I say.

"Our island is rich with resources, and we accumulated a vast amount of money before the war started, which is what has held us over this long," he says.

"Well, other islands aren't faring as well as yours. In my travels, I've noticed an unease among the people of many islands, like they're expecting an attack at any moment, but your people aren't scared to walk the streets. They aren't starving either. I've seen many homeless on the streets of other villages... not so many here, so your chief did something right to sustain for so long. By the way, I'm sorry to hear your father is unwell."

He frowns and says, "Yes, it's extremely unfortunate. We've had healers in and out, but there's nothing they've been able to accomplish. All they've been able to determine is that he's old and ill. I could have determined that myself."

"Norkuz is a talented healer. I'm sure he'd be willing to see if he can do something the others couldn't, if you wish," I say.

"Yes, I'll discuss it with Sir Norkuz," he says.

"Who are you?" I ask.

"What do you mean?" he questions, tilting his head curiously.

"I'll start. I'm Arid Dho'zogg, rightful chief of Likenhallow. Orphaned when I was young. I grew up a petty thief and a traveler. I'm a fighter with blood on my hands. Who are you?" I repeat.

The Lost One: Wrath of the Tyrant

"I see. I am Prince of Zram. My mother ran off three years ago, and my father's days grow shorter by the minute. I haven't wielded a weapon in my life, nor have I wanted for food. I'm a diplomat because my father's a pacifist and taught me the art of negotiation and compromise instead of war," he asserts.

"Hm," I say while staring at him, trying to detect any signs of a lie.

"Lady Arid, I can tell you're suspicious of me."

"I have to be."

"Absolutely. It's natural to be distrusting of others if we've been scorned before," he says while standing and stepping closer to the fire, "I know how it goes. You become close to someone, only to have them rip you apart. Lies, betrayals..."

Prince I'gur has a faint wisp of mourning to his words as he stares into the flames.

"Who have you been betrayed by?" I ask.

"A close friend of mine... one of my guards I'd fallen in love with... and not long before that, my mother betrayed both me and my father. I never felt so broken inside," he remembers somberly.

"I—"

"Well, I'm dismayed to leave in the middle of our conversation, but I should check on my father," he interrupts, dismissing himself.

Chapter Twenty-Three: Agreement

*A*fter leaving the library, a pair of guards stops me in the hall on the way to my room.

"Lady Arid, come this way, please."

"What? Why? Where are we going?" I ask, bewildered.

"You've been requested," he says.

"For what? By whom?" I ask.

"Sir Norkuz and Prince I'gur," he answers.

Something doesn't feel right. They're walking quickly, clearly in a rush. Nalrai grunts nervously as he bounds along behind us.

"Arid," Norkuz breathes out heavily as the guards violently throw open the doors of the chief's chambers.

Norkuz stands by a bedside. Prince I'gur is looking out the window, and an old man is lying in a fancy bed.

"What's going on?" I ask, as the guards step outside.

The Lost One: Wrath of the Tyrant

"Arid, this is Chief Irec. As a healer, I can't do anything to help him, and neither can any of Zram's physicians," Norkuz says.

"That sucks. Why am *I* here?" I ask.

"Your magic," he says.

"My magic?"

I wince at Norkuz, throw an uneasy glance towards Prince I'gur and blurt out, "How is my magic going to help him? I can't control it."

"I know, but you're his only chance. You can heal yourself, so maybe you can heal others," Norkuz reasons.

"I don't heal myself on *purpose*; it just happens," I reiterate.

"What harm could it do to try?" he encourages.

"Oh, I don't know… maybe I'll blow him up instead?" I snip.

"No, you won't. You've got this," he says confidently.

Chief Irec is pale and barely breathing. He is a fragile old man. He looks as though any of his bones might break if I so much as breathe on him, but I take a deep breath and close my eyes, trying to find my magic. To my surprise, the now-familiar tingling springs to my fingertips with ease and spreads through my body.

Heal, I think to myself while concentrating and gently putting my hand on his shoulder.

Raw, hot energy builds up inside me burning every millimeter of my skin, causing my head to pound painfully. I grit my teeth against the discomfort.

Heal him, I think to myself while focusing as hard as I can.

A magical outburst shoots through my arm that feels like a surging, burning sensation. My head hurts, and as the pain intensifies, I quickly withdraw my hand from the chief's shoulder in reaction to the severe sensation. The tingling stops, and I feel tired all of a sudden.

"Your... your eyes. They were glowing blue, and my father... his complexion seems slightly less pale. This is incredible," Prince I'gur says.

"*This* hurts," I complain, head pounding in pain, while gently blowing my breath on my irritated skin in a failed attempt to soothe it.

"I've never seen magic before," Prince I'gur says.

"Only a few have it. It's a rare gift," Norkuz says, while checking on Chief Irec.

"A rare *curse*," I say sourly, "Ma'roog is the only person I know to be glad he has magic."

"Ezzut said once you know how to use it, you won't have to put forth as much effort, and it won't be as painful or tiring," Norkuz says.

"And what does *Ezzut* know?" I ask.

Norkuz gives me a concerned look and asks, "Are you okay?"

"No. I want to talk to you," I say.

"Not a problem. Let me finish evaluating the chief's condition first," he says.

"Soooo?" Prince I'gur says, pressing for an update on his father's condition.

"He has a bit more life in him, but I don't know if it's enough to save him. The only magical healing I've seen is when Arid cures herself. She heals rather quickly, but it's not always instant. By looking at him, I can't tell if the chief is recovering or not, so for now, we'll just keep an eye on him," Norkuz frowns.

"Talk. Now," I say, gesturing to the door.

"Right," he says.

Norkuz follows me out into the hall, and I glare at the guards, pulling him several meters away from them.

"Why did you tell them I have magic? That's not your secret to share," I say.

"What else was I supposed to do? Let him die?" he says defensively.

"Death never seemed to bother you before!" I accuse.

"Arid, I'm a healer. When I can, I much prefer to save lives than take them. I understand that war means we can't always play the hero, but I can't express how much I wish that wasn't the case! I promise you, I'm not as unfeeling as I sometimes act," he says.

"Sure," I say sarcastically.

"I didn't kill them. If that's what you think," he says.

"What?" I ask.

"My brother and the warriors with him. We didn't kill them. We took them to a healer's clinic and left. I wanted to kill him, but I couldn't," he says.

"Why let me assume you were a murderer then?" I ask.

"It didn't matter," he says.

"It didn't *matter*?" I shout.

"No, not really. It didn't change our goal. He's not our concern. You may have thought me a murderer, but you still came along with us... and why? Because the only person we need to be worried about killing is Ma'roog. Look, I'm sorry I told them about your magic. And thank you for trying to help him regardless of that. Now, are you okay?"

"Nothing I can't sleep off," I say.

"Great. If you need anything else, I'll be keeping an eye on the chief for a while."

<<<>>>

The next evening, a feast was held, but I did not attend.

"You didn't show up for the feast," Nokk comments, while walking up to me on a balcony as I stare out at the village.

"No, I didn't," I acknowledge.

"What's going on?" he asks.

"I didn't feel like joining you all," I say.

"Clearly, you'd rather mope. Well, you missed the announcements. Chief Irec died, and Prince I'gur is willing to sign an agreement to help us," he says.

"What's with Prince I'gur? He's either manipulating us, or he's far too trusting for his own good. He didn't question our honesty, and he allows us to waltz around his home freely with our weapons and dragons, without so much as an escort," I question.

"Some people want to believe in the good of others, I guess. Besides, I think he has a crush on Brezmard," he adds after a moment.

"How'd you come to that conclusion?" I ask.

"He won't stop staring at him, for starters. Anyway, are you okay? Because there's normal checking out like when someone gets distracted by a random thought during a conversation, and then there's staring off to the edge of the universe deep in thought checking out like you're doing now," he says.

"What's it to you?" I ask.

"I know I'm probably not someone you really want to talk to, but I want to apologize properly. I don't expect your trust or forgiveness, but I'm sorry. I didn't want to hurt anyone. I realize I was a bit of a jerk, even before you knew I was a spy, but I was trying not to be friends with you because I didn't want *another* friend I had to lie to," he says.

"You're right. I don't want to talk to you, and I don't trust or forgive you. But Brezmard was right. You were trying to live, so I'll do my best not to hate you for it," I say.

"Fair enough," he says.

As we stand on the balcony in silence, I think back to before the battle on Clearhallow, before Nokk tried to kill me, there were moments when he was intolerable, but since then, it's like meeting a different person. He's quieter, nicer, and actually, not so bad. I noticed on the flight here that his neck and arms still have the fading, healing, yellowish indications that he recently took a beating.

"So, what's with the bruises?" I ask.

227

The Lost One: Wrath of the Tyrant

"Oh… Chief Firestride doesn't like it when you act out during your trial. You're supposed to leave all talking to your lawyer," he says.

"Why didn't you?" I ask.

"The lawyer wasn't even trying, and I didn't want Ak'dech to be hanged," he says.

"You must be a good brother because that's not the first time you've put yourself in harm's way to protect her," I note.

"She's protected me my whole life. I owe it to her," he says.

"I understand. Nalrai did the same for me, and I'd risk my life to save him in a heartbeat," I say.

"Exactly," he says.

"Ak'dech seems terrified of Ma'roog," I say, recalling her anxiety.

"Who isn't? She can't let go of her trauma. Watching her parents being murdered in front of her haunts her dreams, even when she's not asleep sometimes. She relives it, and it's so real to her that she doesn't always know that it's *not* happening again. She usually does well at hiding the flashbacks and anxiety, but sometimes, she can't because her symptoms get worse the more stressed she is," he says.

"Do you think she's crazy for hearing and seeing things that aren't there?" I ask.

"No, not at all. Soldiers come back from war with the same symptoms. I think it's part of human trauma sometimes, regardless if we understand it or not. Your nightmares don't make you crazy. They mean you're still hurting."

"How long does the hurt last?" I ask.

"How long does it take to recover from a head injury? I don't think there's a known answer to that. Sometimes it's better in a day, and sometimes, you never fully recover. We don't know why. We just know that's the way it is," he says.

"I didn't know you had it in you to sympathize so well with others without judging or mocking them," I say.

"I was a little busy *acting* like a jerk," he says.

"It's strange seeing the difference," I say.

"It feels strange too, but I don't have to pretend any more. No more lying to people, knowing it would hurt everyone I cared about when they found out. No more secrets to defend."

"Are you glad about that?" I ask.

"Yes, I'm more at peace than I've ever been," he says.

"Good, I'm glad *someone* can find some peace. So, what exactly is included in this agreement with Zram?"

The Lost One: Wrath of the Tyrant

"Prince I'gur will travel east in an effort to convince his allies to join us. We'll go west and gather as many armies as possible. We'll all return to Zram when we're done," he says.

"Simple enough. When do we leave?" I ask.

"Nightfall," he says.

Chapter Twenty-Four: Hatchlings

*A*k'dech, Nokk, Brezmard, Norkuz, myself, and all our dragons have been flying for about two days, and I don't think I've heard a single word in that whole time. Everyone's been lost in their own head. I never thought it'd bother me to fly in silence; after all, that's what I've done my whole life, but it feels strange this time, especially since it carried over onto the rocky islet we decided to rest on. I wouldn't exactly call it an island, but we're resting on a dry part of the islet next to a clump of black rocks jutting out from the ocean. There is little vegetation here, but we manage to find a small amount of broken sticks along with some things we brought to fuel a fire. The night is silent, except for the crackling of the campfire and the sound of the waves hitting the rocks. There's no real shelter—we're completely out in the open—but the dragons are in desperate need of a break after flying from Zram. We've been here maybe an hour, and they've all been asleep for at least three quarters of that. The black rocks we are sitting on jut out the ocean just above the surface of the water, and since the moon isn't out, it makes the night seem even darker than it is. The fire illuminates a small circular glow around it, and the light only reaches so far in the dark night. It gets very dark very quickly the farther one moves away from the fire because the light is quickly swallowed up by the nighttime. Brezmard sleeps under Kemoss's wing, and Nokk sleeps fitfully by the fire. Norkuz sits next to Quldriag, fiddling with a bracelet around his wrist and throwing an occasional glance at Ak'dech, who sits at the edge of the circle of light with her back turned, separate from everyone, hugging her knees and staring into the darkness. Nalrai keeps moving around in his sleep, and I sit beside him observing everyone else. Eventually, I stand up, walk over to Ak'dech, and sit beside her. She sniffs and hurriedly wipes tears from her cheeks.

"Wh-what are you doing over here?" she asks.

I shrug and say, "I don't know, actually."

The Lost One: Wrath of the Tyrant

I guess I expected a response, maybe even a joke, but I haven't seen her smile since the battle on Clearhallow.

"It's chilly this season. Winter will be particularly cold this year, I imagine," I mention.

"It's uncharacteristic of you to *seek out* a conversation," she says.

"I don't know. I guess it didn't... feel good to let you sit over here alone, and it feels strange traveling with you all and not hearing any talking," I say.

"Do you mean you *feel bad* for *me*? Because you don't show empathy very often, especially not toward someone who's wronged you," she says.

"Yeah, weird," I concur, "Also weird how it actually hurt when you betrayed me. I've always been good at not letting anybody get close enough to hurt me. I guess I thought of you as a friend, and despite all that, it doesn't feel right to let you suffer alone after you sat with me in my own guilt after I attacked Xymrar."

"Thank you," she says.

"Do you know Norkuz has been trying not to stare at you for the past hour?" I ask.

"Doesn't surprise me. He's conflicted. It was his idea to save Nokk and I, and he's probably torn between pain and forgiveness. Norkuz has known me longer than anyone else, save Nokk and Qombaryth, obviously. We were put in the same unit after training before either of us were considered for Brezmard's group. He's actually the one who recommended me after he got promoted.

We were really close, so I know he was crushed to find out I was a traitor," she says.

Nynnu, the dragon closest to us, snorts and wakes up with her ears swiveling around. In fact, all the dragons are waking up and looking around, ears perked. Nokk and Brezmard wake, disturbed by the dragons.

"What is it?" Norkuz asks his dragon, standing.

"What's going on?" Brezmard asks.

"We don't know," I say, getting to my feet with my hand on the hilt of my sword.

Nynnu cautiously sneaks away from the fire towards the darkness as Nalrai bounds in front of her leading the way. I listen for whatever they're hearing, noting only the waves and fire. I step away from the flames and away from the shore until it's so dark I can't see in front of me. I'm surprised the warmth of the campfire reached as far as Ak'dech and I were sitting because it gets colder as I step away.

"Nalrai," I say, holding out my hand.

Instead of coming back to guide me, fire bubbles in his throat as he opts to illuminate his surroundings. Nokk runs ahead of me, trying to catch up with his dragon, who's crouched on top of a boulder about a hundred meters away with her tail flickering back and forth. She reaches a claw down behind the rock carefully then jumps back and growls before scooting closer again, sniffing. I run after Nokk to assess the situation, but he stops dead in his tracks when he reaches the boulder. Even in the dim lighting, I can see his face lose all color.

The Lost One: Wrath of the Tyrant

"What is it?" I ask, as everyone else catches up.

"Hatchlings," Nokk gags, while leaning against the rock beside him, breathing in and out deeply with his eyes closed.

"Hatchlings?" I say, as I run over and similarly stop when I see them heavily injured and crawling over the corpse of their mother. I swallow to keep from throwing up.

"Why did *these* hatchlings catch our dragons' attention? Creatures live and die all the time. That's nature," Brezmard says.

"You hear that sound they're making? It's a distress cry. It must have caught their attention," Ak'dech explains.

Four metallic silver dragon whelps crawl over the gruesome carcass of their mother while the body of a fifth hatchling lays off to the side dead. The rest of them are all covered in blood and injured. One of them is missing an eye and is barely able to move. He's hardly breathing. I kneel beside them, reaching out to the weakest hatchling that wheezes with every shallow breath. As I cup my hands together to pick him up, he doesn't have the strength to struggle and lies limply in my palms. It's so cold he should be shivering, but he's too weak for even that. I hold him tenderly, stroking his scales. He gives a pathetic attempt to resist, then he squeals and spends all available effort to open his wings and scratch at me with his claw. Nynnu pokes at the rest of the whelplings gently with her snout, occasionally giving a small lick to a wound.

"They're freezing," I say.

"They're in bad shape," Norkuz agrees, picking up two of the stronger whelps that squirm as he does.

Norkuz hands one off to Ak'dech and grabs the last hatchling from behind the boulder.

"There should be another one," I say.

"What do you mean?" Norkuz asks.

"I know this breed. They always hatch in a brood of six, and they live in much warmer places than this. They don't like the cold," I say.

"I don't see a sixth hatchling," he says, "Let's get them away from here and warmed up."

A layer of sweat shimmers on Nokk's face, and he's even paler than before.

"Nokk, are you okay?" Ak'dech asks.

"I wouldn't have thought you'd have a weak stomach after all the battles you've seen," I comment.

"I've witnessed battle… nothing like this," he says shakily.

"Have Nynnu give you a ride back to camp," Norkuz says.

Nynnu snorts, strutting away from Nokk, focusing her attention on the whelplings.

"I don't think she wants to do me any extra favors at the moment," he says, "It's fine. I can walk. It's not far."

The Lost One: Wrath of the Tyrant

I listen to the hatchling's wheezing and soft gurgling as we walk back to the campfire. Once we get there, I keep the one I'm holding in my hands. Norkuz and Ak'dech set their whelps by the fire, and the stronger hatchlings squirm and try to climb closer to the flames as they feel the warmth. Norkuz then grabs medicine supplies out of his healer's kit and mixes together some sort of salve.

"Hold him still," he tells me.

"Way too easy," I say.

Norkuz softly cleans the blood out of the hatchling's empty eye socket with a cloth dipped in the salve, which causes it to squeal in discomfort. He then spreads the ointment over the rest of the young dragon's wounds.

"He has a broken wing, a broken leg, and part of his tail is displaced, but I'll tend to those after I assess the other hatchlings. He needs a break before I address the other wounds," he says.

Nynnu sits by the fire with her wing over the other three hatchlings, cuddled up to them.

"Do you think they'll live?" Brezmard asks Norkuz.

"I'll do my best to see that they do," he says.

"So we're going to bring them along with us to all these different islands?" Ak'dech asks.

"Why not? They should be fine as long as we keep an eye on them. When they get better, we can take them back to Clearhallow and raise them ourselves," Norkuz says, while reaching under Nynnu's wing to grab the next hatchling.

"Assuming they'll get better *and* assuming we'll be able to return home? That's quite optimistic of you," Brezmard says.

"They wouldn't like Clearhallow," I say.

"No? All our other dragons do," Norkuz says.

"As I said, they hate the cold. They'd freeze with how much snow the north gets," I say.

"We'll find somewhere for them," Norkuz says.

"Are you already attached to them?" Brezmard asks, amused.

"Are you not? They haven't done anything to deserve this," Norkuz argues.

"Don't worry. We're not abandoning the adorable baby dragons," Brezmard says while rolling his eyes.

"Arid, how do you know so much about these dragons?" Nokk asks.

"I spent a few weeks in the far south while running from some pirates I robbed, and I met a dragonologist studying them. They were common to the area, and she was... *eager* to share her findings with anyone and everyone," I tell.

The Lost One: Wrath of the Tyrant

"I wonder what they are doing here," Ak'dech says.

"I don't know, but we should stay on alert. When these dragons mature, their scales are hard as granite. They're among the more formidable dragons I've encountered, so whatever killed their mother has to be dangerous," I say, petting the hatchling's neck.

"We'll be out of here as soon as the dragons are rested," Brezmard says, "Norkuz, are you okay staying up for the rest of the night to watch the hatchlings?"

"That's fine," Norkuz says.

"The dragons need to focus on resting up. The rest of us will take shifts keeping watch. Ak'dech and Arid first, then Nokk and myself," says Brezmard.

Norkuz rubs something inside one of the hatchling's mouths and takes her resistant bite without so much as a flinch. She calms down as soon as he spreads the substance behind her teeth. Then she commences chomping and licking at it.

"What's that?" I ask.

"A treat. Jelly, with a bit of dragon nip mixed in. I would have given it to the other whelp if he were more responsive," he says.

Quldriag's ears perk up when Norkuz mentions the jelly, and he bounds over, sticking his head right into Norkuz's neck.

"Quldriag, are you jealous?" I laugh.

"Not right now buddy. They need special attention," Norkuz says, while pushing away his dragon that snorts and struts away taking offense.

"Keep that away from Nalrai. He has a bad reaction to dragon nip," I say.

"Okay. No jelly for Nalrai," he says, petting the hatchling a few times before switching her out for the next.

Chapter Twenty-Five: Dungeons of Ioneot

*I*t's the next day, and our first stop after resting the dragons is an island called Ioneot. Their guards keep close tabs on us as we approach, but they allow us to talk to the chief. These people are much less trusting than Zram; and apparently, they're much poorer than Zram too because their village is falling apart. Supposedly, they made a business investment with Clearhallow that didn't work out in the past, and it left them struggling. They never recovered from it. The only place they could offer us to stay while they consider the alliance is the dungeon. They also allowed us to keep the hatchlings with us, but the grown dragons are out back in a stable. The dungeon hasn't been used in over a decade, which is easily apparent by looking at it. It used to be a prison, but I could tell the bars were ripped out the decaying cells, probably because the stone that used to hold the bars in place was crumbling. It's well enough lit down here, but it's no warmer than the outside. It reeks of dampness and rats, and water drips down the cracked walls into muddy puddles on the dirt floor. We were provided straw mats, dry rations, and old, woolen blankets filled with holes smelling of animals and filth. The hatchlings squeak in complaint at the cold. Norkuz gathers them together on his mat and throws a blanket over them. He then sits down and digs through his rations, holding out a handful of dry crackers for the baby dragons.

"You should've been a dragon trainer," I say.

"I enjoy being a healer. Besides, I would have grown too attached to the little ones and been devastated each time a dragon went to a new home after I trained them," he says.

As Norkuz is speaking, one of the whelps climbs closer to him, trying to find a way into his warm cotton doublet. He wraps the dragon up in a massive hug and rubs his finger under its chin affectionately.

Ak'dech laughs and says, "Looks like you've made a friend already. What *will* happen when we find a proper home for them?"

"That's not a problem for today," he says, checking on the hatchling's wounds.

I go to sit by Norkuz and the hatchlings and watch.

"They're so terrified and confused," I say, as they whimper and crawl over one another.

"I'm sure. They're without their mother, injured, and being carried around by strange creatures. I'd be scared, too," Norkuz says.

"Norkuz has practically adopted them. We should name them," Ak'dech says excitedly.

"No, we can't name th—" Brezmard starts.

"What do you think, Nokk? What should her name be?" Ak'dech asks while grabbing a hatchling.

The dragon squirms, nipping at her fingers unsuccessfully.

"Tsavoz," Nokk says without hesitation.

"Why Tsavoz?" Brezmard asks, distracted from the fact he was trying to say no to naming them moments earlier.

"It's from an ancient myth. It means *little goddess*," I say.

The Lost One: Wrath of the Tyrant

"Tsavoz was the goddess of good fortune," Nokk says.

"This is coming from the man who tried to fight the last person who mentioned gods and religion?" Brezmard scoffs.

"It's a *story*. I don't believe in the goddess of fortune, but I enjoyed the myth," Nokk defends angrily.

"So, what's that little one's name? The one attacking Norkuz," Ak'dech says.

"Acanix," Norkuz says immediately.

"The bright god... bringer of the sun and stars," I say, noticing a pattern forming.

"How do *you* know all our myths?" Brezmard asks.

"I've read a *lot* of books. You do realize they're not *your* myths? They were translated from the Ancient Tongue, meaning they were written long before Clearhallow was settled," I say, annoyed.

"Oh," he blushes in embarrassment, looking away.

Ak'dech reaches for the healthiest hatchling.

"You can be Sari, goddess of the night," she says, but quickly lets go as the whelp bites her hand forcefully.

"Ow!"

"Did she draw blood?" Norkuz asks, reaching for her hand.

"It's fine," she says, clenching and releasing her fist.

"If she pierced skin, you need to cleanse it. Hatchling bites tend to cause fever if you don't wash them," he says.

"Okay, *I'll* clean it," she says.

As Norkuz and Ak'dech argue about who's going to clean the bite, I grab the weakest hatchling. He tries to resist, but he's still too weak to effectively wiggle free. I hug him, tickling his neck and the underside of his good wing. He relaxes, resting his head on my arm.

"What's *his* name?" Ak'dech asks me as Norkuz tends to the bite on her hand.

"Ascez… god of strength," I say.

"Let's hope so. He *needs* a godly amount of strength to survive those wounds," Norkuz says, "It'd be great if he could start eating, but so far he's refused."

"He's too scared to eat," I say.

"What? How do you know?" he asks.

I shrug and set Ascez in my lap. The movement startles him, so I soothe him with more gentle scratches. Then I reach into my ration pack and pull out a cracker, crumbling it in my hand.

The Lost One: Wrath of the Tyrant

"Could I get a scoop of jelly?" I ask Norkuz.

He plops some into my palm. I mix it with the cracker and hold my hand in front of Ascez's nose. He sniffs at it and starts licking it off my glove.

"Wow. That's impressive," Norkuz says.

"The lightning beasts liked you too, *and* you calmed the cave dragon," Nokk says.

"Dragons are easy," I say dismissively.

"Dragons are ferocious beasts who naturally want to tear you apart and have you for lunch. Dragon catching and taming are more dangerous than any battlefield position. A medium-sized dragon could rip through your chest like a piece of parchment. So no, wild dragons aren't *easy* to deal with," Nokk says.

"Well, *I've* never had a problem with them," I say.

"That's my point!" he says.

"How do you prevent them from biting?" Ak'dech asks.

"They'll only bite if they feel threatened, or if they're playing," I say.

"How do you tell which one it is?" she asks.

"Many clues. They're already scared and not well enough to play just yet. Also, she was quick to draw blood, which means she is trying to scare you off," I say.

I reach a hand out to Sari, who is the most aggressive and distressed. She instantly attacks my hand, scratching and biting. A frightened growl comes from her throat as her teeth latch onto my glove. The bite is surprisingly powerful. I pick her up and hug her firmly so she can't move. She squirms desperately, panting quickly. Eventually, she calms down, but her muscles are tense, with an occasional fit trying to escape. I can feel her heart racing, fluttering harshly against her chest.

"She'll take a while," I say, holding her still.

Ascez snoozes, wheezes, and shivers in my lap. Acanix frequently attempts to burrow deeper into Norkuz's cotton doublet, whimpering. Tsavoz lets out a lonely cry since she's been left under the blanket by herself, so Ak'dech picks her up. Tsavos screeches shrilly as she's lifted, however, she doesn't resist or try to break free despite her scream. Instead, a soft, high-pitched whine continues with each breath out after she's wrapped securely in Ak'dech's arms.

"Are you *sure* Clearhallow's too cold for them?" she asks.

"*Now* who's getting attached to them?" Norkuz laughs.

"If autumn *here* is too cold, then winter *there* would kill them. We can't bring them back to Clearhallow. You shouldn't have named them. Stop falling in love with them," Brezmard says grouchily.

Ak'dech stands up, walks over to where Brezmard is sitting and says, "*You* watch them then."

The Lost One: Wrath of the Tyrant

"What are you—"

"I haven't seen *you* helping out," she interrupts, placing Tsavoz on the back of his neck and shoulders.

Brezmard jumps. Then Tsavoz shrieks and scurries down his arm, whimpering, but Brezmard catches her as she's about to run off his arm.

"What are you doing?" he splutters, face turning red in anger.

"Well, *obviously*, you're much more capable of not growing fond of them. Therefore, it makes more sense for *you* to take care of them," she snipes, irritated, "And don't hold her like that. She has a broken wing."

He holds her out away from his body and says, "Take her back."

"Why?" she asks, crossing her arms stubbornly.

"Because… I said to," he says.

"Convincing," Ak'dech snorts sarcastically.

Tsavoz chirps in distress. Brezmard brings her to his chest in response, trying to quiet her.

"She's… shivering," he sounds surprised.

"Uh, yeah. What do *you* do when you're cold?" she says quizzically.

He holds her even closer, trying to keep her warm. Ak'dech shakes her head as she heads back over and sits next to me again.

"He's not letting her go, is he?" Norkuz whispers.

"Uh, no," Ak'dech whispers back while glancing at Brezmard, who's doing absolutely everything he can to make Tsavoz comfortable.

<<<>>>

I wake up with two hatchlings cuddled up against me—two more than I fell asleep by. I expected the holes in the blanket to make feeling warm throughout the night hardly worthwhile, but there's plenty of heat beneath it with the whelps. Despite the warmth under the blanket, I get a chill down my spine... something's not right. The torches that kept the room lit earlier are burned out, and... someone's watching me. I sit up slowly on the mat and ease onto my knees with my fingers already around the handle of my dagger. I can feel Vrarg breathing beneath me. I can hear hollow footsteps pounding all around me. I feel eyes staring at me through the dark, and an icy breath crystalizes on the back of my neck. I twist around, dagger swinging—nothing but air. The motion upsets whatever is in the room, and loud wailing starts up, filling the dungeon. I can't pinpoint a specific point of origin of the sounds, but it seems to bounce around the walls and come from everywhere at once. Cold wind spirals around the room. I jump as a hand reaches from behind me and grabs my wrist.

"Don't," Ak'dech says, as she wraps my own arms across by body to opposite shoulders, pulling me into a hug.

"Wh-what?" I shudder.

247

The Lost One: Wrath of the Tyrant

"Put your dagger down. You'll hurt someone," she whispers.

"That's the point," I say, looking around for the intruders, ready to throw Ak'dech off me to fight.

"There's no one here to hurt," she says.

"You… you don't hear that howling?" I ask nervously.

She shakes her head and says, "Arid, it's in your head."

"No… no it's not. Not this time," I deny, shaking my head as the pitch of my voice rises, "You don't hear them? You don't hear the footsteps or wind?"

"Shh, calm down. You're okay. Breathe," she says.

My heart's racing, and my eyes sting with tears that refuse to fall. A ghostly scream blasts in my ear. I can't see anything that could have caused the sound, but the wails are coming from my right. I react by trying to swing my dagger at it, but Ak'dech holds my wrist firmly and says, "Give me the dagger."

"You reacted to it. I saw you. You looked at it," I say, convinced she heard the screams and howling before I did.

"Arid, the dagger," she says calmly, twisting my wrist slightly.

"I don't trust you," I say.

"If there were howling, wouldn't the others wake up? Even the hatchlings are asleep, and you know dragons are fairly light sleepers, even as babies," she says.

I look around again. It's very dim in here, but not pitch black. Enough light from outside torches spills in through the barred windows. Norkuz is asleep with the other two dragons slumbering beside him, and one of them kicks fitfully and makes an occasional whimper of distress. Nokk and Brezmard are fast asleep, too. My fingers are clenched tightly around the dagger's handle. I hesitantly release it, then Ak'dech grabs the dagger and puts it aside before putting her arms back around me, hugging me from the back. I move my legs from underneath myself as my feet start to tingle.

"But... I saw you react to it," I say.

Ak'dech doesn't say anything.

"So, why are *you* up?" I ask.

"Do you believe in ghosts?" she asks after a second.

"What? No... I don't know," I shake my head in confusion, "What does that have to do with anything?"

"There's something not right with this dungeon, is all. I never made it to sleep, and I've found no indication we're in danger. But there's... *something* here," she says uneasily.

"I can almost *feel* their footsteps," I say, reaching for my dagger.

"You're okay," she says reassuringly.

The Lost One: Wrath of the Tyrant

I take a deep breath as my heart slows back toward its normal pace. I can still hear Vrarg breathing, but the howls and footsteps have grown fainter and fainter until there's peace in the dungeon. I've been careful not to kick or brush against the small hatchlings near my feet, and luckily, they are cuddling together, sleeping peacefully. The room is filled with a grim magic hanging stagnant in the air. Ak'dech must be right. This dungeon is haunted by something, but Vrarg remains serene and doesn't mind the grimness in this place, as a more peaceful magic swirls gently through the ground, causing a dim spark of magic I've never noticed before to radiate softly around us as Ak'dech keeps her arms around me in a comforting hug.

Chapter Twenty-Six: Do You Hear Me?

We've been waiting in the dungeon half the morning for the chief to announce his decision on an alliance. The guards have brought us more rations and assured us our dragons are being well cared for, but we can't check on them ourselves because we're not allowed to leave the dungeon without an escort. Allegedly, the guards are "too busy" to take us anywhere. I'm not sure if we're guests or prisoners at this point, but I don't like being trapped in this dungeon. It doesn't feel right after last night. Since awakening, the hatchlings have been loud. Even Ascez manages a chirp here and there because they miss their mother, and they've been doing nothing except cry out for her, which transmits a lonely mourning echoing in the chamber. We've done our best to comfort them, but there's only so much to be done.

"Come on, Acanix. Eat... please?" I plea to the one that's been attached to Norkuz, while offering a chunk of stale bread that came with the morning rations.

Acanix doesn't even acknowledge me but repeats his cry over and over, looking for his mother. This is the hatchlings' second day since we've found them, and they spent all of yesterday sleeping on the way over. They haven't had time to call out to their mother for her to find them.

"Poor babies," Ak'dech says.

"What is that horrendous screeching?" Chief Miglec flinches as he walks into the dungeon.

"They're scared," I say.

The Lost One: Wrath of the Tyrant

"Shut up. I will not be spoken to by a female I have not addressed," he says.

"Excuse me?" Ak'dech says, offended.

Norkuz shakes his head at her.

"Apologies, Chief Miglec. It's not in our culture to shun our women," Brezmard says sourly, "Have you come to a decision?"

"Get those *things* to quiet down," he sneers, "Then we'll talk about my decision."

"We've been trying to quiet them all morning. They won't—" I start.

"Silence! I will not hear from *that* creature, either," he says, waving his hand toward me in a demeaning manner.

"The whelplings won't quiet. They're scared and miss their mother. Perhaps we should talk somewhere else while Lady Ak'dech and Lady Arid tend to the hatchlings," Brezmard suggests.

"That is acceptable. You two, stand guard to the entrance of the dungeon," Chief Miglec orders, snapping his fingers at two of his guards while glaring in Ak'dech's and my direction.

"What an arrogant, little prick," Ak'dech says, a few seconds after their footsteps fade.

"As long as they come to an agreement, and hopefully—soon—so we can get out of here," I say, lying down on my stomach, "The chief's a jerk. Their village is falling apart, and their dungeons are haunted. The sooner we leave, the better."

"Right. So, how do we help *them*?" she says, tickling behind Tsavoz's ear.

Tsavoz draws away from Ak'dech's hand, continuing her incessant chirps, and her little dragon eyes stare blankly around the room.

"I... don't know," I say.

I pick Tsavoz up and hold her close. Her chirping hurts my ears, but it starts to quiet down after a few seconds and fades to a whimper.

"At least you're gaining their trust," Ak'dech says.

"You don't have any of Norkuz's dragon nip jelly, do you?" I ask.

"No," she says.

I put Tsavoz next to the others and throw a blanket over them, hoping they'll go to sleep. Surely they're tired after crying the last few hours. *I'm* tired after their crying, and my head hurts from the noise. They finally start quieting a bit, and the time between the silence and each chirp increases little by little. I watch a lump crawl toward me under the blanket, then it pokes his head out and rests its snout on my arm.

The Lost One: Wrath of the Tyrant

"Hello again, Acanix," I say, running a finger down his snout.

He whines sorrowfully for a while as he starts to fall asleep, then he jerks awake immediately after he drifts off and crawls closer to me. As he climbs from under the blanket, he tries to find the best spot to lie on me.

"Cuddly," Ak'dech says.

"Yeah," I say, scooping him into my arms.

Acanix settles there comfortably, drifting off to sleep in seconds.

"Finally, their cries are silenced at last," Ak'dech whispers, as the hatchlings all fall asleep.

"Yeah, finally," I agree, "Hey, uh… thank you."

"Don't mention it," she brushes off the conversation, immediately knowing I was talking about last night's strange episode, "I wasn't about to let you stab anyone, especially not these cuties," she nods at the blanket.

I look up as footsteps approach. It's Brezmard and Norkuz stepping back into the dungeon, escorted by a couple of guards.

"Where's Nokk?" Ak'dech asks.

"Don't worry, he's fine. He's talking with the guards to figure out as many details as he can about a particular problem they've been having, and they want us to help them before they agree to help us," Brezmard says, "Arid, we need to catch some thieves. Any tips?"

"They need help with thieves? What kind of thieves?" I ask.

"Uh, the ones that steal things," he stares at me cluelessly.

"Apparently, violent ones. They're not afraid of murdering a few guards to get away. They've killed a handful of them already," Norkuz says.

"I'll take care of them," I say, jumping at an opportunity to get out of this dungeon for a while.

"The chief—"

"The chief will have to deal with it. I'm going," I say, getting up and handing Acanix to Ak'dech.

"Fine," Brezmard says, "What help do you want?"

"You said Nokk's learning what they know? I'll take him with me. That should be more than enough," I say.

"Take her to Sir Nokk," Brezmard orders the guards.

They bow, then glare distrustfully at me before starting off down the hall.

The Lost One: Wrath of the Tyrant

"So… who hurt your chief? Why doesn't he tolerate women?" I ask the guards.

"Women can't be trusted. They're inferior in every way… utterly powerless, and those without power eventually try to take it," one of the guards says.

"Then why withhold *all* power from them?" I ask.

"That is not our doing. That is nature's determination," he says.

"That's ridiculous," I say.

"Your friends choose to defy nature by allowing women into their ranks, giving them an illusion of power. This defiance will be your army's downfall."

"Okay," I say, deciding it's not worth arguing about.

We don't have to like their army. We just have to cooperate until Ma'roog is defeated, I think to myself.

When we arrive at a study, Nokk is at a small table talking to some guards. The chief is thankfully nowhere to be seen.

"So, if you know who they are, why not go to their homes and arrest them?" Nokk asks.

"They don't have homes. They're never in one spot for long, so we don't know where to find them. Besides, they are dangerous. Two of them carry knives on them, and the third uses his size as his weapon," a guard answers.

"Are you here to help us out?" Nokk asks me.

"Ah, yes," the guard says, "A female traveler is weak and defenseless. We can use her to lure them into a trap. She will make the perfect bait!"

"Actually, I was thinking *Nokk* would be the bait. We can get him a change of clothes so they're not scared off by him being a trained soldier," I say. Then I start directing my words toward Nokk, "Between how scrawny you look and how young you clearly are, *I* wouldn't give a second thought to robbing you if I were in their shoes. You'd make a convincingly helpless victim. Besides, that necklace you think is well hidden will make an enticing prize."

"This was my mother's necklace," Nokk frowns, "It's the only thing I have from my parents."

"You'll still have it at the end of the day," I promise.

Nokk caught me up with the details on the way to the market, which is one of the thieves' favorite places to steal from. It makes sense though: lots of people and lots of items. As I break away from Nokk to move forward with the plan, I stay far back so it doesn't appear we are together, but I'm in close proximity just in case he needs me. Nokk's doing a good job of pretending he's not nervous. He's carrying on with his fake shopping trip with his necklace dangling freely in front of his tunic. He occasionally stops at a shop and looks around or asks the shopkeepers a question. He looks naive and carefree. I crouch behind an abandoned stand, peering over it to keep watch for anything suspicious. The guards—who stayed back by the palace in order not to discourage the thieves—gave a description of the robbers, but there are many people who could fit their description.

The Lost One: Wrath of the Tyrant

It could take days to draw them out, so if they don't show, I'll find another way to track them down, even with the vague idea of what they look like. I suddenly notice an oddly alert girl watching Nokk out the corner of her eye. She watches him for several minutes as she goes about her usual shopping, then she stops by two men at another stand, talking to them for a moment and nodding slightly at Nokk. They look around to locate him. The girl and the smaller guy both have daggers sheathed by their belts, and all three match the descriptions the guards gave. Without waiting, the larger man charges at Nokk, not bothering with an attempt at stealth and tackles him. The two with weapons keep the crowd away with the threat of their daggers, and they are ready to react to anything that goes wrong with their robbery.

"Nice necklace, pretty boy. Have anything else for us?" the gigantic man growls, reaching for the ruby hanging around Nokk's neck.

I walk over to the attempted mugging.

"Back off, kid. This is *our* loot," the girl says, pointing her dagger at me.

"Get off of me!" Nokk grunts, impressively rolling off his back, managing to get enough leverage to switch places with his attacker and throw his elbow into the man's neck.

The thief's hands fly up to his neck as his throat surely swells from the hit. The smaller man rushes at Nokk while the girl stands hesitantly in front of me threatening the dagger. I can tell she instinctively wants to go with him to ensure the jewelry doesn't get away, but she stays with a lazy attempt at keeping me and the crowd at a distance.

"Hey, do you need help?" I ask Nokk.

He angrily screams as he wrestles the other thief to the ground. They said these thieves were tough and dangerous, so I wasn't expecting him to take out the first thief so quickly and easily. It makes me wonder if Ioneot's army is even worth recruiting.

"Back off!" the girl says as I inch closer to help Nokk, then she lunges at me with her dagger.

I duck and grab her arm, pull her forward, and drive my knee into her stomach. She takes the hit well, pulls her arm free, and swings her elbow into my ribs, followed by a quick swipe with her dagger. The sharpened edge finds my arm and slices it painfully.

"Ow! You nicked an artery. That's not nice," I say, as blood immediately spurts from the wound, spraying down my arm and hand.

She tries to return the shot to the stomach I gave her and brings her knee up toward me. I grab under her knee and yank up toward the sky. She lands on her back hard, curls up, and grasps at her leg in pain. Nokk has both thieves pinned down, too, and they are all too injured to get up and run.

"That's a lot of blood," Nokk mentions, as I walk toward him.

"Yeah," I agree, feeling lightheaded, "I might need to sit down for a moment."

He breaks my fall as my legs give out and yells, "Arid!"

"Fine, I'm fine," I mumble.

The Lost One: Wrath of the Tyrant

For autumn weather, it's been a little chilly lately, but as I lay in Nokk's arms, I feel like I'm freezing. Even so, I can feel sweat all over my body as Nokk tries to stop the blood from gushing with his hands.

"Arid! Hey, you have to heal yourself, okay? Use your magic to heal yourself because I can't get you to Norkuz in time. *Do you hear me?* Arid!" Nokk shouts.

Chapter Twenty-Seven: The Streets of Rhargrim

"This is what you get for letting a woman try to do a man's job. Incompetence and weakness lead to higher casualties."

That's the first thing I hear from Chief Miglec as I wake up on the couch in the palace's study surrounded by books.

"Ow," my arm twitches as Norkuz sews my skin together with needle and thread.

"Sorry. I'm almost done," he says.

"Thanks, but don't worry about it," I say, grabbing the thread from Norkuz and ripping the stitches from my skin.

"What are you doing?" he asks, grimacing as my skin separates from itself, exposing the open gash that I made worse.

"She is absolutely insane... another reason women shouldn't be on the battlefield," tsks Chief Miglec.

"I'm sorry, but I didn't see *your* men doing anything about the thieves after all these months. It took her one day to 'clear up this particular problem' for you," Nokk mocks the chief's voice, irritated.

I get to my feet and feel my muscles knit back together. My skin connects and heals over the muscles, and a pink scar replaces the gaping wound in seconds.

The Lost One: Wrath of the Tyrant

"Huh... okay, I won't bother bandaging you in the future," Norkuz says dejectedly.

"I appreciate your effort. Besides, I may be in control of it at the moment, but who knows about later? I may still need your help," I say.

"W-Wh-Wha—" Chief Miglec seems unable to form a complete sentence, or even a word, while staring at my arm.

"Well, now that your thieves are taken care of, I assume you don't need us for anything else? We will talk to Zram about the financial assistance you requested, including the cost of moving your troops, along with food and pay. We look forward to your army joining us," Norkuz says.

"Bu-but... she..." Miglec stutters and stares in disbelief, trying to understand what he saw.

"Yes, it's amazing, but we really would like to move on if that's alright. We have more islands to consult with, and we're trying to get this over with as soon as possible. So unless you have anything else to discuss, we're going to get moving," Norkuz says.

Miglec nods, speechless.

It's been almost three days, and the baby dragons are about the length of an average forearm. Ascez is nestled against my leg, sleeping in front of me as we fly smoothly, with minimal turbulence, toward the next island.

The Streets of Rhargrim

Norkuz hasn't become any more certain about this little dragon's chances of survival, but his breathing sounds less strained than it did when we found them a couple days ago. He's much less stressed around me than he is around the others, but even I can barely get him to eat. We've been flying two days straight. Last night was cold, and today promises it'll only get colder. We purchased blankets from the market, and at least they're in better condition than the old, wool holey ones from the dungeon, but it's going to require constant work to ensure the hatchlings don't freeze to death. Between the blanket and Nalrai's warmth, Ascez is comfortable enough for the moment, but the sun will go down. Even more, the clouds have been gathering as we fly closer to our stop. That signals there may very well be a storm. On a few occasions, I have visited the island of Rhargrim before, and I honestly don't have hope for them providing us with much assistance. Their people have always been friendly, but it's a small village that has never seemed particularly organized in any manner. I've noted from conversations off the streets that their government's absence is a common complaint, but they're not as poor as Ioneot. Rhargrim's buildings are much better taken care of, however, they have significantly fewer people, a smaller military, and less food and supplies. On Ioneot, we were greeted by guards well before we had officially reached the island. Here, we land at the edge of town, and no one approaches us to ask questions. On Ioneot, their structures were spread out, but Rhargrim has everything close together. Their whole village could be walked around in no more than three or four hours, and there's no obvious central marketplace. Instead, there are signs hanging from various windows that invite customers to walk in and shop. There are also unlit torches placed along the street, waiting to light the way when it becomes dark. I'm used to hearing conversations around me as I walk through an inhabited village, but I find those are few and far between. It's been like this every time I've visited, and it's honestly one of the reasons I come back. There's a quiet, slow pace about the village... a little dreary, but I've always enjoyed the calm. As we walk through the town, I see no guards or soldiers, and no palace or mansion. There's no obvious place where the chief may reside.

"Excuse me," I stop a woman on the street.

The Lost One: Wrath of the Tyrant

"Hello. Are you travelers?" she asks, looking at our dragons.

"Yes. We're looking for a chance to speak to your overlord. How do we find the chief?" I ask.

"My dear, no one's seen the chief in months. He doesn't interact much with the citizens, or even his guards, rumor has it. It's doubtful you'll find the opportunity to visit with him," she says sweetly, touching my shoulder lightly.

"We're looking to make an arrangement with him. It would help if you pointed us in the direction of his dwelling, and we'd be more than happy to work it out with the guards," Brezmard says.

"Well, if you're set on it, I could show you where to go in the morning. For now, you all look tired and in need of a place to rest, especially your dragons. My friend works the only inn around, and I'm sure she would be willing to accommodate your group. It'll be tight with all of you, but it'll provide shelter from the cold. We may get the first snowfall of the season, and you'd be best off indoors," she says.

"That would be much appreciated," Norkuz says.

"Are the streets usually this empty?" Brezmard asks.

"They're a tad more empty than other days. Between the cold blowing in and a fever that's been spreading through town, trips outside are kept to a minimum. We stay inside as much as we can to avoid both. I'm only out and about today to shop for food and herbs. My husband is unfortunately starting to show signs of the fever," she says.

"Do you have physicians or healers?" Norkuz asks.

"One, but he's far too busy to tackle this mass fever situation on his own. Only the rich get to see that physician," she responds.

"You said no one has seen the chief in months? Why is that?" I ask.

"Who knows? I've heard he greatly prefers to spend his time alone. He does what is required to keep the basic necessities accessible to our island. We're lucky to have luxuries such as firm dwellings and warm clothing, but other villages hold public events to keep up morale and entertain the people. There isn't much energy dedicated toward community activities here: no celebrations or festivities held by the government, no tournaments, no plays, no public form of gatherings or recreation," she says.

"That sounds… dull," Brezmard comments.

"Yes, it can be. However, I don't know one person who's ungrateful to live here… at least we're not starving," she says.

I notice a young girl coughing on the side of the street playing with an old doll. She's hurriedly rushed inside by who I'd assume to be her mother. She wraps her own coat around the girl as a second layer of protection from the cold while looking around anxiously.

"How many are surviving the fever?" Norkuz asks, eyes following the young girl inside.

There's a short silence before the woman answers, "Some."

"It's not safe for us to be here," Ak'dech says.

The Lost One: Wrath of the Tyrant

"Hold on. We can't leave. We need as many people as we can get, and *they* clearly need help as well. If we can get a few physicians sent over here, I'm sure it'd help them out a great deal," Norkuz negotiates.

"You could help us?" the woman asks.

"We can't have disease spreading through the ranks. We could lose all these armies we're trying to bring together. You remember what happened during the training exercise near the Brirzik monument, don't you? Imagine having that happen on a level a thousand times larger, and potentially deadlier than that. All our efforts would be in vain. This island should be quarantined," Ak'dech argues.

"We can't let them *hope* their island survives this!" he insists.

"Brirzik monument?" I inquire.

"It's near one of our training grounds. Norkuz and I went on an exercise there, and it was a complete nightmare. We lost a lot of knights to sickness," she explains briefly.

"Brezmard?" Norkuz pleas, looking to his friend for a decision.

"When you said *some...*" Brezmard asks our guide.

"I'm afraid your friend's assessment is right. If you're here to recruit our army, you might be better off moving on without us. I don't know what you're planning, but I wouldn't want this fever to spread to your people," she says, looking away.

"Brezmard, *they need help*," Norkuz says pleadingly.

"I'm sorry, ma'am. We have to go. We can't take that big of a risk right now," Brezmard apologizes.

"Don't worry about us, sweet child. We'll pull through," she says.

"Norkuz, let's go before we get infected," he says.

"I'm not leaving," Norkuz says.

"What do you mean?" Brezmard asks.

"I'm staying to help these people. If you want to leave, that's fine. I'll meet you back on Zram after I've done what I can. I'll wait on an empty island for a few weeks until I'm sure I can't spread anything I may get sick with, then I'll join back up with you. I'll also see if I can get their chief to agree to help us, and then I'll tell his soldiers to isolate if their chief signs on. You don't need me to negotiate with the next islands," he responds firmly.

"Please, we don't want to cause any divisions between you. You're free to leave. We've survived this long. I'm sure we'll figure it out on our own," the woman speaks up.

"We need you," Brezmard says to Norkuz.

"No, you don't. I'm one knight. If I don't make it back, you can fight the war without me," he says.

"No, you're coming with us. That's an order. You're our only healer on this trip. We *need you* with us," Brezmard stands his ground.

The Lost One: Wrath of the Tyrant

"They don't have enough medical care available to them! Ak'dech knows enough medicine to take care of the hatchlings and any minor wounds you acquire. I'm going to help these people, Brezmard! I'm a healer! I can't stand by and let a whole village run around without help. Send over physicians from Zram to help us, and any other healer who agrees to an alliance with us, then I can come back and fight," Norkuz raises his voice.

"I gave you an order!" Brezmard yells.

"And what authority do you have over me?" Norkuz says coldly.

"I... Norkuz..." Brezmard says softly, "You're my best friend. I need you. You can't get sick and die. Let's go. Please."

"I'm sorry, but I'll be okay. I need to see that they have someone they can turn to for medicine," he says.

"Okay. You can stay here... for a *few* days. Meet with the chief, then get out. We'll wait for you on Khaudkur, and we'll see if they can spare any physicians. We will send them medicine as soon as we can. You can help whomever you need to while you're waiting for the chief's decision, but then you *get out*. And someone's staying with you to drag you back if you don't comply, or if you get yourself sick," Brezmard determines.

"Okay, fine. I'll leave after I talk to the chief, but you don't have to risk someone else getting sick. I'll be alright on my own," Norkuz compromises.

"I'll stay," Ak'dech volunteers.

"No, you know more medicine than we do. Besides, you need to watch the hatchlings, like he said," Brezmard admits, then he thinks for a moment, "Arid, are you okay staying here?"

"We can't risk Arid getting sick," Norkuz says.

"I'm not scared of a fever," I say, "I'll stay and make sure he gets out of here alive."

"Be careful… both of you," Brezmard says, as he settles in his saddle.

Chapter Twenty-Eight: Melancholy

few hours later, Jar'kog, a guard of Rhargrim, tenderly knocks on the door to the chief's chambers and says, "Chief Ark'lir."

"What is it?" the chief answers.

Jar'kog cautiously opens the door, and the room on the other side is dark. The chief lies in a large bed. I believe he is staring up at the ceiling.

"You have visitors... the Dragon Knights. They've come to speak about a potential arrangement to rid the world of Ma'roog's tyranny. They're also willing to help with the fever running through town," the guard says.

"Have Kiz'nor take care of it," the chief says.

"Sir, this is big enough that we need you out here. It could mean the end of *both* plagues wreaking havoc on our people," Jar'kog says.

"Fine. Send in my squire and have Kiz'nor and the visitors wait for me in the conference hall," the chief groans.

"Very well sir," the guard says, shutting the door gently.

"Is the chief ill?" Norkuz asks.

"Not with fever, but he's been depressed since he was a boy. He doesn't enjoy *anything*. He leaves his chambers only to consult with Kiz'nor, his head advisor, or to eat and bathe... and sometimes those last two happen very seldom. We've had periods where we've had to drag him to eat," Jar'kog says.

"Melancholy," Norkuz says.

"Yes, our physician uses that word for it too," Jar'kog says, "Kaz'rogg, go fetch the squire. Send him to the chief's chambers," he tells another guard as we pass him by a door.

"Yes, sir," Kaz'rogg runs off.

"Ten years ago, there would have been a court jester to keep you entertained while you wait, but Chief Ark'lir was displeased with all of our previous jesters. He had them fired and never bothered to hire a new one. I'm going to track down Kiz'nor. Should you need something while you wait, Sir Khi'rax is the guard outside the door," Jar'kog says, while leaving us in the conference hall.

"Why were you so adamant about staying?" I ask Norkuz after Jar'kog leaves.

"They need help," he says simply.

"Lots of places need help. Disease is not localized to this tiny village, and even more dangerous than any fever is the Rul Coilband," I say.

He looks away from me, silent for a moment, and then says, "I know. It would have probably been a wiser decision to leave, but that sick kid on the street reminded me of my little sister."

The Lost One: Wrath of the Tyrant

"You have a sister?" I ask.

"*Had*," he corrects.

"Did she die from illness?" I ask.

"No, although, she almost did when she was the same age as that girl. She got very sick, and I was impressed by the physician that tended to her. He saved her life, and that's why I chose to become a healer when I joined the knights. Long story short, I failed her a few years later, and seeing that girl was like looking at my sister. I stayed because of the guilt," he says.

"What happened?" I ask.

He sighs and says, "We were out being dumb by some cliffs on the northern edge of Clearhallow. I was a few years older than her. I was supposed to be responsible and make sure she stayed safe. However, there are a couple of trees on the top of the cliffs. I challenged her to a race to see who would make it up faster. She slipped and landed at the bottom of the cliff, on to the beach. I couldn't do anything to save her. I should have never challenged her to a race. The trees were too close to the edge of the cliff. I knew better. I knew it wasn't safe. I might as well have pushed her off. I was fifteen. She was *twelve*. That's too young to die. Anyway, that day was hard. We were close. She was a sweet kid, and everyone loved her. Zir'grog, my brother, was never the same. He adored her as much as anyone else, and her death sent him spiraling. He'd just been inducted as a proper Dragon Knight, but he betrayed them and joined the Rul Coilband's army. My parents were disappointed in him, and when he returned home, they shunned him for being a traitor. That's the event that jarred him enough to murder my parents," he says.

"I thought you said it was jealousy," I say.

"It was. He'd always been jealous of me. He hated my guts, but my sister's death left him unhinged. He was always... different after that... almost mentally unstable. He couldn't understand why my mother and father forgave me so easily, and it enraged him to hear them praise me while he endured their scorn. It was a couple years down the line, but according to the village, my parents were constantly gushing about how proud they were of me for joining the Dragon Knights Army. They were even happier about my return home and were planning a celebration, and that's when he killed them. He let that be the first thing I walked in on when I got home from training," he says.

"You blame yourself for your parents' death?" I ask.

"Yes... all their deaths."

"And that's why we're here, because you're willing to put your guilt above your safety? Do you really hope this will make you feel better?" I inquire.

"Yes," he says.

Jar'kog enters the room again, accompanied by an old man.

"Meet Sir Kiz'nor, the backbone of Rhargrim," he introduces.

"Nice to meet you," Norkuz nods, bowing.

"Likewise... Now, before the chief gets here, I have a few inquiries to get out of the way," Kiz'nor says, jumping straight to business.

"By all means," Norkuz says.

"You're here on behalf of Clearhallow?" he asks.

"Not exactly. We're traveling with Prince Brezmard of Clearhallow, who... had a minor disagreement with his father that we are hoping to clear up soon. We're here on behalf of Zram. Ioneot has also joined us," Norkuz replies delicately.

"So, you personally aren't in charge of anything?" Kiz'nor raises an eyebrow skeptically.

"I'm Prince Brezmard's second in command," Norkuz says.

"We'd prefer to speak to someone in a *real* position of power... a prince or a chief. If you're traveling with this *prince* of yours, then why is he not here?" the old man asks.

"You have a fever running rampant through your streets. I'm not going to allow my prince to expose himself to a sick island," he says.

"Fine. I suppose that will have to be well enough. Who is your friend with you?" Kiz'nor asks.

"A survivor from Tiendys. She would have been chief if Ma'roog hadn't razed her village," he answers.

"Hm. Very well."

We wait in awkward silence for several minutes before the chief shows up. He's a middle-age man with a beer belly and a death-like hollowness in his eyes. He's excessively pale, moves slowly, and hobbles through the door as though he has back pain.

"Why is this so heavy?" says the chief, grabbing the top of his metal chest plate and glancing back at a skinny boy following him timidly.

"It's made of metal, sir," the boy—his squire, I'd assume—pipes up squeakily.

The chief waddles over to a chair and sits down, slouching as deep as the wooded seat and his armor will allow. His squire scurries skittishly to the farthest corner of the room, sitting on the floor.

"Excellent to see you, sir." Kiz'nor says sitting near the chief, inviting us to sit across from him.

"What business is there to take care of?" the chief says, rubbing his eye.

"Chief Ark'lir, are you feeling well today?" Norkuz asks.

"I'm feeling as I usually would. Get on with it. I want to return to my chambers," the chief snaps irritably.

"We're trying to end the war, and we'd like your army to join us. As I understand it, you're sorely lacking physicians to handle the epidemic you're experiencing. We can send some over to help," Norkuz says.

"Sounds good. Any objections, Kiz'nor?" Chief Ark'lir asks, looking at his advisor.

"Sir, this is a serious matter. I ask that you at least *pretend* to be interested in the details," Kiz'nor asks, annoyed.

The Lost One: Wrath of the Tyrant

"I *am* interested, believe it or not. This war is going to ruin us if it continues, and we would greatly benefit from more physicians during this plague. I don't see a downside," Chief Ark'lir says.

"If we send our army away, it leaves us unprotected in the event of an attack from the Rul Coilband," Kiz'nor says.

"You really think our soldiers could stop an invasion? Our fighting force is small. It wouldn't matter if they were here for an attack. As I see it, our best odds are to find allies and get the war over with. We don't have enough soldiers to make a difference on our own, but if the Dragon Knights think we can be of assistance, then what could it hurt? We're all dead if we sit here waiting around. Our only chance is to join forces," the chief says, letting out a bored sigh.

"So be it," Kiz'nor agrees unhappily.

"Unless you are unable to work out the rest of the details yourself, Kiz'nor, I'll be off to my chambers," the chief says.

"I'd prefer to work with you, if you wouldn't mind, Chief Ark'lir... someone who's in a *real* position of power," Norkuz says.

The chief groans, "Fine."

"Actually, might I have a word with you alone?" Norkuz says.

"Why?" Kiz'nor asks, throwing a scathing look at Norkuz.

"I'd like to address a private matter," he says, "A guard can remain, but I'd like everyone else gone."

"Even me? I'm here to make sure you don't get in trouble and you make it back safely," I say.

"Even you Arid," Norkuz says, encouraging me to leave with a trusting glance.

The chief's squire stands up from his corner and heads towards the door after receiving an approving look to leave the room from the chief.

"Your friend better not try anything funny," Kiz'nor grouchily grumbles to me as I follow close behind them into the hall.

"I don't know what he's doing, but he won't hurt your chief. Besides, your guard is in there, and we'd be able to hear a commotion from here," I say.

"What's it like on Clearhallow?" the squire chirps up curiously.

"Now's not the time for pointless questions, Aar'muq," Kiz'nor scolds as the boy pouts.

"Why not? We're going to be standing here in silence while we wait for them to finish talking," I point out.

"Is it big?" Aar'muq asks eagerly.

"I don't know much about Clearhallow. I haven't seen much of it," I say.

"Oh," he says, deflated.

The Lost One: Wrath of the Tyrant

"Aar'muq idolizes the Dragon Knights. He thinks they're heroes for some reason. They're arrogant, is what they are… preaching their ideologies to all others they come in contact with, and trying to enforce their own laws on other lands. They try to spread their culture to islands that want to be left alone. They're almost as bad as the Rul Coilband," Kiz'nor snorts.

"They have that reputation, yes. Their chief is… set in his ways and thinks he's always right; even so, I don't believe the knights can be compared to the Rul Warriors because the Dragon Knights are not conquerors. When Prince Brezmard is chief, they'll change. He's not as arrogant as his father. He'll be a better leader," I say.

"Miss, do you think that knight would do a sword fight with me?" Aar'muq asks.

"We'll be busy while we're here, I imagine, but there's no harm in asking," I say.

"Aar'muq, there's no time to worship that hero of yours in there. You'll have to stay here in case the chief needs you," Kiz'nor says.

"No wonder Chief Ark'lir has melancholy with *you* around all the time," I say to Kiz'nor.

"Excuse you?" he gasps, flabbergasted, "You need to respect your elders."

"Oh, sure, but you don't need to respect anyone else? Not everything has to be down to business all the time. I realize this situation is serious, but let the boy have a chance to dream for a moment. If you don't allow those around you to smile, it's no wonder the chief is sulking in his room all the time.

Maybe instead of firing his court jester, he should have spent the time finding a new advisor," I say.

"Who are you to speak to me like this?" he asks.

"Who are *you* to tell Aar'muq he absolutely cannot partake in a duel? Surely, a few minutes could be spared for him," I retort.

"How dare you question me, *whelp*! You do not know the things I have experienced in my time. I have learned more than I expect you will ever live to see and experience," he barks, finding a way to look down on me despite being shorter than I am.

"What harm could come about from a brief duel?" I ask, "It makes sense you're the one keeping the island running. Your citizens have food and shelter but nothing beyond the basic needs. They're grateful for what they have, but your people aren't happy. It'd be a much cheerier place if you held tournaments every now and again."

Norkuz opens the door to the conference hall.

"Chief Ark'lir, I want this woman kicked out to the streets *immediately*," Kiz'nor demands.

Norkuz raises an eyebrow at me.

"In this cold? These are our new friends, Kiz'nor. We shouldn't throw our friends out in the snow. Aar'muq, go to the physician and tell him to come here. While you're at it, make sure my coat is ready to go out. We're taking a venture into town," Chief Ark'lir says.

The Lost One: Wrath of the Tyrant

"Yes, sir!" Aar'muq says, as he sprints down the hall at full speed to fulfill the order.

"What is this?" Kiz'nor asks the chief.

"I'm going to assist our guests with handing out tea and medicine to those who need it. Sir Norkuz suggested that it might help with morale for the citizens to see me about the streets," the chief says.

"That's madness. If his prince can't negotiate with us due to the fever here, then it's far too dangerous for you to be out and about in the snow," Kiz'nor says.

"Isn't it my job to serve the people?" Chief Ark'lir questions.

"Your job is to rule," the advisor says.

"Kiz'nor, there's no difference between ruling and serving," Chief Ark'lir says, "The way things have been done, I feel like my life has no meaning. I'm supposed to be chief! I'm supposed to ensure the well-being of my people, but ever since I've been in this position, *you're* the one who's been doing everything. I've been sitting around like a useless sack of rubbish. I want to go and see their faces, and I want to see that I've made a difference. I want to see to it that they feel safe and cared for. Isn't that my job... to protect those under my rule? To give them what's needed to build a proper home here? What good am I doing sitting between these same drab walls day after day? I want to go out and see my village. I want to hear laughter and chatter. I want to assure them that we're doing what we can."

"Your job isn't on the streets serving out tea. Your job is to sit behind a desk and direct *others* to do that," Kiz'nor says.

"My father was perfectly happy to do that, but it hasn't been working out for me so well. Clearhallow's prince is out training with his knights every day. He's personally seeing to it that his village is safe. That's what I want to do," Chief Ark'lir says.

"We are not Clearhallow! We have been doing this *our* way for generations, and we have survived everything that has come our way! I have been here longer than you have been alive, and I have watched both your father *and* your grandfather keep this island together," Kiz'nor shrieks.

"Kiz'nor, you're fired," Chief Ark'lir frowns, "Kaz'rogg, see him to his chambers so he can pack up. I want him out of here by tomorrow evening."

"Yes, sir," the guard says, stepping forward to escort the flustered old advisor to his chambers.

"Sir, it's good to see you stick up for yourself," Jar'kog remarks.

"I'm sick of his degrading attitude. Thank you for the suggestion to do things my way rather than allowing others to speak for me, Sir Norkuz. I can see how your advice may help me feel better with time," Chief Ark'lir says.

"I hope you *do* feel better," Norkuz says.

"What's the plan?" I ask.

"My physician will tell Sir Norkuz everything he knows about this sickness, then we'll go out and get medicine to as many as we can," the chief says.

The Lost One: Wrath of the Tyrant

"We'll stay a few days to hand out medicine and teach the others how to care for their sick loved ones, then we'll leave to join the others. That'll have to suffice until we can get more physicians out here," Norkuz finishes.

"Oh, before we leave, that squire thinks you're a hero and wishes he could be a Dragon Knight," I mention.

"Aar'muq claims you're the greatest warriors in the world," Chief Ark'lir says.

"He would like a sword fight with you," I smirk.

"I think I can manage that," Norkuz says.

Chapter Twenty-Nine: Quarantine

For the past couple of days, Chief Ark'lir has been figuring out how to get medicine to all who need it more quickly, but so far he's been recruiting healthy volunteers to deliver it door to door. Norkuz and I have been walking in the snow visiting the sick, and in order to cover more dwellings at once, Rhargrim's physician split away from us to visit other locations. While we help the sick, our dragons follow us around town from a distance because although no one has said anything about them, we can tell by their faces that the people are uneasy around them. The villagers are much more comfortable when the two beasts are flying far away from our interactions. As we walk from house to house, Norkuz compassionately checks the symptoms and instructs the sick people in town on how to improve their chances of recovery. After two days, we complete the visits throughout our designated side of town and head back to Chief Ark'lir's mansion.

"How are things going here?" Norkuz asks Chief Ark'lir, as we walk into the conference room accompanied by his squire, the owner of an herbal shop, and a couple of guards standing around.

"We don't have enough medicine," Chief Ark'lir says, frowning at the keeper of an herbal shop he's been purchasing medicine from.

"I'll make sure more gets sent over. In the meantime, we can improvise. Comfrey and licorice for coughs," Norkuz says, "Coriander for fever. Lavender, rose, or sage for headaches and body aches."

"Add the whole stock of those herbs to the order," Chief Ark'lir says to the herbal shop owner.

"Of course, Chief Ark'lir," he says.

"You should announce an official quarantine. No one allowed to leave their home unless authorized, such as those delivering food or medicine," Norkuz suggests.

"I'll see to it," Chief Ark'lir nods.

Aar'muq coughs. The shopkeeper takes several steps away from him.

"Aar'muq..." Norkuz says, crouching in front of the boy, putting his hand on the child's forehead, "Are you feeling ill?"

"No, I'm fine," Aar'muq denies adamantly, jerking away.

"Aar'muq, now's not the time to be tough, okay? You're feverish. Go to your room and rest. You'll have food and medicine brought to you. Don't leave your quarters until a physician says you can, and I need you to make sure you get lots of rest, drink lots of fluids, stay warm, and take the medicine they bring you, okay?" Norkuz says.

"N-no," the child refuses fearfully.

"You'll get others sick if you're around them," Norkuz says.

"Bu-but... I don't want to stay in my room! I don't want to be alone in there!" the boy shouts.

"What's wrong with your room?" Norkuz asks.

"I don't like being alone," Aar'muq squeaks.

"You're brave. You'll be alright. Think of it like a mission. You need to fight off the disease like a soldier fights off the enemy. You'll be keeping everyone else safe by staying in your room. It won't be forever," Norkuz says.

Aar'muq thinks about it for a moment before he nods and says, "Like a mission, huh?"

"I'll talk to you from the hall if it'll help," Chief Ark'lir tells the boy.

"Yes, sir. That'll help," Aar'muq says.

"Alright. Run off to your room, soldier. Someone will check on you soon," Norkuz says.

"Thank you for the sword fight and teaching me how to get better," Aar'muq says, as he hugs Norkuz briefly before running off.

"Is there anything else we can help you with before we're off? We need to make sure enough medicine gets sent over as soon as possible. There isn't much more I can do for anyone with the shortage," Norkuz tells the chief.

"No, you should be off. I know you have much more to do than sit around and get sick. Thank you for the advice. I will take it to heart. You are welcome back any time as an honored guest," Chief Ark'lir says.

"You're a good person, chief. Go show that to the world," says Norkuz.

The Lost One: Wrath of the Tyrant

As Norkuz and I leave the mansion, I ask, "So, are we headed to an empty island to quarantine ourselves?"

"Yep," he says, as we mount our dragons and fly away from Rhargrim.

It's been about five hours, and we finally arrive on an island with no human inhabitants, just west of Rhargrim. My feet sink through the snow with every step, and usually my dragon suit does well enough when the temperature starts to drop in the fall, but I've never seen it get so cold so fast. It doesn't help that my suit has rips and tears and holes from all the injuries I've sustained since joining forces with the Dragon Knights, and with all the combat I've endured during traveling, I haven't taken the chance to get it repaired yet. I've been far too preoccupied with other woes to prepare my gear for the winter, but now I'm regretting it. We have now been here for two days, and Quldriag moves snow around so Norkuz can pack cracks and holes to our temporary quinzee shelter we built. While I prepare to go hunting, they are making repairs to the snow mound's domed chamber after a windstorm damaged it. Norkuz says we'll only be in quarantine for a few more days if neither of us shows signs of illness, but surviving on this island is going to be rough with the snow. There are no fish to be seen, and most of the animals are hiding from the cold. Nalrai and I have split up to hunt for food in different parts of this island's forest. I'd prefer to hunt with a bow, but all I have is my sword and dagger. My feet are numb, and my fingers hurt. My mask protects my face from some of the harsh wind, but not well because my eyes are fully exposed. Flakes of snow stick to both my suit and skin, and even my covered nose and ears suffer from the extreme cold. I've been out hunting for about ten minutes, and I finally spot the first animal. It's a white rabbit, and it sits relatively still, looking around with its ears and nose twitching. I stop, watch it, then adjust my grip on my dagger, but instead of reaffirming the grip, it falls from my numb fingers, startling the rabbit. I dive at the critter, but it springs away before I can get my hands on it. I punch the ground in frustration.

"Dammit," I huff.

An inhuman screech shakes the trees. I scramble over to my dagger and look around for the source of the sound. Something massive runs through the trees, clumsily breaking branches.

"Quldriag!" I yell, recognizing him as he tries to stop in front of me, but he slides and slams into a tree instead, "Hey, what is it?" I ask.

He screams at me, anxiously prancing a few steps back in the direction of camp. I step toward him, and he takes off running.

"Hey!" I yell, running after him.

The snow makes it exceptionally difficult to run. It's been falling all day and comes halfway up my shins. My footsteps don't reach above the top of the snow. Instead, it drags me through the slippery whiteness, slowing me down. Quldriag rushes over to Norkuz in the snow fort we built and throws his snout into the healer's chest without hesitation. Norkuz pats his neck, reassuring the dragon.

"I'm alright. You didn't have to go get help," he says.

The snow fort shelter has been patched up a bit, and the fire's burning hot. Nothing seems particularly out of place, but Norkuz is sitting by the fire, sweating and shivering.

"Everything good?" I ask.

"Everything's fine. He's overreacting. I'm a little tired, so he got all concerned," he says.

The Lost One: Wrath of the Tyrant

"Quldriag is one of the calmest dragons I've ever met, albeit a little grumpy at times. I wouldn't expect him to freak out over nothing," I say, pulling my gloves off and scooting close to the flames, trying to thaw out.

"There's safety in numbers. He's probably on edge because he isn't used to traveling with a small group. He's almost a bit like Aar'muq. He gets anxious without people," he says, while petting his friend's scaly neck to pacify him, "Quldriag, if I hadn't given the jelly to Ak'dech for the whelps, I'd give you some. It'd help you calm down, wouldn't it?" he teases his dragon.

Quldriag lies down, puts his head in Norkuz's lap and stares up in concern at his knight.

"I'll head back out to find food as soon as I've taken a moment to warm up," I say.

"Take your time. I'm not all that hungry," he says.

"What do you mean you're not hungry?" I ask suspiciously.

"It's snowing pretty hard, and I doubt there's much out to find anyway."

"I did see one psychotic rabbit hopping about, but it was much faster than I am."

"We can eat what's left of the rations from Ioneot," he says.

"You mean you actually managed to save food all this time? You must have only eaten *six* rations instead of ten?" I say mockingly.

"It's never a bad idea to pack extra food when traveling. Besides, you normal-size people are always assuming I could live off the ridiculously pathetic portions you eat. It's astounding. I think Brezmard's pet mouse ate more than you," he says.

"He kept a mouse as a pet?" I ask.

"It was a ludicrous phase. I was newly appointed as his personal guard, and it was an *interesting* experience, to say the least. He acted like a spoiled child *constantly*. After weeks of trying to get the servants to trap the mouse, he caught the rodent himself then promptly had special gloves made so he wouldn't get bit. He even had one of the handmaids sew a sweater for it, and he carried the poor critter around everywhere. It didn't last very long though. He got annoyed at it one day because it was extra hard to hold onto the mouse. It refused to be held. It consistently squirmed and tried to get away. He fed it to Kemoss and never mentioned it again."

"Quite frankly, that's horrifying," I say.

"It was only a year ago. We're all glad he's grown up now," he says.

"You made that story up, didn't you?"

"I'm not kidding. After his mother's death, he was going through a rough time, and he didn't have much to help him handle it. You saw how well the chief listens to him. It's not like he could go to his father for guidance. He staved off melancholy with a shield of anger, violence, and an arrogant sense of entitlement, and he has always pretended he was ok and hidden behind one facade or another… until now," Norkuz says, trying to suppress a cough.

The Lost One: Wrath of the Tyrant

"You're sick, aren't you? That's why Quldriag's worried," I piece together.

"I've never been prone to illness, but I'll be fine. The symptoms will pass in a few days, I'm sure of it. It might be a good idea for you to keep your distance though. There's no need for you to catch it too," he says.

"I told you… I'm not scared of a fever. I promised to keep you alive. There's no way I'm going to tell Brezmard about your death. I don't think he'd react well to that," I say, putting my gloves back on and scooping up snow to pack into the cracks of the snow shelter, "So stop making excuses to get me to leave. We're in this together. I won't leave you here to die."

Nalrai lands next to me, returning with a dead hog in his claws.

"That's a nice catch," Norkuz remarks.

"Thanks, buddy. I appreciate it. That *is* a nice catch," I praise Nalrai, patting him on the head as he releases the hog from his claws.

He makes a noise almost like a cat purring, plops down by my feet, and rolls around in the snow on his back, insisting on belly rubs.

"At least *someone* seems at home," Norkuz comments.

"Unlike Quldriag, Nalrai is used to traveling with just me, so this is closer to what he's used to… just the two of us trying to survive out in the wild," I say, giving in to Nalrai's request for belly rubs.

Quldriag drags the hog closer to the fire while Norkuz sits in the snow by the flames, grunting as he struggles to get to his feet so he can start preparing the meat, but he pauses on his knees and takes deep breaths. Quldriag growls and snaps his teeth at Norkuz.

"I agree with Quldriag. You need to sit," I say.

"I got it," he says.

"No, *I* got it," I correct, walking over and grabbing two of the hog's legs.

I drag the heavy beast to a nearby tree and search through the pouch around my waist for rope, but I can't find any.

"Here," Norkuz says, reaching into Quldriag's saddlebag and pulling some out.

"Thanks," I say, as Nalrai carries it over.

I slit the hog's throat and hang it from a branch by its feet so the blood can drain out of the neck.

"I don't think it's fair for you to do everything yourself. Let me do something," Norkuz says, trying to get to his feet again, but Quldriag growls at him disapprovingly.

"You know what you *could* do? Follow the advice you gave all the sickly on Rhargrim: Eat some food, drink plenty of fluids, and get some damn sleep," I say, tossing a pack of rations at him.

"Thank you, I appreciate your concern," he says.

The Lost One: Wrath of the Tyrant

"Yeah, whatever," I say, rolling my eyes.

As I pack more snow onto the fort to reinforce the cracks, Quldriag lies on his belly next to Norkuz in the snow and wraps his wing around the knight to cuddle.

It's nighttime, and I'm lying down in the fort on a blanket, unsure if I'm awake or in a vision. I float weightlessly in the air surrounded by a cloud of blackness, and then an onslaught of chaotic screaming sounds, shouting, and images of fire and battle threaten to break into my head. I take a deep breath and calm myself. I'm in control this time, not the magic.

"You're learning," Maroog's voice commends me in my head, *"But don't make the assumption you're in charge because you're able to tune the chaos out of your head this time."*

"I have questions for you," I say with authority in my head, *"Ak'dech and Nokk, the two young spies you trained after murdering their parents, you spared their life because one of them has magic, didn't you?"*

"You don't ask the questions here, Arid," he says, annoyed.

*"You can sense **my** magic from afar, so it's probably easy for you to keep track of them too if one of them has magic,"* I say accusingly.

"You come demanding answers from me? You might as well be asking the gods to reveal their secrets," he laughs, *"Your confidence is amusing, whelpling, but this is **my** place of power, and I am the terrible nightmare controlling the world!"*

"Oooo, I'm trembling," I say, unimpressed, *"Ak'dech doesn't seem to be an empath. What does her magic do?"*

"Why would I tell you something like that?" he asks.

"Tell me what curse she carries," I demand.

"Let us move on from the concern you carry for your friend. Did you appreciate the gift I sent you, child?"

"Gift? What gift?" I ask, with a sense of dread arising at the question.

His smug, pleased tone is perhaps more haunting than the screams I've finally managed to block out of my head.

*"You **didn't** come across the dragon whelps? How unfortunate for them,"* he says.

"They didn't do anything to you! This isn't their fight! Why involve them?"

*"You're right. It **wasn't** their fight, but you have a special bond with dragons, don't you? You can almost tell what they're thinking… another one of your magical gifts. I bet their pain makes you sick to your stomach,"* he says.

"How did you know we'd be there?" I ask.

"I know a lot of things," he says simply.

The Lost One: Wrath of the Tyrant

"What about the last whelp? What did you do with it?" I interrogate.

*"Ah, you **knew** there was another. I am impressed, honestly. That whelp is a fine reward... my trophy, in fact. He will be a fearsome warrior to inspire obedience in my kingdom,"* he says proudly.

"You mean inspire fear, not obedience," I say.

"Is there a difference?" he skeptically asks.

"You know the difference. You choose not to care," I state.

"Yes. This is the way things have been since the beginning of time, Arid. The strong control the weak. The weak bow down in terror. I, the great Ma'roog, am the hero of my own homeland, Gler, and all will bow down to me. You will not take my glory from me, lost child of Tiendys. I know you are building up an army against me, and I can promise you, it will not go well. You will lose this war, and we will meet again soon," he growls.

As I awake, I can feel warm magic under my skin—tingling, but not burning. I'm angry, but that's under control too. Nalrai's wing is spread over me like a blanket. It's quite warm in the snow cave, almost uncomfortably hot. I hear gasping and wheezing nearby.

"Norkuz?" I call out.

Nalrai twitches as he awakens, and Quldriag stirs as well, concernedly sticking his snout right into Norkuz's face. Norkuz starts to reach toward Quldriag's neck, but he doesn't have the strength to lift his arm more than a few centimeters.

"Norkuz?" I repeat, crawling over to him, "You're okay. You're fine," I say, trying to swallow my sudden anxiety.

"N-no," he gasps.

"What do you mean *no*? You're fine," I say, discarding my gloves to the side and grabbing his hand that's burning with fever, "Come on, *heal*," I plead under my breath, focused on trying to heal him.

A pain comparable to a row of thorns burying themselves in my skin grates down my arms, followed by the sensation of liquid fire. *Heal*, I think to myself, redoubling my effort to focus while ignoring the pain and sweat drenching my face and neck.

"Stop," Norkuz says after a moment or two.

"I'm not letting you die," I say, gritting my teeth.

"I said *stop*!" he yells, and pulls his hand away, "That's enough."

At the same time, one of the dragons tug on the back of my collar in a silent agreement that I had done enough. I feel the pain leaving my arms, although a strong ache now settles inside my skull.

"You good?" I ask Norkuz, trying to ignore the headache and a wave of exhaustion that comes crashing down on me.

"Tired, but fine," he says, already looking better and no longer gasping for air.

"I'm glad that worked. After I couldn't heal Chief Irec on Zram, I didn't know if it would work on you," I yawn.

"Remind me to thank you later," he says, drifting off to sleep, and then I fall asleep shortly after him.

Chapter Thirty: Skirmish on Khaudkur

*N*orkuz felt fine after more sleep, but we stayed another day to watch for symptoms in either of us. Khaudkur, the island Brezmard said he'd wait for us on, is only a few hours from where we quarantined. When we arrive, we get off our dragons and flag down a couple of soldiers patrolling through the streets.

"Excuse us, gentlemen, we're looking for some friends of ours. They should've landed here a few days ago to talk with your chief," Norkuz says.

"The visitors from Clearhallow?" asks one of the guards.

"Yes," Norkuz says.

"That can't be. We just sent guards to escort their friends to the inn," the guard says.

"What do you mean?" Norkuz asks.

"We were told to expect two knights arriving on dragons. They showed up about an hour ago, took a look around, and headed to meet up with the rest of the knights," the guard says.

"What the hell do you mean? We're standing right here!" Norkuz yells, alarmed, "Where's the inn?"

"Sir, we can't take you there. We don't know who you are," the other guard says.

The Lost One: Wrath of the Tyrant

"Those are our friends! You sent impostors to meet them!" Norkuz yells, more agitated than when he argued with Brezmard about staying to comfort the sick on Rhargrim.

"Prove your identity," the guard demands while crossing his arms.

"Prove? How do you want us to do that? You didn't ask the first two to prove their identities, I bet. My friends could be in danger!" Norkuz shouts.

Nalrai's ears perk up. He looks off in the distance, and I see smoke.

"Never mind. We've got the location," I say, nudging Norkuz and pointing toward the smoke, "Get us there quickly," I tell the dragons.

"Hey, wait," the guards yell while lunging at us, but Nalrai and Quldriag are much faster than them.

They snatch us in their claws and take us toward the smoke. When we arrive, we see Kemoss crashing through the wall of the inn, and she gets to her feet in time to engage a dragon twice her size. When she collides with the other dragon, she's pushed backward easily, failing to do any damage as she swipes and bites at the enemy.

"Quldriag," Norkuz yells for his dragon to help out.

Nalrai flies low to the ground, and I land on my feet, stumbling, as Nalrai soars off to assess the situation. One of the enemy dragons force Ak'dech out of the large hole in the wall that Kemoss crashed through earlier, and she forcefully tumbles through the streets.

"Get in there," Norkuz orders me, as he rushes over to Ak'dech, who lays motionless on the ground.

I run in the hole created by Kemoss and Ak'dech's violent exit, and Nynnu is at the entrance twitching on the ground, out of the fight. The room has taken heavy damage and is partially destroyed. The parts of it that are still intact create a tight space to fight inside what's left of the room. Even though Qombaryth has a drastic size disadvantage, she viciously fights another huge dragon on the far side of the room and makes the most of the limited space and moves more easily than the larger dragon. Brezmard is fighting the two human impostors on his own—losing—while Nokk stands in front of the hatchlings, guarding them, but it's easy to see he's itching to join the fight.

"Brezmard," he says, ready to jump in and help.

"No! Stay there!" Brezmard says firmly.

These Rul Warriors seem to be much better fighters than any I've ever come across. Even so, I launch myself at the nearest enemy, bringing him to the ground. Nalrai blasts past me, slamming into the other dragon to help Qombaryth, and the impostor screams in agony, flailing, as I stab him high in his thigh with my dagger. As blood spurts from his wound, I stand there covered in his blood.

"Bitch! Dammit, just finish me off," he shrieks.

His face is quickly losing color as he loses blood, so I make the same incision as I did on the hog a few days ago and slit his throat with my dagger, causing him to bleed out in seconds. Norkuz enters the room and joins Brezmard against the remaining enemy by delivering an extremely powerful blow to the back of her skull with a large, jagged rock.

The Lost One: Wrath of the Tyrant

They stand over her motionless body as an open head wound gushes onto the floor, revealing solid tissue mixed in with blood and other fluid. Once Nalrai jumps in to help Qombaryth fight, the other dragon doesn't stand a chance. Now the enemy dragon's chunks of flesh hang from Nalrai's teeth and Qombaryth's claws, and its body is ferociously torn apart with innards leaking out similarly to the female warrior's head injury.

"Easy, killer," I tell Nalrai, as he continues to attack the lifeless body.

He snorts, paces around in agitation, and roars angrily.

"Your timing couldn't have been more convenient," Brezmard says, giving Norkuz a relieved hug.

"I agree. It's a little strange how they showed up just before us. How did they know you were here, and how did they know to impersonate us?" Norkuz says coldly while throwing Nokk a distrustful look.

"It wasn't me. I swear," Nokk says immediately as he checks on Nynnu.

"It's Ma'roog, and he's responsible for the hatchlings too," I say.

"How do you know that?" Brezmard asks.

"I saw Ma'roog in a vision. He knows what we're doing. He said the army we're gathering won't be enough to stop him, and he seemed cocky as ever about it. For some odd reason, he had the hatchlings put on that islet because he knew we'd find them," I say.

"*We* didn't know we'd be on that islet. How did *he*?" Brezmard asks.

"Do you really think he told me how he knew?" I ask.

"No, I'd imagine not," he says.

"Where's Ak'dech?" Nokk asks.

"She's outside catching her breath," Norkuz responds.

Nokk walks out and calls back to us, "Ak'dech and Kemoss are still fighting that dragon!"

Nalrai springs out of the large hole in the wall and toward the fight far too eagerly. I've never seen him act so bloodthirsty or upset during a fight. He surges forward swiftly, sinking his teeth and claws into the beast's throat, ripping its airway to shreds in an instant.

"What's with your dragon?" Nokk asks, disturbed by his eagerness.

Nalrai snarls at me, baring his teeth and crouching aggressively.

"Hey, buddy. What's going on?" I approach him cautiously.

He growls and snaps his teeth at me, but doesn't make a genuine attempt to bite.

"Let's go for a flight until you calm down, okay?"

The Lost One: Wrath of the Tyrant

I put my palm on his snout. He flashes his teeth and actually bites at my arm, but I manage to pull away quick enough to avoid it.

"You sure you've got it handled?" Brezmard asks.

"Nalrai, calm down," I command, "I've got it. Worry about your own dragon. She's limping."

"What? Kemoss?" he calls his dragon and spots her hirpling slowly behind him.

Nalrai continues growling at me, then he takes a step forward with blood and saliva dripping off his teeth. A distinct odor taints his breath.

"What happened to that jelly we've been giving the hatchlings?" I ask.

"The dragon nip jelly?" Norkuz asks.

"Yes," I say.

"Ak'dech?" Nokk asks.

"Qombaryth's satchel, last I checked," she whispers.

Ak'dech sits with her head in her hands, eyes closed lightly as she takes slow, deep breaths. I step back as Nalrai takes a step forward. I try to place my hand on top of his head, but he tries to grab my arm with his teeth.

"Sorry, bud," I apologize, then I grab his ear and tug down on it, digging my nails into a soft spot behind it. I punch him on the nose with my other hand. He wails in pain, stunned by the blow, then I take advantage of his daze and push his head toward the ground until he loses his balance. I put my knee under his jaw in order to lean against his throat. He struggles briefly before realizing that resisting makes the pain worse. I put more pressure against his neck until he loses consciousness. During the chaos, the innkeeper must have run off to find guards because now he has returned.

"See! Look what they did to my inn! The whole wall has been torn through, and there are people unconsciou—"

His word is interrupted by a shrill scream as the innkeeper realizes the warriors aren't sleeping off the fight.

"Gods, that was a loud scream," Ak'dech complains.

"Sir! Sir, we'll deal with this. You go make yourself some tea to calm down," one of the guards says to the innkeeper as they stand in the damaged room by the gaping hole in the wall.

The man appears to be too shaken to make himself tea, so the guard's partner escorts him out of the room and away from the aftermath of the battle.

"Prince Brezmard, explain this mess," the other guard says, gesturing around to the two dragons and two humans who have been very gruesomely killed.

"Lady Wai'zniff, we were attacked," he says to the guard, "I wish I could say we could pay for repairs, but the best I can offer is to help with some of the cleanup."

"Nonsense. You were attacked as guests in our home. We offer our most sincere apologies that our security let these criminals get so close to you. That is highly unusual. I will bring it up with the chief," she says.

"Of course," Brezmard says.

"There are more Khaudkur soldiers on the way. We'll take care of the remains. You're all more than welcome to visit our physician if needed," she invites.

"We just may do that," Norkuz says, looking around at all the wounded knights, "How much experience does your physician have with dragons?"

"We can get a specialist out here if you'd like," she offers.

"That would be appreciated," he says.

"I'll send the first available runner to take care of that," she nods to Norkuz.

"Nokk, go take care of Nynnu and keep an eye on the hatchlings," Norkuz orders.

"But Ak'dech needs—"

"What are you going to do to help her?" Norkuz cuts him off.

"I'm fine," Ak'dech snaps irritably at both of them.

"I'm sure," says Norkuz, "But here's some peppermint leaves to chew on anyway, and I don't want you up and about. Sit there and rest, or take a nap or something, alright?"

<<<>>>

It's been three hours since seeing the physician, now it's time to recover from battle because our months of traveling have finally caught up with us. Most of us walked away with injuries, and utter exhaustion plagues our group as we settle in a stable, which was the only space left for us to rest after the inn was shut down due to the attack. Ak'dech is stumbling, unable to keep her balance, as she wobbles into the stable. Nynnu can barely walk, but she shuffles inside the stable's door, just out of the way of the entrance, lies on the ground, then immediately drifts off to sleep. Brezmard has a sore knee, and he's limping much like his dragon. Nalrai is still drowsy but much calmer, and he is ill from the dragon nip, which we found splattered all over one of the dead dragons. That jelly definitely caused a reaction and was the culprit to Nalrai's aggressive behavior. As Norkuz helps Ak'dech walk, Qombaryth and Quldriag boost along the other weakened dragons and support them by taking some of the weight off their injuries as they try to move around. While they are doing that, Nokk and I carry the hatchlings into the stable. It's amazing how they have gotten stronger since I saw them last. In fact, a couple of them are filled with energy and are difficult to keep hold of. They're curious about their new environment, wanting to play and explore. It's actually a relief to set them down after carrying their squirming bodies from the inn to the stable. As soon as I place the hatchlings on the ground, Sari sprints to the far side of the stable and starts exploring every corner she can reach. While she's darting around the stable, the double doors open after a brief knock, and an elderly woman and two guards walk in. I grab Sari as she tries to run right up to them, and I receive bites to my wrist and forearm for my successful attempt.

"Good afternoon, Chief Ti'arfoz," Brezmard greets respectfully, giving a brief bow.

The Lost One: Wrath of the Tyrant

"Good afternoon, Prince Brezmard," she says tiredly, "I heard about your scuffle earlier and wanted to check in for myself. You and your allies are doing alright?"

"A little banged up, but a bit of rest will go a long way," he says.

"You're more than welcome to stay as long as you require," she says.

Her voice stretches beyond tired. She sounds like she's already lived a hundred lifetimes filled with all manner of terrors, and her sunken eyes tell the same story.

"Do you think we have a chance, Chief Ti'arfoz?" I ask.

"To win this war? We better have one! Regardless, Prince Brezmard was right when he presented this alliance idea to me. We don't have any other choice but to join forces to fight against Ma'roog. I have watched the rise and fall of a dozen dictators. I've watched my government fall apart with a civil war not unlike the one that tore your two islands apart, but never have I feared more for the state of the world with Ma'roog in power. This man destroys all that's around him," she says.

"We *will* win," Ak'dech says with conviction, as Nokk sits quietly in solitude.

"I certainly hope so. This world has seen too much war. If there is anything I can do beyond sending my army to help, let me know," she says.

"Actually, this voyage has taken longer than expected. If you could possibly convince the island of Vazgut to join us, it would be a great help," Brezmard says.

"I'll send a delegate," she agrees.

"Thank you," he says.

"I'll leave you to rest," she nods.

"That leaves us with Drahid and Clearhallow," Ak'dech says as Chief Ti'arfoz leaves.

"I think Chief I'gur from Zram should negotiate with Clearhallow. I doubt Chief Firestride will be too eager to listen to any of us," Norkuz says.

"Chief I'gur is young and inexperienced... brand new to the position he holds. Chief Firestride isn't going to listen to him, but I think *I* can earn his respect... or at least his attention," I say.

"Let me come with you," Brezmard says.

I shake my head and say, "This doesn't need to be complicated with a messy family reunion. If you come, his focus will be on you."

"He's *my* father. I want to speak to him, and I want to ask if I can come home," he says, longing obvious in his tone.

"Later. Now's not the time to worry about that," I say.

As I contemplate my plan for Clearhallow, Nalrai wraps himself around my ankles, curling up to sleep.

The Lost One: Wrath of the Tyrant

"What's that?" Ak'dech asks, pointing at Nalrai's saddlebag hanging partially open.

"Oh, uh…something I… *picked up* on Lokk," I say, pulling a book out of the bag.

"You stole it?" Nokk blurts out, finally breaking his silence.

"Maybe," I shrug.

"What's in it?" Ak'dech asks.

"Math or science or something. I don't know. It's supposed to be a bunch of disproved theories, but I found it useful. It helped me find Glul'gur, somehow. It's like my magic connected with it and showed me where to go," I say.

"Do you mind if I take a look at it?" she says while reaching for it.

"Be my guest. I don't understand it," I say, handing it over to her.

Chapter Thirty-One: Guilty Verdict

*I*t took some convincing to get Brezmard and the others to let me split off on my own to talk to the chief of Clearhallow, but I finally got them to agree. As I approach, the Clearhallow guards recognize me immediately. I remember training with some of them back when Brezmard thought I could teach his soldiers how to fight better, but without resistance, I let them arrest me today and request an audience with the chief. Instead, two Dragon Knights escort me to the courtroom for a trial… my trial. I assume this case has something to do with my previous crime allegations, but I guess they've already determined the outcome of the hearing because they have an insignia on the sleeves of their surcoats that reads: Executioner.

"Word of advice: don't speak unless you're answering a question. We have specific… *guidelines* in place on how to handle misbehaving prisoners, and the chief has been, uh, *frustrated* lately," one of them whispers to me before we enter the courtroom.

"Where's my lawyer?" I say.

"The legal trial system has gotten worse since you were last here. You aren't being provided a lawyer. The chief decided we no longer have a use for them," he says.

"Thanks for the warning," I say.

"I apologize in advance. It's nothing personal," he says.

"I understand," I say.

The Lost One: Wrath of the Tyrant

"Stop talking," the other knight says.

When we enter the courtroom, I notice the floors are stone, and there's a desk at the front of the room, sitting on a raised platform. Chief Firestride is already sitting there, hands sternly clenched together atop the desk. The guards bring me in front of him, and my knees crack as they forcefully shove me to the ground. Then they tie my hands tight with rope around a t-shaped pole that's been added to the floor. It's so tight I can feel my hands tingling within seconds.

"Where is my son?" the chief shouts, slamming his palms into the desk and standing up as spit flies from his lips and his face burns red with rage.

"Strange of you to assume I know," I snort.

I receive a kick to the ribs.

"I know you know!" he yells.

"Safe! He's safe," I say resentfully.

He calms down a little then asks, "But *where* is he?"

"That's not my right to say. I didn't bring him away from here. He made his own decision. I don't owe you anything, but I have enough respect for him not to betray his trust. If he wanted to be here with you, he would be," I say, earning a smack across the face.

"Lies! I know my boy! He would never turn his back on me!" he screams.

"You never *listen* to him!" I shout back, and then I receive another kick to the ribs as I force out the words, "He sent me here to discuss an important matter with you."

"He would come himself if he had something to tell me," he says, pointing at something or someone behind me.

I hear the footsteps of the second knight walk to the other side of the room and back, retrieving something, probably.

"You're going to listen to me, *chief*," I spit the last word.

"You're in no position to be making demands, *thief!*" he says, giving a nod to the executioner.

A whip cracks down across my arm.

"You are going to listen to me!" I yell, breaking the rope around my wrist as anger flashes through me.

The knights scuttle away in shock as the chief freezes in place.

"Gu-guards," he stammers, afraid.

"We need your Dragon Knights to join us in finishing this war. We have gathered the armies of the world to stand against Ma'roog. Send them to Zram, and Brezmard will take command and lead them into battle. You can either have him fight with the knights by his side... or without them," I say, stepping up to his desk.

"The battle will be futile. Ma'roog cannot be killed. He will slaughter us," he utters, shrinking back as I approach.

311

"So, we'll be without you then?" I question.

"That's my son you're sending to the front lines," he says.

"*I'm* not sending him anywhere. He's *choosing* to fight. You should be proud. He's brave enough to follow his heart, and despite him missing his father, he chooses to do what he thinks is right instead of following what you told him to do," I say, "Now, will you or won't you stand behind him?"

"How'd it go?" Brezmard asks me as I'm escorted to one of Zram's outdoor training arenas where the knights are sparring with each other.

As I enter the arena, I notice Ak'dech is sitting out on the ground with her back against one of the walls in the stone pit coliseum, and Brezmard still carries a limp. I clearly hear anxiety in his voice as he pressures me for details.

"How's my father?"

"We made an arrangement. He'll be sending knights over soon," I say.

"So he's doing okay then? I imagined he'd be upset about my continued absence," he says.

"Oh, he most definitely is upset. He's turned to absolutely barbaric treatment of his prisoners, and none of the knights seemed comfortable around him," I say.

"What do you mean by 'barbaric'?" he asks.

"They no longer punish with just boots and fists, but whips as well. Oh, and he fired all your lawyers," I say, "But enough about my near mutilation, how'd it go on the Isle of Drahid?"

"Fine. No problems there," Norkuz says, as he stops sparring with Nokk to join in on the conversation.

"Chief I'gur has yet to return from Rekluz, the last island he was designated to visit, and the palace staff are running things right now. We already have soldiers from Ioneot showing up, so we're cramming as many people into guest rooms as we can and setting up tents in the pastures. We failed to plan out space and rooming accommodations, so we're going to struggle with a place to put troops and supplies as more soldiers show up," Ak'dech says, standing to her feet.

"We can move the extra soldiers to an empty island," I say.

"How about Tiendys?" she suggests, "It's in the middle of Rul Warrior territory, and they have no reason to have a bunch of troops there because there's nothing to conquer or seize. It's a desolate island with nothing but sand and ruins. Besides, after leafing through that book of *debunked* theories from Lokk, I want to check out a hunch I have, and I'll have to travel to Tiendys to do so."

"Tiendys won't provide much food other than fish," I say, "But it'll be warmer and easier to keep the troops and their dragons from freezing to death. In fact, there's a small island about 30 minutes east by dragon that's rich with vegetation and wildlife, and there's lots of empty space to camp and train nearby. No matter where we go though, Ma'roog's going to know. What do you expect to find there?"

"The entrance to Draug… and perhaps your people, too," she says.

"*What?*" I ask.

"My top suspicion is that Tiendys has to have the entrance to Draug on it based on what the scientists who wrote the book says. Now, I must admit, Lokk's research *is* shaky, but when you're studying a field beyond science, like magic, you can't expect it to be perfect because magic doesn't follow the rules of science," she says.

"Arid, will you be okay going back to Tiendys? Last time you seemed kind of… out of it," Norkuz recalls.

"Whatever it takes, especially if there's a chance that's where my people are. From where I'm standing, it looks like Tiendys is a better option to station the troops than any place else," I say.

"Ioneot's agreement with us and Zram was conditional based off of financial support, so we'll start sending soldiers to Tiendys and confirm Chief I'gur's alliance because Ioneot's soldiers are ready to head back to their island the moment he gets back if he can't agree to the financial arrangement. The palace staff has already brought forth complaints about the attitudes of their troops. Therefore, this is going to be a rough couple of weeks with everyone training together. I anticipate disagreements and arguments, but we need as much harmony and cohesion as we can achieve," Brezmard says.

"You're going to be chief some day. Listening to complaints and sorting out disagreements among your troops is something you should be able to handle," I say.

"Yes, but the people of Ioneot are so… *stubborn*. I don't know that I'm a skilled enough mediator to settle all the disputes I suspect are going to come up," he says.

"Good thing you have friends," I gesture to Norkuz and Ak'dech, "And Chief I'gur has far more training in negotiating than he does in battle. I doubt he'll be much help on the front lines, but in diplomatic matters, I expect he'll be a valuable ally."

"That's *if* the Ioneots are willing to cooperate at all," Brezmard grumbles.

"Where are the hatchlings?" I ask.

"Within the warm walls of the palace, being cared for by the servants. They grow stronger by the day, so I'm confident they'll all recover fully," Norkuz says.

"Good. Maybe they'd like it here. It doesn't get as cold as Clearhallow," I say.

"Maybe so," Ak'dech says, "And maybe I'll stay with them if they live here."

"What do you mean?" Brezmard asks, "Aren't you coming home to Clearhallow with us?"

"Us?" Norkuz asks, "We're traitors. I'm pretty sure you're the only one who will be allowed back without an execution. At the very least, we would get lifetime imprisonment."

"Norkuz, if I'm allowed back, you will be too. I'm guilty of the same crime you are," Brezmard frowns.

The Lost One: Wrath of the Tyrant

"Yes, but *I'm* not the prince," he responds, "Brezmard, I have no doubt you'll go home, but if you think we can go with you, you're wrong. It'll be a death sentence."

"And the alternative is exile?" Brezmard says, sounding distressed.

"Zram seems like it'll be a nice place to live," Nokk chips in while playfully elbowing his sister.

"Zram *is* halfway between Clearhallow and Tiendys. Currently, there's nothing but sand and space, but I'm sure the whelps would love to visit the village of Likenhallow once it's rebuilt and there's a place for people and dragons to stay. Besides the southern dragonlands, which are inhabited solely by dragons at the very south end of the planet, the island of Tiendys is one of the warmest places. Come to think of it, Tiendys is somewhat close to Zram, so I'd be down to help rebuild Likenhallow too," Ak'dech says thoughtfully.

"I'd gladly welcome your assistance rebuilding my village," I invite.

"Look at that sis! You already have the chief's approval," Nokk says while clapping his hands together in excitement.

"Don't call me chief. That's weird," I say uncomfortably.

"Better get used to it. What do you think *your people* are going to call you?" Ak'dech says.

"I'm not going to be chief," I say.

"You're going to defy all odds, win a war, find and save your village... only to deny your birthright? That'll go over well," she says sarcastically.

"Your father was the chief. It's your responsibility to lead your people. You don't get to choose," Brezmard says, "But you're all going to be welcome on Clearhallow. You're my family. We'll always be together. I'll convince my father, you'll see, but I'm not going home without my friends. And of course, Arid, you'll be more than welcome to visit any time. Clearhallow would love an alliance with our cousins."

"When you're chief, you can bring us home, but even if we *do* go back, we're still criminals. A pardon doesn't cleanse our sins. No one's going to look at us the same way. No one will trust us. We'll be outcasts no matter what you do or say, but your name won't be tarnished. I guarantee your father has done everything in his power to make sure you're free from blame," Norkuz says to Brezmard.

"I was going to have you as my advisor," Brezmard says.

"I won't turn you away if you need me," he replies, giving him a pat on the shoulder.

"I... I think I need to go for a flight with Kemoss," he says, motioning his dragon over.

No one says anything as they fly away.

Chapter Thirty-Two: Variable

*I*t's been a couple of days, and Chief I'gur came back with as much success as we did because the world is desperate for Ma'roog to see his final day. We've settled the financial matter with Ioneot, and Chief I'gur agreed Tiendys would be a better place to situate the united armies. However, he's staying behind on Zram with a handful of his soldiers until all parties have been informed of the change, and the hatchlings are staying on Zram, too. I'm currently meditating in the forest on Roldraak, which is the island near Likenhallow outside of camp, but I'm close enough to be disturbed by the nearby rustling of soldiers as they set up camps on both Tiendys and Roldraak. When the rest of the allied soldiers get to camp, the majority will be set on Tiendys, but for now, they're setting up base on Roldraak and gathering as much food and water as they can in preparation for the arrival of more soldiers. For now, I sit in the forest of Roldraak, tuning out the cracking of branches as soldiers move around nearby. It's hard to focus on the quiet behind the clumsy movements of the troopers, and it's a struggle to keep my temper under control because Ioneot's soldiers are getting on my nerves with their loud, misogynist comments. Their boisterous troops have scared off all the wildlife, and it's hard to meditate and focus on the sounds of nature with all their rowdiness.

"Mind if I join you?" Ak'dech asks.

"Be my guest," I say, opening my eyes.

She sits across from me, frowning as she stares intensely off into the distance.

"You're annoyed, too?" I inquire.

"Very," she says.

"Take my hands," I say, stretching out my arms.

She takes my hands, closes her eyes, and starts breathing in her nose and blowing the air out of her mouth as we try and meditate together, but her arms twitch every once in a while.

"What was that?" she gasps and jumps, startled, as another branch cracks nearby.

"Someone stepped on a stick," I say, standing up.

I offer her a hand again and say, "Let's go for a flight... get away from the noise."

"Qombaryth won't appreciate being disturbed for a random favor right now because she's too busy prancing about with a new dragon friend from Zram," she says.

"Nalrai won't mind flying us both," I say, "Let's go take a look around Tiendys. You can test out whatever theory you've come up with, and maybe we can find Draug."

"That sounds lovely," she says, "But first, let me tell Norkuz or Brezmard that I'll be with you and Nalrai so they don't get worried."

Nalrai bounds over to us as he hears his name, and I talk to him while Ak'dech goes to find them.

"You think we'll find Draug?" I ask Nalrai.

He snorts, then licks my face.

"Ugh, gross! What is *that* supposed to mean? I'll take it as optimism," I say, pushing him away and wiping saliva off my cheek.

Ak'dech returns a few minutes later. I hop up on Nalrai and pull her on the dragon behind me.

"What are you going to do if we find the entrance?" she asks, putting her arms around me comfortably.

I almost shrug them off but resist the urge to do so, reminding myself that *she's* the one in need of a hug this time because I can tell she is upset and something is on her mind.

"It's easy. If we find the entrance, we go through it and find my people," I say.

"I have a feeling it's not going to be that simple," she says.

"Me, too. It's *never* easy, is it?" I ask.

"No," she agrees, "If Ma'roog knows where we are, what we're doing, and where we're heading, why hasn't he attacked us yet?"

"He's had twenty years," I return, "I don't think he's ready for this battle, or he would have taken the entire world by now."

"Good point," she says.

"I have a question for you," I say awkwardly.

"Okay?" she says.

"Have you ever noticed… anything *different* about yourself? I mean, something that's totally different from other people?" I ask.

"What do you mean?" she says.

"I mean… anything *magical*?" I ask.

"No. You're the magical one," she answers.

"Right. Of course," I say.

"Why?" she asks.

"I was wondering why you were the only one who felt the dungeon was haunted," I say.

"I was the only other one awake," she reasons.

"I suppose," I say, not knowing how to tell her that I suspect she has magic, especially when I haven't noticed anything particularly magical about her.

"This flight was a good idea. It's nice to get away from those arrogant asses on Roldraak," she says, "Flying has always been relaxing to me."

"Same for me. Nothing bothers you in the sky often. It's quiet, and the air is much colder at flying altitude than on the ground. It gets chilly and a bit hard to breathe, but not even the cold, thin air can bother me much up here in the calm," I say, "Ak'dech, are you okay?"

"Fine. Why?" she says.

"You were more than just annoyed at those soldiers back there," I speculate.

"You noticed?" she says.

"Don't act so surprised. I've known you for months now," I say.

"I'll be fine. I don't want to talk about it," she says softly, hugging me tighter.

The flight from Roldraak to Tiendys is much shorter than the ones we're used to, and I initially took it intending to clear our heads. We spend most of it in silence with a few stray comments casually slipping by here or there... but nothing meaningful. When we land on Tiendys, a small handful of soldiers are setting up tents on the shore. Ak'dech leaps off Nalrai onto the beach, and when I hop off Nalrai my feet land heavily in the black sand. I hesitate and hold my position, reluctant to take a step forward because of the panic attack I had the last time I was here.

"Come on... you're stronger this time," Ak'dech says, taking my hand and stepping forward in the sand with me.

"What makes you think I'm stronger?" I ask.

"We've been traveling together for months. It's obvious that you have gotten stronger, mentally and magically," she says.

"Obvious, huh? Well, how are we supposed to find Draug? We didn't see anything last time we were here, even with a thorough search. I don't even know where to start. It could take days," I say.

"It could. Good thing we'll have time while waiting for our forces to show up," she says, "So tell me, how did you see Glul'gur the first time? Maybe we can find it that way," she says.

"I had the vision of the map when I was holding the book from Lokk," I say.

"Here, I'll draw a rough map of this area in the sand and—"

"Don't bother," I say, digging my hands in the sand, "Vrarg is very loud here... *very* present. It's like it feeds into my own energy. It's no wonder I was overwhelmed last time we were here."

This time though, I'm ready, but Vrarg's magic is so strong that it's a bit shocking and disorienting. It takes a moment to figure out how to adjust to the powerful burst of energy Vrarg is pouring into me, but...

"It's by the volcano," I say, sensing the energy.

"What? How'd you—" she starts in shock.

"Let's go," I say, walking toward the foot of the mountain.

The Lost One: Wrath of the Tyrant

Ak'dech follows close behind, and Vrarg feels more alive with every step I take toward the volcano. It feels as though I'm getting closer to the source of a powerful energy, almost as though the crater at the top was an opening into its very soul and I'm approaching the core of its being. The only other place the magic has felt this strong was on Glul'gur, except Glul'gur was peaceful—until Ma'roog got there—but Tiendys feels like it's in turmoil. Although the magic here feels like bright light, warm and welcoming, I sense a cold or black magic forcing its way in, and there's a faint shimmer in the air around the mountain, like how Glul'gur appeared when Nalrai and I first approached it.

"Do you see that?" I ask Ak'dech.

"See what?"

My feet feel heavier as I try and hurry through the volcanic rocks and sand at the base of the mountain to approach the shimmer at the top. Shadows and invisible wisps that I sense more than see flit away from the shimmer when I arrive. If I believed evil could possess a place, this would be where it showed itself based on the intense sense of dread I feel. As I step up to the shimmer, a wooden door takes shape and becomes visible. As with the dark wisps, the door is more of a feeling than a visible sight, but the closer I get to it, the more real and solid it becomes. I can hear whispers coming from the other side, so I reach toward the door and place the tips of my fingers against it. I think this is it! I found Draug, and I shiver as the cold energy of Draug's magic spreads through me. As soon as I put my entire hand on the door, the shadows that flitted from the shimmer when I first got here streak toward me, wrapping around my arm like a sheet of invisible fire. The shadows are so cold they burn, and the whispers from the other side of the door scream in my head louder than any dream, making the door unbearable to touch for more than a moment, so I withdraw my hand quickly, grateful for the strength of Vrarg protecting me this far.

"We... we found it," I say, with a short laugh of relief escaping my lips, "I can't believe it's here."

"I don't see anything," Ak'dech says.

"No? Maybe only sorcerers are meant to see it," I say, "But Ak'dech, I think we just found hell, and it'll take a vast amount of magic to step through safely."

"Are your people in there?" she asks.

Hesitantly putting my hand back up to the door I say, "There's... screaming in there."

"How'd Ma'roog get them through the door if it's so dangerous?" she asks.

"I don't know. He knows more about Draug and magic than I do. Maybe there's a trick to bringing people through," I say.

"Will that be a problem getting them out?" she asks.

"I... don't know," I frown, "I'm... not sure I'm ready to go in there."

"We have time to look for a way to bring them through. The book was pretty vague, but I can go through the book more and see if there's anything about getting them out safely," she says.

"I wonder... how did the scientists find the entrance? You couldn't see it, so I'm assuming nobody else could... unless they were sorcerers like me," I ponder.

The Lost One: Wrath of the Tyrant

"In the book, the scientists said they noticed… fluctuations in natural laws… places on Vrarg that weren't quite consistent with our understanding of the world. Fluctuations in things science deemed as constant, such as gravity or other laws of physics, were changed, and scientific laws were broken. Actually, there are a lot of places with these fluctuations. This could've been something else entirely, or nothing at all, but I took a guess on this one because your people were already here. The scientists must've traveled for *years* searching for their hypothesized portal to another world, but their findings were probably discredited because as I said earlier, their research itself was shaky and inconclusive," she says.

"There's more than Glul'gur and Draug?" I ask.

"As I said, it was very vague, but most of Clearhallow falls within these regions of fluctuations and inconsistencies. I have no way to tell if that's what each spot on the map means, but Glul'gur was marked as one with fluctuations. So was Draug. That's two for two. I'm hoping we can explore the entire planet of Vrarg and figure out where they all are after this war," she says.

"Ha, as if we'd have the time…. but we'll see," I say.

Chapter Thirty-Three: Smile

*7*wo days have passed. I have been doing a lot of meditating trying to figure out anything about the door, and Ak'dech has been going through the book to see if she can decipher anything that will help. More islands are showing up to set up camp and train. Ioneot, Zram, Khaudkur, as well as two islands Chief I'gur recruited, Qele and Ikuh, have arrived. Between Roldraak and Tiendys, there's plenty of space, but our biggest issue at the moment is food and water. Ak'dech is testing a spring to see if the water is safe for consumption, and many of us are being sent out in hunting parties to find as much food as we can. Nokk and some other soldiers who are more knowledgeable about the habitat are gathering edible plants, and Norkuz leads a crew to set up a field hospital with supplies sent from Zram in case of training incidents or sickness. We have dragons out catching fish, and everyone who isn't currently occupied with another task is training under Khaudkur's leader, Chief Ti'arfoz. I'm with Brezmard and a handful of soldiers from various islands, and we are on the way back to the main camp with a successful haul from hunting. Nalrai, the one dragon we have with us, is carrying back a couple of deer and a few rabbits we killed, and there's a soldier from Ioneot who has been particularly vocal, saying anything that comes to mind and getting on everyone's nerves in the process. He likes to state his opinion on everything, and he loves arguing. Any decision the soldiers make, he'll argue against, and anything that catches his attention, he'll give his opinion.

"Haha, look at them over there, gathering herbs. Losers," he laughs, as we pass a couple of the gatherers.

"They're making sure we don't starve," a soldier from Zram says, "Why do you find that funny... or insulting? It's not anything less than what *we're* doing?"

"Gathering herbs is a *woman's* job," he snorts in response.

The Lost One: Wrath of the Tyrant

"Eat crap then. Enough comes out of your mouth to sustain you," I say sourly.

"Oh, are you a little *upsetty* that I said that? Did I *offend* you?" he scoffs childishly.

He waits for a response but doesn't receive one and says, "You know, I could see you being really pretty if you just smiled mo—"

Before I know what I'm doing, I can feel my fist cracking against his jaw. He crumples to the ground, grasping his face, and I yell, "Want to say that again, you asshole? Come on! Get up and say it again, you piece of sh—"

Brezmard interrupts my infuriated screaming and sternly says, "Arid!"

"*What?*" I yell defensively.

"Make sure he's okay," he tells another soldier in the group.

The soldier makes a grimacing face but checks on him.

"Come here," Brezmard motions to me, stepping away from the group.

"What?" I demand as I follow, "He deserved it."

"I know. He's been asking for it all evening. Just… take a deep breath. We're not trying to start *another* war. We need our troops to be healthy and cooperative, regardless of whether we like them or not," he says.

328

I take a frustrated breath and say, "So they get to say whatever the hell they want?"

"Your job isn't discipline. It's *my* job to keep people in line and keep the alliance from falling apart, okay? Anyone gives you a hard time, bring it up to me or Norkuz. We'll set them straight," he says.

I glare at him and say, "Fine."

He puts his hands on my shoulders and asks, "You good?"

"Yeah, sure," I say, taking a step back away from him, "Let's get back to camp. The sun's going down."

"Hey, Arid... it's important to keep up the well being of *all* our troops... that includes morale. Keeping troops happy, or at least not miserable, is important to the health and functionality of an army. Remember, you can talk to me about anything, okay?" he says.

"Uh-huh, I'll keep that in mind," I say dismissively.

Since when does he care? I think to myself while the other soldiers check on the guy I punched.

"I think his jaw is broken," a soldier says.

The injured guard moans in agreement, unable to speak.

"We'll take him to the field hospital when we get there," Brezmard says, "And we'll get it taken care of. Keep walking," Brezmard commands, waving all the soldiers onward, then he steps in front of the injured guard and privately says, "You don't speak to people that way, understand? While you're part of our alliance, you follow *our* traditions. Let that broken jaw be a lesson on speaking respectfully," Brezmard says firmly with a threatening edge to his tone as he stands tall and gives him a small shove on the shoulder to ensure he gets the message.

"Nnn," the guard growls in what sounds like disgruntled agreement.

"Anything like this happens again, and I'll personally see to it that you'll *never* talk again," Brezmard warns.

"Nnn," responds the guard, unable to close his jaw.

"Let's get you to a healer," Brezmard sighs.

It's much quieter the rest of the way back to camp, and most of the hunting party breaks off when we get there because all the work is done for the day, and they are free to work on anything they want. As we reach the field hospital's tent, I ask Brezmard, "Where do you want this?" nodding to the food my dragon is carrying.

"Ask Norkuz," he says, while heading into a large tent they've set up while we've been out.

I follow Brezmard into the tent, and Norkuz is laying out thin sleeping mats on the ground in preparation to take patients while Ak'dech leans casually against a pile of rolled beds made of straw.

"About time you got back," Norkuz says, "More people have been showing up. Rhargrim sent who they could, but it's only a handful of soldiers because that disease is devastating their island. The physicians are doing what they can, but most of the army was infected."

"We'll take anyone we can get. I hope the sickness passes quickly for the sake of their village," Brezmard says, then he clears his throat and declares, "We have a casualty for you."

The Ioneot soldier steps up.

"What happened?" Norkuz raises an eyebrow, taking a look at his jaw.

"He took a fist to the face," Brezmard explains.

"That's going to make it hard for you to eat anything for a while. You'll have to grind up what you can with a rock, or whatever you can find, and drink your meals. It's a bit out of place. Hold still. This is going to hurt," the healer tells the soldier.

There's a scream of pain as Norkuz twists his jaw almost violently.

"Bmch," the soldier tries to speak.

"Yeah, talking will be hard too. Take these and suck on them or make some tea… might help with the pain," Norkuz says, handing him some herbs, then wrapping a bandage under his chin and over the top of his head, "Try not to move the bandage and your jaw too much until it's healed up a bit. Having a broken jaw is going to suck for a few weeks, if you're lucky."

"Lumcky?" the soldier murmurs.

"Yeah. Lucky. No guarantee it'll ever heal completely," Norkuz says, "But if that bandage starts to get loose, come see me to fix it. That's all I can do for you."

If looks could kill, I would be dead the way the soldier glares at me on his way out, but lucky for him, he doesn't try anything revengeful.

"How's the water supply coming?" Brezmard asks Ak'dech.

"I'm waiting for signs of contamination to show. It can take a few hours because I'm running multiple tests to be sure. It looks promising though," she says.

Brezmard thinks for a moment and asks Ak'dech, "Why are you here? There are plenty of other things you can be helping with instead of standing around in the tent."

"I'm just checking in with Norkuz for a moment to see how things are going while I'm waiting on the tests," she says, moving quickly to leave, "I'll get back to work."

"Right… keep me updated," Brezmard says.

"Will do," she skips away.

"Clearhallow has arrived here too. They're putting up tents and getting settled in," Norkuz says.

"Clearhallow? Is my father with them?" Brezmard asks.

"Yes. He demanded to see you. I told him you'd be back soon," he says.

Brezmard takes a deep breath and says, "Okay. Anything else while I'm here?"

"No, that's it," he says, "If you need a mediator, I can go with you."

"No, I don't think that will help much. I'll grab Kemoss and hope she can keep me out of harm's way. She will protect me or fly me to safety if it comes to violence. Wish me luck," Brezmard says.

"Holler if you change your mind. I'll be there in a heartbeat," Norkuz replies.

"No doubt you would be. You're still my personal guard," Brezmard says, heading towards the exit of the tent.

"Soon-to-be advisor," he reminds Brezmard, "Here, let me show you where to put that," Norkuz tells Nalrai, leading us outside to a hole dug into the frozen ground, "So, Arid, that look the Ioneot soldier gave you as he left suggested that maybe you had something to do with his jaw. I take it *you're* the one that punched him?"

"Don't worry. Brezmard already scolded me," I say.

"I wasn't going to. I saw the colors on his surcoat. He's from Ioneot, and from the experiences I've had with their soldiers, there's no doubt he deserved it. Actually, I wanted to check in on you. Ak'dech said you found Draug."

The Lost One: Wrath of the Tyrant

"*Did* she now?" I ask icily, as Nalrai drops the food by the pit, "I haven't seen you two talk much lately, until now, all of a sudden. I thought you were still holding a grudge against her?"

"I don't know the outcome of this battle. I don't know if any of us will survive. I love her. I've always loved her. If either of us die, I don't want it to be while I'm pretending I hate her," he says.

"Wow. I forgot you were the sappy guy. Oh, and nobody was buying that you actually hated her. What did she say about Draug?" I ask.

"She says you don't know if you can get them out safely," he answers.

"And do you have a solution?" I ask.

"No," he says.

"Then I don't want to talk about it. I'll figure it out. I'm getting better with my magic. I can heal on command now, and I think I'm figuring out how to activate and boost my strength. So, unless you have a solution, leave the door to hell for me to worry about."

Chapter Thirty-Four: Ceremony

7he anticipation of the upcoming battle has been building throughout the army. All the islands have shown up, and we've been training in shifts, making sure we're all rested and fed as well as possible. Tempers are running short between various soldiers from different islands due to cultural clashes, and stress about the upcoming battle is high. It's been hard to maintain the peace, but Brezmard and the other leaders have been doing well at keeping everyone in order. To our surprise, Ezzut tagged along with the Dragon Knights. After Brezmard, Norkuz, Ak'dech and Nokk fled the island to find me, Ezzut had no choice but to stay in Clearhallow. Since then, he has been training with them and helping keep the peace using his ability to empathize and sense emotions, which makes him a great asset here because he has been a major help with reducing tension among the troops. However, Ezzut is upset that we left without telling him and didn't invite him to be part of the group. Despite the tensions, though, I've seen progress in troop cohesion and teamwork, thanks to him. Chief I'gur, the diplomat from Zram, has insisted on learning swordsmanship so he can fight alongside us. It's a suicide mission, but he's relentless in his quest to learn. Brezmard's been tutoring him, and his determination is very apparent, often trying to go far beyond his limits. Norkuz has told him on several occasions to take a break and sleep, but undeniably, he's improved over the last few days. The majority of us have moved to Tiendys, while a support group remains on Roldraak, but anyone who plans to fight is here by the volcano. I've been trying to figure out the magic at the doorway, but it leaves me drained and in a bad mood because I haven't made much progress. Since I've been here, I've had vivid dreams. They're not visions brought from my magic, but there's a magical variable to them I can't explain. It's like the dreams are tinted... stained... with a faint aftertaste of magic. In the dreams, fire eats at the dwellings of my village, and my parents die in front of me. Ma'roog was right. I don't remember which one died first, and the dreams are different every night. Sometimes, there's the faint echo of a crying baby.

The Lost One: Wrath of the Tyrant

What's wrong with my head? I think to myself, confused and upset because I can't remember which parent died first.

"Arid, you have a moment?" Brezmard asks, as I make my way to camp from Draug's passageway door.

"Why?" I ask, joining the small huddle of soldiers chosen as leaders.

"I want your input on our plan of attack," he says.

"I'm not really a strategist," I say.

"Right, but you have the most difficult job… fighting Ma'roog," he says, "So, when we invade Gler, we're going to go in waves. I'll lead the main attack head-on. We'll have two groups flanking from the side and rear, led by Sir Ek'dzem, who is one of my knights from Clearhallow chosen to help lead the charge with my father, Chief Firestride. Behind me, we'll have whatever archers we have, headed by Sir Daz'rir from Zram, as well as a second and third wave that will be following as soon as we disrupt the front lines. You'll hang back until you have an open path to Ma'roog."

"Great," I say, "Anything else?"

"No, that's it," he frowns, "I thought you'd be more interested."

"No, not really. This is the part where I take your word for it and hope you know what you're doing," I say.

"Arid! Come here. We have something for you," Ak'dech grins mischievously, walking beside Nokk.

"What is it?" I ask.

"We'll show you. Come on!" she says, grabbing my arm and leading me toward one of the smaller camps.

"I'm not sure I trust this," I say grumpily.

"Hopefully this will help with your bad mood," Nokk says.

"Mm," I grumble unhappily.

Nalrai seems curious about whatever they're leading me to. He prances along much more cheerily than I do. Nalrai's unworried attitude makes me think they told him about this. He'd never trust a situation like this if they hadn't.

"You're in on this, aren't you?" I ask him, feeling slightly betrayed.

Ak'dech laughs and says, "Brighten up. This won't take long. He's just excited because we promised him free snacks and a belly rub."

"Are we taking a detour or something? I feel like we've taken more turns than necessary. I don't need the scenic route," I whine, as Nalrai gets more excited at the mention of treats.

They lead me to a campfire, and obviously, Brezmard took the quick and direct path because he's sitting by the fire next to Norkuz upon my arrival. Nalrai sprints over to Norkuz, licks up a handful of fruit hungrily, and lies next to him.

The Lost One: Wrath of the Tyrant

"Welcome," Nokk says, patting my shoulder then taking a seat on Brezmard's other side.

"What's going on?" I ask, as suspicious as before.

"It's called a party," Brezmard says.

"Lame party. I've seen better," I crack.

"We want to extend an invitation for you to be officially knighted," he says, ignoring my comment.

"What?" I blink blankly.

"I can make you a Dragon Knight. We don't usually allow foreigners as official members of our ranks, but I've convinced my father to make an exception, albeit reluctantly," he says.

"Why?" I ask.

"We don't want you to feel like you're going into this battle alone, regardless of whether you find a way to get your people out of there or not. The Dragon Knights are a family. We don't want you to think you don't have one," Norkuz says, scratching Nalrai's underside.

"What's involved?" I ask.

"Usually a large initiation ceremony with a crowded party, but we thought maybe you'd prefer something smaller should you accept. It's also tradition that if a knight is expected to take an exceptionally dangerous mission, we lend them gifts, which will either be burned with the knight's body or returned upon their success. These are usually items that may prove helpful in the task at hand, or it can be a valuable item or expensive gift, which are typically only given to nobles and royalty as a sign of respect to honor the knight and show respect for their bravery. We'd like to combine both ceremonies if you take us up on the offer," Norkuz says.

"As a Dragon Knight, you'd be expected to fight for the good of Clearhallow and its allies... and protect your fellow knights. It's like a pact. We fight alongside you, no matter what," Brezmard says.

"You said it's like... family?" I say.

"The knights are the only family I have," Norkuz says.

"Well... no grand, fancy business, alright? And no long dramatic speech or anything. Keep it short and sweet," I say, accepting their alliance.

"We'll keep it to a minimum," Brezmard says, standing and drawing his sword, "Kneel, cousin."

"Short and sweet," I mutter the reminder under my breath as I lock eyes with Brezmard.

"Arid Dho'zogg of Likenhallow, I welcome you into the ranks of the Dragon Knights of Clearhallow. May we fight beside each other with honor and loyalty," he says, tapping the flat end of the sword against both my shoulders, "You may stand."

The Lost One: Wrath of the Tyrant

"So that means you officially outrank me now?" I question.

He smirks, amused, and says, "Of course. That was the whole goal," he jokes.

He takes a moment to put on a more serious expression and says, "I offer you leather arm guards. I would've liked to give you a full metal chest plate, but I haven't had the chance to have one made."

A streak of Clearhallow's blue runs down the middle of the leather arm guards.

"Thank you, I'm sure they'll be useful," I say, struggling to fit them on because I'm inexperienced with armor, and there is an overabundance of straps I can't figure out.

Brezmard helps me strap them to my forearms, then he gives me a hug.

"Stay safe," he whispers.

"I was lucky to get this. This will purify any water. I've been holding onto it for a while in case of a real emergency, but it seems like an appropriate gift. Filter the water with cloth or moss or whatever you can, then add a couple drops per liter and you'll be set," Ak'dech says, holding out a small vial as soon as Brezmard releases me.

"Sounds expensive," I say.

"I expect to see this returned, Arid Dho'zogg!" she says sternly, placing it in my palm and giving me a tight hug.

I thought I understood the weight of the upcoming battle, but it feels heavier with each gift. I might never see these dorks again, and the thought is admittedly rather gloomy.

"Dried willow bark... stronger than peppermint. It'll help numb pain if you need it. Chew it just like the peppermint leaves," Norkuz offers.

"So you've been giving me the weak stuff this whole time?" I say, feigning offense.

He hugs me instead of giving me a verbal answer, then he says, "Welcome to the family, runt."

"Um, I know this isn't practical like the other gifts," Nokk says awkwardly, then he grabs the twine around his neck and pulls off his necklace.

"Isn't this your mother's necklace?" I ask.

"Yes. I lend it to you as a sign of respect," he says.

"I'm honored you would lend me something that means so much to you. Are you *sure*?" I ask, grabbing his shoulders, holding him an arms-length away to closely watch his reaction.

"Just promise I'll still have it by the end of the war," he says.

"I promise I will do everything that I can to get it back to you," I say, hugging him.

"Arid! Lady Arid!" Ezzut scrambles into the camp.

The Lost One: Wrath of the Tyrant

"Ezzut, weren't you on Roldraak? What are you doing here?" I ask.

"Don't you feel it?" he asks, winded from running, "Listen to the magic. It's screaming that Ma'roog is approaching."

Ezzut seems to be in pain and grasps his head as tears slide from his eyes. I take a moment to listen to my surroundings and tune into Vrarg's magic to sense what's going on. Dread takes the place of my curiosity once I realize that Ma'roog is indeed getting close. I can sense his magic and proximity strongly.

"The battle will be here. Tell the soldiers to get ready. We have *hours* before Ma'roog arrives," I say.

Chapter Thirty-Five: Battle of Tiendys

7he troops are prepared. There's only one problem we're scrambling to resolve... Draug... how to get in, and how to get my family out. As I stand at the invisible door of Draug at the base of this dormant volcanic mountain, I have to admit, I'm hesitant to go in and look, and my hesitance goes beyond the uncertainty of not knowing if I can get them out. I don't want to be disappointed if they are not in there, and if they *are* in there, this will be an enormous change. It feels surreal to think that maybe I can finally have them back. I don't know what to expect.

"Arid, you'll go in and free them. Kias, one of my Dragon Knights, has been assigned to lead the evacuation mission with you," Brezmard briefs, nodding to Kias so I know which knight it is.

"So after I get them out the door, I'll just send them to *him*—"

"*Kias* uses the pronoun *her*," Nokk interrupts me.

"Oh, so I'll send them to *her*, then she'll make sure they get to Roldraak safely?" I ask.

"Yes. She'll wait outside the doorway to direct them to an evacuation party. Norkuz, Ak'dech, Nokk, and I will be busy making sure any final preparations for battle are in place," Brezmard confirms.

"Right, easy enough," I say, hoping desperately I can get them out.

The Lost One: Wrath of the Tyrant

Nalrai butts against me to let me know he's worried. I give him a rub under the chin.

"Good luck," Brezmard says.

I take a deep breath, reach for the doorknob, and endure the strange, tingly cold feelings of the magic. All the other times I attempted to go through the door, I hesitated because of the intense sensation from the magic, but honestly, I was scared I'd be disappointed that my people wouldn't be there. However, time is running out before Ma'roog arrives. I have to do this now, so this time, I do not hesitate. The door opens, and I step through it into a dimly lit hall lined with prison cells on each side. It's quiet, and a smoky mist fills the air like cold fog. I see people behind the locked jail bars, but there's no keyhole on the lock. Each cell is tightly crammed with prisoners who look weak, filthy, and malnourished, and they all notice my presence as I walk down the hall. They seem mentally beaten down, and only a few manage to express any level of hope in their expressions.

"Who are you?" a woman asks.

"Ae you from Likenhallow?" I ask, walking up to the cell.

"Yes, all of us are. Are you here to... I... who are you?" she hesitates, unable to bring herself to say her thoughts.

"I'm here to free you. Do you know a way out of here that's safe?" I ask.

"I'd wager we can walk right out. That door was meant to keep us *out* of Draug, not in, because this place is for magical beings and powerful sorcerers so we don't belong here, and Draug knows it very well. It doesn't even want us here. It was being locked in the cells by Ma'roog that kept us in all this time, so I don't believe this place will prevent us from walking out that door," an old man says.

"You can just... *walk out*?" I say, finding that hard to believe.

"I'd stake my life on it. I can go through first if you'd like to test out that theory," he says.

"I've been looking for a way to get you through safely this whole time, and you can just *walk out*?" I repeat, stunned.

"You're the chief's daughter, aren't you?" he asks, "Arid Dho'zogg?"

"Yes," I say, mouth dry from heightened adrenaline levels and nervousness, "Hold on, I'm going to try to get you out, and when I do, there's a friend on the other side. She'll tell you where to go."

I put my hand on the lock and concentrate, begging my magic to work. To my surprise, it takes little effort to get the lock to click open.

"Thank you," the first woman says, putting her hand on my arm for a moment before following the old man out the door.

They appear to go through safely. I look down the hall. There are dozens of cells. It's going to take all day if I go through and open them one by one.

The Lost One: Wrath of the Tyrant

Please let this work, I silently plead, putting my hand on the wall and focusing with all the concentration I can find.

Draug's magic feels stronger and more intense than Vrarg's magic, but I wonder if I can connect with it and use it the same way, or better. Out of curiosity, I put my other hand on the hall's wall and try to tap into Draug's power source to boost my own magic, then I hear clicks echoing through the hall as all the locks pop open, freeing the prisoners. Draug's power feels strong and amazing, like a rush of euphoria and confidence. It feels, for a moment, like I can do anything.

"Come on! This way!" I call, ushering people toward the invisible wooden door.

I'm sending a very large group of people out the door. I hope Lady Kias can keep up and evacuate them as quickly as possible before the battle starts, but if Brezmard is confident in her abilities, I have faith she'll handle it. Surely Brezmard put her in charge for a reason. Suddenly, a hand grips my wrist urgently.

"You're the chief's daughter, you said?" a middle-age woman gasps.

"Yes. The exit is this way," I say, trying to lead her over.

She shakes her head and says, "There's a room at the end of the hall. I've heard his screams. Ma'roog keeps him in a special cell. You need to go free him," she says.

"Who?" I ask.

"Your brother!" she says, seemingly confused that I don't know.

"My… my *what?*" I stare at her.

"You don't remember him? Your little brother. Go save him," she says, letting go of my wrist and joining the crowd.

I sprint down the hall against the flow of people to a wooden door at the end. I pause and take a breath before I open the door, with a dim memory of a crying baby ringing in my ears. Behind the door, the room is much darker than the hall with no visible light source.

"Hello?" I call out.

It's a couple of seconds before I get an answer.

"Who are you?"

I follow the voice to a metal cage sitting in the center of the room. The only thing else in here is a bloodstained table, which sits just beside the cage.

"My name is Arid. I've come to free you," I say, squatting on the outside of the cage to talk to him at eye-level.

A boy sits in the corner of his cell, hugging his knees, because the cage isn't tall enough for him to sit upright. He has long, white-blond hair that's knotted, tangled, and goes halfway down his back, and he has a scraggly beard tangled down to his easily visible collarbones. He wears no shoes, and what are supposed to be his shirt and trousers are bloodied rags. Bruises cover his skin, the majority of which are yellow, but his arms are a deep purple from more recent trauma. His pale skin is barely visible behind the injuries, and a film of dirty, black filth is smeared over his body and clothes from years of grime.

The Lost One: Wrath of the Tyrant

He stares emptily at me with pale blue eyes that don't quite focus on my face, and he looks like he could be the ghost of a starved and beaten child.

"Free me? I don't understand," he says, "This is my home... a safe haven. I'd die if I step foot outside these walls."

"No, this is a prison," I say.

"Ma'roog said there's nothing left out there. He keeps me safe here," he says.

"Ma'roog lied to you. Do you feel safe *here*?" I argue.

"I... don't know," he says.

"You're starved, beaten, and more malnourished than the other prisoners. I can see it! He's torturing you," I say.

"This is the only place I've ever known. The outside is dangerous. He's not a liar! He's the only thing I have left!" he shouts.

I put my hand up to the lock to open it. His eyes do not acknowledge the movement, but he jumps at the sound of the lock opening. As I reach for his hand, his eyes never focus on me, or my hand.

"Were you born blind?" I ask, noticing his lack of response to movement.

"No, I... I used to see," he says, "But Ma'roog said I didn't need my sight. He took it because I angered him."

"Come with me. I need to get you out of here. I won't hurt you," I promise.

"No! It's dangerous out there!" he yells.

"I will drag you out of here, and I doubt there's much you can do about it. Please... come willingly," I warn.

"I'm... not a fighter. I won't fight you," he says.

"I'd imagine not. You've been trapped in a cage your whole life," I say, taking his hand and pulling him to his feet, "What's your name?"

"Shythilulth," he says.

"It's nice to meet you, Shythilulth. You're the chief's son?" I ask, guiding him gently through the hall.

"The chief is dead, so I'm the son of a dead chief of a dead village. Doesn't matter though. I don't remember him," he says bitterly.

"It does matter. That makes you my brother. I didn't think I had any family left, but Shythilulth, I'm your sister."

He stops in his tracks and says, "I don't have a sister. Ma'roog never said anything about me having a sister, living *or* dead. He said my parents were murdered, and he saved me from the same fate."

The Lost One: Wrath of the Tyrant

"Did he ever say who killed them?" I ask.

"A bad guy," he says.

"Ma'roog killed our parents, Shythilulth. He's not protecting you from anything. He's a monster," I say tenderly.

"Stop lying to me," he says.

"We're going to go through a doorway. It might feel weird, and everything on the other side is different. There's a battle coming, but we're going to get you on a dragon to safety. It's all going to be new and probably terrifying, but I promise we're trying to help. Don't freak out, okay?"

"Why are you so... what's the word...? Oh forget it. If it's so *safe* out there, why are you warning me and making it sound so dangerous?" he says.

"I don't want you to be scared. Hopefully, if you know what to expect, it'll help you be less afraid," I respond, "We're stepping through the door now."

As we exit the portal, the trip through the magical doorway makes him dizzy, and he loses his balance and grasps my arm tightly, gasping as we reach Vrarg.

"Is he the last one?" Kias asks.

"Yes," I say.

"I'll get him sent out to Roldraak," she says.

"Give me a moment," I request.

She nods.

"It's cold," Shythilulth states.

"They'll take care of you. They'll give you a blanket and sit you by a fire," I say.

"Arid, what does it mean to be brother and sister?" he asks.

"I... I guess it means whatever you make of it. I have two friends who are siblings. They'd do anything to protect each other," I say, while gently handing my brother over to Kias.

"Including leaving each other to go fight?" he asks.

"Yes," I say, "I have to. Ma'roog is destroying the world."

"I don't want Ma'roog to die, but I... I want to have a sister. That would mean I have family. I want to know what that's like. Ma'roog always said it was a bad thing, but sometimes the voices in the hall would talk to me, and they said family is important and good," he says.

"I want to have a brother," I say, giving him a hug, "I promise, if you make it through the battle alive, I'll make sure I survive too."

"Do you *have* to fight him?" he asks.

The Lost One: Wrath of the Tyrant

"Yes, but don't think about it. Shythilulth, I want you to promise me you'll make it out of here alive," I say.

"I promise," he says.

"Good. Kias is going to make sure you get out of here. Follow her instructions, and you'll be fine," I say.

"Can you see?" she asks Shythilulth, noticing his blank stare.

"Not since I was five," he says.

"It might be a bit difficult getting on a dragon for the first time. Come with me," she says, guiding him onto her dragon, "Oh and Lady Arid, I saw Brezmard and the others pass by a moment ago. I don't know exactly where they are now, but they should be nearby."

"Thanks," I say, distracted by the strong gust of magic I sense in the air.

Ma'roog is close. I can feel it, so I say to Kias, "You need to get the rest of them out of here *now*."

"Will do. Good luck," she says.

I hop on Nalrai and track down Brezmard on the shore.

"They'll be here soon," I say, as Nalrai lands beside him.

"I know. You see that cloud out over the ocean? That's not a cloud. It's a horde of warriors surrounded by their dragons' smoke.

One of our patrols confirmed. The enemy is ready for battle and prepared to spit a lot of fire. We're hoping they don't send warriors to Roldraak now that we're sending civilians over there," he says.

"They better not touch my people," I growl.

"That's the goal… for them to never hurt anyone again," he says.

"I have a brother," I say.

Brezmard looks away from the incoming horde, shocked at what I said.

"I didn't remember him. He must've been a baby when Ma'roog attacked. If I don't make it back and you do, keep an eye on him for me," I say.

"You will make it back," he says, gaze returning to the enemy.

"But if I don't, make sure he's okay. I trust you with my life. Now I must trust you with his," I say.

"I give you my word," he says.

"What do we do now? Sit here and wait?" I ask.

"Yes," he says.

"Where are the other knights?" I ask.

The Lost One: Wrath of the Tyrant

"Nokk, Ak'dech, and Norkuz are doing final checks to make sure the soldiers are ready for battle," he says.

"I'm going to wait somewhere there are less people... try to lead Ma'roog away from as many people as I can," I say.

"Good luck," he says.

"To you as well," I return.

I don't want to make myself an easy target by being at the top of the volcano, so Nalrai flies me partway up. While strategizing, I envision multiple scenarios of how this battle could go, and I'm wondering who will benefit more from the magic being so strong here... me... or Ma'roog? Maybe the strength of the magic here will give him an advantage. Or maybe it'll provide *me* with some much needed help. I'm not sure, so I watch for Rul Warriors to arrive and try to sense exactly where Ma'roog is located. The wait is agonizingly long, and I impatiently watch as the first Rul Warriors reach the island, greeted with swords and arrows from our knights. Then suddenly, Nalrai growls as Ma'roog's dragon—a massive, heavily scarred monster—lands in front of us.

"I have been waiting for this," Ma'roog says, sliding off his beast, glaring in my direction.

Nalrai steps in front of me, and I say, "No, Nalrai. Back up. This is my fight."

I'm fairly certain this is a suicide mission because Ma'roog is much more experienced than I am with magic, but I'm not going to watch my dragon die before I do.

"Which of your parents died first?" Ma'roog asks.

"It doesn't matter," I say, swinging my sword at him.

"Right to business huh?" he asks, swiping my sword away with a flick of his wrist.

"You can't hold my childhood over me like it's some sort of weapon. You took my village from me when I was barely old enough to talk. So what? I'm done being the victim," I say.

"You and your family will always be the victim. The past has a tendency to repeat itself, whelpling. I clearly remember the attack on Likenhallow where I burned your village to the ground. It was a quick battle they had no chance of winning, and this one will go the exact same way. It'd do you well to learn from your history and surrender," he says, pushing off my next attack with a flick of his wrist as though he's bored.

"My past doesn't define my present. I do. I'll be the victor this time," I say, tapping into Vrarg's excessive magic, which helps me deliver an invisible blow to his chest.

Ma'roog stumbles back then says, "Enough games," sending me flying sideways into the wall of a rocky ledge with the flick of his wrist.

The volcano's wall cracks, but I jump up and go toward him with my sword, letting magic guide my hand like intuition. It's like my magical instincts direct me where to strike to break down his defenses. He parries the attacks with his sword, but I can see him starting to sweat.

"You're out of breath? We've only just begun," I taunt.

The Lost One: Wrath of the Tyrant

Instead of doubting my magic, I need to trust it, so I close my eyes and use Vrarg's massive source of power, along with my own, to sense weaknesses Ma'roog may have and attacks he may be getting ready to make. I can feel Vrarg in every rock and grain of sand below my feet. I can also feel Ma'roog and his dark magic and evil intentions toward me, so I rush at him with my sword and dagger with super speed and strength. It takes a couple of attempts to reach him because he keeps dodging the blades, but I get a hit in magically and send an invisible blow to the back of his neck.

"I said *enough* of your games!" he yells, knocking me backward and pinning me under a crushing, invisible force.

I can't take in a breath of air, and I struggle to break free, trying to push against the invisible wall. I can feel sweat dripping down my back while my lungs burn, starved for air. All my power is focused on trying to get out from under the immovable wall, but I can't get enough of a power boost from Vrarg to free myself. I don't think Vrarg's magic is going to be enough to save me, especially with Ma'roog and I using its powers at the same time. As the wall applies more pressure to my chest, I reach out to Draug in desperation to tap into its power so I can have two sources of energy feeding into my magic to make me stronger.

Help me, I plead in my thoughts to Draug, realizing I can't overpower Ma'roog with the magic of Vrarg alone.

Draug responds immediately by sending a flood of magic into my veins, and I've never felt more power in my body before. I feel supercharged and unstoppable, like a god, and I break free from the crushing wall, shattering it with the borrowed magic from Vrarg and Draug, along with my own. Tiny lightning bolts zap between my fingertips, but I feel no pain. I have the all-consuming magic of two worlds—Vrarg *and* Draug—flowing through me. They each have vast amounts of magic, almost unlimited, which is flooding through my body, and I don't want to let go of the power.

I want to feel like a god forever as the light energies of Vrarg and the dark energies of Draug swirl together in my chest, coursing through me at the same time. It's starting to feel chaotic and tumultuous, like the two energies are not mixing well together, and I can sense that Draug and Vrarg are at war and constantly fighting. They can't be free from one another, but they can't be one with each other, either. I can also feel the entirety and insight of both planets as their magic flows through me. Vrarg is a bright energy and has been damaged by the war Ma'roog waged and wants him gone. Draug is shrouded in darkness and is specifically designed for sorcerers like Ma'roog and wants to imprison him.

What's this feeling? I think to myself as an electrifying sensation comes over my entire being.

The common enemy must be enough for them to set aside their own war for now. They are coexisting in order to help me defeat Ma'roog, and I finally see fear in the eyes of the man who has tormented the world with no remorse as lightning zips between my fingertips.

"What did you do? How are you doing that?" Ma'roog demands an answer.

"Draug is more powerful than I thought," I say, as I feel Draug's shadows wrapping around my mind.

Draug and its shadows more than willingly offer me more power and strength than I have ever found from Vrarg. I'm tempted to hold on and keep this god-like power forever, but it feels like Draug's magic is trying to corrupt me—claim me—maybe even imprison me.

"You can't use Draug's magic like you use Vrarg's… it doesn't work. I've tried. It's different," he laughs, sending a barrage of invisible attacks at me.

The Lost One: Wrath of the Tyrant

Ma'roog's assaults are weak and nothing more than an annoyance compared to my own power. It's like being hit with a soft pillow rather than a fist or weapon.

"That *stings*," I sarcastically say, knocking him to the ground with a flick of my fingers, then I walk over to him and put my foot on his chest.

"You can't... no one can touch me," he says.

"I can do what I want. I am a god," I say, kicking him into the crack my own body made in the rocks earlier.

The side of the volcano cracks even more as my foot applies pressure to his chest, and I notice another entrance to Draug underneath the crack I'm pushing him through. Being connected to Draug allows me to see that this dormant volcanic mountain is riddled with passageways to hell, and I can feel the magic energy seeping through the crevices. Most of the entrances require a bit of digging since they are buried underneath rock and sand, but they are much clearer to see now that I am in sync with this place.

Ma'roog laughs and says, "You're not meant to use Draug's magic. It's poisonous and corrupts the mind until there is nothing left of the consciousness. Look at you. You're power-hungry, and it took only *seconds* for it to corrupt you," he chortles.

I stomp my foot down on his chest, sending him through the crust covering the passageway. I hear him scream as he falls through, and I feel sick to my stomach... must be a side effect of the magic. I know he's right about it taking over the mind because I feel like I'm losing control, and I have an intense hunger for power. I also feel the tension between the two worlds, Draug and Vrarg.

They are occupying the same space and are trying to force each other out of its spot, but there's a reason Vrarg is at war with Draug: Draug's magic isn't meant for our world. It's dangerous and is an exclusive place for powerful sorcerers to be imprisoned. I can feel it ripping me apart trying to get out of my body.

"Take it back," I whisper to Draug, fighting every urge in my being that wants it to take over my mind, but it doesn't listen nor withdraw its magic from my body. Like a malicious spirit, it's still trying to possess me.

"Take it back! You've helped with what I needed!"

Ma'roog's dragon ran off as soon as I beat its master, and Nalrai paces back and forth beside me anxiously as he sees the rapid sparking of lightning bolt magic around my entire being. He doesn't like it, but we're both distracted by a blood-curdling scream nearby. It's a voice I recognize. I look over to see Norkuz slaying a warrior and quickly kneeling beside Nokk who has blood shooting from a slit across his neck.

"Nokk!" I yell, running towards him.

Maybe I can use the extra magic to save him. It'll be more than enough.

"Arid!" Norkuz shouts as he spots me on the mountain running toward them while he's trying to stop the blood from spilling out of his friend's throat.

I'm about three steps away from saving Nokk when a hand reaches up from underground, and I fall forward hard as it grabs my ankle. I can feel energy draining from me. It feels like the magic is being sucked out of my body.

The Lost One: Wrath of the Tyrant

"No, let go!" I shriek, kicking at the hand.

Its grip is as firm as steel, and it drags my leg under the black rocks.

"*Arid!*" Norkuz yells, leaving Nokk's side to come save me.

I claw desperately at the ground, but the gravel slips through my fingers as I sink deeper into another one of Draug's entrances.

This mountain might not be as dormant as I thought, I think to myself.

It's not erupting, but I can feel the heat of the magma cooking my flesh even under the dragon scales I'm wearing. Nalrai reaches me first and grabs the back of my dragon suit, trying to pull me up, but the suit tears away in his teeth. Norkuz reaches me just in time to grab my hands, but they slip through his bloody grasp.

Epilogue: Draug

7 land on my feet, but I'm disoriented.

Where am I? I think to myself.

I twirl around to get a look at my surroundings. It's an empty desert, nothing but sand dunes as far as I can see. The sky is filled with dark clouds, and wind spins the sand in circles through the air. I can feel Draug's magic surrounding me... familiar magic, but dark. I can tell I'm not on Vrarg anymore. I can no longer feel its energy.

"That's not fair! I don't belong here! Take me back! *I want to go home!* I gave everything I had to save them, and now that I finally did, you're going to rip them away again?" I shout to the sky.

A deafening roar splits through the air, shaking the ground, and I hear footsteps pounding toward me. I can make out a massive form in the distance, but I don't know what creature it is. It's the biggest I've ever seen though. In fact, the cave dragon I fought was a dwarf in comparison. I'm used to dragons breathing fire, or even ice, but whatever this is spits shadows and exudes powerful magic I can sense from a distance. My own magic tingles in my arms, but without the boost from Vrarg and Draug, I don't know how powerful I'm going to be since I relied on them to supplement my magic. I don't feel connected to either world, so I don't even know if I can use my sorcery here or not. As it is, I'm worn out from the battle because all that magic took a toll. I'm sore and utterly exhausted. Even so, the creature is definitely coming at me. It speeds up, running toward me, and I take off running, sprinting as fast as I can away from the monster.

The Lost One: Wrath of the Tyrant

"Dammit, dammit... *dammit!*" I yell, trying to find a place to hide.

I can't outrun it because its legs are as long as a redwood tree. I know nothing about this environment other than it's dark and dusty. I have my sword and dagger, but I doubt they would do much good against the creature given its gargantuan size. Out of the corner of my eye, I can see other creatures chasing me... different ones. They're not nearly as large, but they're about as big as I am. They have pointed claws, jagged fangs, and glowing eyes. They're also faster than I am and keep up with me easily. They are about twenty meters off to either side, waiting for an opportune moment to strike. Then a snake-like monster pops up in front of me, bursting through the sandy ground. I shriek and instinctively hit it with my sword. Then I plant my foot into the ground hard to push off and quickly change direction so I can run past it. I spot a cave ahead of me and charge toward it. The furry creatures running on my sides change course to run *at* me instead of parallel. I'm only a few steps away from the mouth of the cave before they catch up to me. I grab my dagger and force it into one of their chests, and an ungodly screech emits from its throat. I can feel blood dripping from my ears as intense ringing sounds in them. The ringing... is all I can hear... all other noises are drowned out. I throw the squealing, lanky beast into the other creature and skid into the cave, spinning around to defend the entrance.

I should have checked the cave when I entered. That's the dumbest oversight I made. I think to myself, as I keep my dagger up and dart my eyes hysterically at the mouth of the cave.

An arm locks around my throat, pulling against my airway. It's a human arm. I reach up, grab the assailant's shoulder, lean forward, and throw my attacker off of me. It's Ma'roog. He shouts something at me, but all I can hear is a shrill ringing. At this point, the first giant creature I saw has arrived, and its footsteps are heavy enough to shake the ground, enough to cause a landslide. The cave trembles as rocks fall and cover the entrance, then the snake-like creature bursts through the rocks at the mouth.

I don't care what Ma'roog is trying to say. I race farther into the cave, trying to find refuge. Instead of a tunnel, I reach a dead end and press my back against the farthest crevices of the cave, holding out my sword, looking around wildly for intruders. I need to find a way back to Vrarg. I'm an experienced survivor. I've fought off mermaids and hydras. I've lived off meals made from the dust of dragon scales and the blood of fish. I beat the most notorious tyrant Vrarg has ever seen. Never have I encountered such terrifying circumstances as I have in the past few minutes. I've seen no source of water. I don't have Nalrai by my side. This world is wild and dangerous, and Ma'roog, he is a concern—but he is the least of my concerns. I focus on my magic, feeling it buzzing lightly in my veins, but the dark magic of Draug, now set against me, is apparently far stronger than any weapon or use of magic I could procure in this new environment. If I want to survive, I need to learn how to fight off these monsters fast and use my magic more effectively, even with Ma'roog by my side.

The End of
The Lost One: Wrath of the Tyrant

Arid's adventures will continue in *The Lost One: War of Gods and Dragons*

Scan to Leave a Review

About the Author

Nick Wickens is a certified emergency medical technician who has been writing for over nine years. Nick's goals are to have fun with writing, as writing is a way for Nick to escape the present and anything that's troubling in the moment, making drama and darkness Wickens' favorite themes to write about. Nick is passionate about acting and is working toward a degree in drama. Nick has also been playing the piano for 17 years and interests range from the gym, long car rides, music, writing, and artistic things in general.

For upcoming books visit:
https://www.nickwickensbooks.com/index.html